NEW WRITING 11

New Writing is the best showcase for outstanding fiction, poetry and non-fiction by established and new authors alike.

New writers, new writing, new books: here is writing that leaps into its own time, that crackles with now. Our cities, our journeys, our love affairs, our familiar landscapes, are at once immediate and awry, recognizable yet unexpected.

In this eleventh edition of the annual, *Picador New Writing 11* highlights both new writers and selections from works in progress by well-known writers. Chosen by Andrew O'Hagan and Colm Tóibín, this is an idiosyncratic and exhilarating collection.

Andrew O'Hagan's debut work was the highly acclaimed *The Missing*. His first novel, *Our Fathers*, was published in over a dozen languages. He lives in London.

Colm Tóibín was born in Ireland in 1955. He is the author of *The Blackwater Lightship*, which was shortlisted for the 1999 Booker Prize. He lives in Dublin.

D1717495

Also available from Picador

New Writing 10

By Andrew O'Hagan

The Missing
Our Fathers

By Colm Tóibín

Fiction

The South
The Heather Blazing
The Story of the Night
The Blackwater Lightship

Non-Fiction

Bad Blood:
A Walk Along the Irish Border

Homage to Barcelona

The Sign of the Cross:
Travels in Catholic Europe

NEW WRITING

11

edited by **ANDREW O'HAGAN**
and **COLM TÓIBÍN**

PICADOR

In association with

First published 2002 by Picador
an imprint of Pan Macmillan Ltd
Pan Macmillan, 20 New Wharf Road, London N1 9RR
Basingstoke and Oxford
Associated companies throughout the world
www.panmacmillan.com

ISBN 0 330 48597 0

Typeset by Intype London Ltd
Printed and bound in Great Britain by
Mackays of Chatham plc, Chatham, Kent

Contents

Introduction

The street called after Picasso in Barcelona is a street full of trucks and traffic, with the Parc de la Ciutadella on one side and ordinary buildings on the other, some of them run-down. Passeig de Picasso is close to the port and close to the railway station. It has no obvious glamour; it is often deserted; it is never entirely safe. It is easy to imagine Picasso wandering around here, as indeed he must have done in the last years of the nineteenth century, delighted with it all, the dinginess, the shadows, the city noise, and ways of escape close by.

If he walked on the park side of the street, moving towards the railway station he would find a monument to himself, a tribute to him from the city of Barcelona done in the late 1980s, a work which does not appear much in guide books to the city or posters or postcards. It is a glass case and it is meant to have water running down the sides into a pool which surrounds it. But the glass is often broken and the water hardly ever works. This, too, might have delighted him, the local vandals and the local dust and leaves combining to destroy a public monument, adding to its strangeness and isolation and mystery.

It was designed by the Catalan artist Antoni Tapies. Inside the glass case is a huge old hall stand and some other furniture with metal girders running through everything. All is askew and shaken about. There are old sheets lying in the middle of everything and there are ropes. There is no logic, no clear meaning, no obvious reference to Picasso. There is something written on the sheets, but it is impossible to read. It could be a room after a bomb, but it could also be a room after a dream.

It is easy to stand back and read the monument once you are prepared to grant it its ambiguities. It is a monument to the imagination itself, to our ability to create images, to work from the nervous system, to create something which in its intensity and newness makes our experience in the world seem denser and more mysterious and harder to explain.

You can shut your eyes and imagine Picasso trying to get inside the glass box, move things around, add new colours and shapes. You watch him as he runs a yellow line down the glass, or you imagine Tapies as he conjured up this dream in a glass box, and you know that these gestures and plans come from the deepest and richest parts of the self, mixing instinct with skill, mixing dream with the concrete.

This collection of new writing allows thirty writers inside the glass box. None of them, we hope, can fully explain why certain, and indeed uncertain, themes or phrases or rhythms were chosen. They have nothing obvious in common, representing no groups or movements or nations or provinces, representing only the primacy of the imagination and the power of language.

Yet Joyce said that memory is imagination, and you may discover a habit in this year's anthology, a habit for strong personal voices and irrepressible pasts. At any rate many of the poems and prose pieces take an interest in matters of place. This is an anthology of comings and goings, but a firmness of location may be evident in the language, even when, as so often, dislocatedness is more to the point. While the glass box is imagined territory, the railway station is real.

We invited some of these writers to contribute to this book. Others submitted work for which we are grateful. We wish to thank Sarah Hemmings of the British Council, and Maria Rejt and Peter Straus of Picador.

Andrew O'Hagan and Colm Tóibín

Mary-Kay Wilmers

My Cold War

1. Waiting in the Car

At the villa in Coyoacan where in August 1940 Trotsky was murdered, there are two cats: a ginger one called Trotsky and a black one named after his murderer, Ramon Mercader. The villa has for many years been a museum and for a while visitors could wander about as they pleased; they could lie down on Trotsky's bed or sit where he was sitting when Mercader struck him with the most famous murder weapon in modern history. Today the rooms where he'd been living with his wife and grandson for the previous year and a bit are protected by a glass partition running along the corridor at waist height. The partition is 'alarmed' and every time a visitor leans over it, which most visitors inadvertently do, the alarm goes off. The walls of the main bedroom, still spattered with holes, mark a first, failed, assault in May 1940; and on the floor of the study where, three months later, Mercader got his man, large red bloodstains look as if they've been rubbed into the stone.

Out in the yard, a red flag flies at half mast over the Old Man and his wife Natalya's grave – a nine-foot slab of concrete with a hammer and sickle and his name carved into it. The yard isn't big but there's room for several tropical trees and some very large cacti. With the jacaranda in bloom and the two cats nestling against each other in the spring sun, it seems quite idyllic. Only the sound of the alarm reminds you that in 1940 this was less a villa than a fortress, that the tower in the corner looking out on the street was a real watchtower, not a place for Trotsky's grandson to play, that visitors were barred and most of the Old Man's entourage carried guns: that, in short, an emissary from Stalin was at all times expected.

1

Ramon Mercader, unaccountably, struck Trotsky with the broad end of the ice pick. Trotsky cried out – 'a long, endlessly long "aaaa"' – bit Mercader, was pushed to the ground, got back on his feet. Picking up whatever was to hand – books, ink pot, a Dictaphone – he threw it at his assailant, before wrenching the ice pick from him and finally staggering back, his face covered in blood, his blue eyes, Natalya said, 'glittering' behind his spectacles. Though they'd been living in anticipation of this moment for more than a decade, the rest of Trotsky's household didn't immediately understand what was happening and three or four minutes went by before they came running into the study, fell on Mercader, and began to beat him with the butts of their revolvers.

Natalya, seeing that Mercader's life was in danger, asked her husband what was to be done with him. 'Tell the boys not to kill him,' he said. And then said it again: 'No, no, he must not be killed.' Trotsky wanted Mercader to live so that he could tell the world on whose orders he'd been sent. But Mercader spent twenty years in a Mexican jail, six in solitary confinement, and in that time never let on that he'd acted on the Kremlin's instructions, pretending throughout that he was a follower of Trotsky's who'd lost faith in him.

Trotsky died the next day in hospital in Mexico City. Stalin, he had said, sought not to strike 'at the ideas of his opponents but at their skulls'.

Had he died straight away and in silence Mercader would have escaped. That at any rate had been the plan. A car was waiting close to the villa, its engine running. Inside it were Mercader's mother, Caridad Mercader del Rio, and the Soviet agent in charge of the operation, a man of many aliases but in the KGB hall of fame referred to as Leonid Eitingon. They heard Trotsky's 'aaaa', heard the screams and cries and sounds of running feet inside the villa, realized that something had gone wrong and drove off. Some say that Caridad and Eitingon were lovers, others insist that they weren't, that Caridad wasn't good-looking enough for Leonid; and some say – though it hardly matters – that they were waiting in separate cars which took off in different directions. Whatever the exact arrangements and whether or not they were lovers, Caridad's presence at Coyoacan was a warning to her son of the danger she'd be in if he failed.

Pravda announced Trotsky's death three days later, on 24 August. He died, the paper said, 'from a fractured skull received in an attempt on his life by one of his closest circle'. Stalin had been waiting – or, more precisely, preparing – for this moment for a very long time.

2. Objectivity

'*Eto fakt?*' (Are you sure?)

'*Eto fakt.*' (No, it's true.)

My father didn't like it when my mother talked to her family on the phone. He had mixed feelings about the Eitingons – that was one problem. Another was the problem of her speaking a language he didn't know. Although he was, in general, good at languages and spoke several without any trouble, he had no interest in learning Russian. A question of snobbery perhaps, but, more likely, of pride and his own dignity. For the forty years of his marriage the only Russian words he knew were the usual pair, *do svidania* and *spassibo*, and that all-important word, *fakt*. He thought it very amusing that Russian has no word of its own for the incontestable units of what he cherished most deeply: 'objective reality'.

He valued rationality and everyone agreed that he was a very reasonable person. But reasonable isn't the same as rational, and like most people who think of themselves as rational my father took it for granted that objective reality and his own thinking were coterminous. The problem for me was that my belief in him was rather extreme, and it wasn't until after he died that I saw myself as having something that could be described as my own way of thinking and that it was different from his. I began to resent the years I'd spent under his spell: one consequence is that I now regard even the words 'objective' and 'objectivity' as instruments of oppression, as scarcely more than a way of saying: 'I'm right and you're wrong.'

But can you, logically, dismiss objectivity and at the same time recognize its lack? I think not. What to do? On the one hand, my father, who saw 'things as they are'. On the other, my mother, who never saw things the same way twice. ('Snake in the grass' was what she called me when, as a child, I would unamiably point out that what she was saying today was the exact opposite of what she'd said yesterday.) After my father's death, when I was able to see her character more clearly, it seemed that 'post-modern' was the only epithet that could adequately describe a character of such radical volatility.

Genuinely unswayed by his own emotions, my father, without realizing it, was overpowered by my mother's and too much a positivist to see how wayward her influence could be. Not given to intimacies, he relied on her to take care of all necessary human transactions. 'Your mother's wonderful with people,' he would say, confusing charm, of which she had a great deal, with under-standing, which she had only intermittently and never when either his interest or hers was at stake. In a sense perhaps my parents weren't all that different from each other: his reasons and her feelings were equally incontestable. What neither of them left room for was uncertainty.

For that reason and others I doubt that my father would have seen the point of these stories, which only on rare occasions fit under a rubric of objective reality. Little is known for sure and the evidence I have been able to find is often thin and even more often contradictory. As for my mother she had at times a highly attractive recklessness and it led her at first to enter into the spirit of the enterprise. Then she changed her mind and told me that I must drop the whole thing. What had been a good idea became a bad idea overnight. As always with her, there were no inter-mediate stages, no transitions. Someone, I imagine, told her that they didn't like what I was doing and, snapping from one mode to another, she adopted that person's sentiments as if they had been hers all along.

3. At the Lubianka

In November 1991 someone told me that the KGB now had a press office. The idea of the KGB wanting to put its best foot forward was rather appealing. (Around the same time, in London, I'd had reason to ring the very recently unbanned ANC. 'ANC. How can I help you?' said the person who answered the phone. That, too, was surprising in a world-historical way.) The press office was sufficiently like a press office to have both a listed phone number and no one in the office to pick up the phone.

I gave up and went into town, hoping that some other way of making contact would occur to me. It was three o'clock in the afternoon and already getting dark. I wandered around, past the rows of women standing outside Detski Sad, the children's shop, cradling one or two old toys that they were hoping to sell. There was nowhere to sit so I bought a pie from a stall to eat in the street and then wandered some more. The bronze figure of Felix Dzerzhinsky, Leonid's protector, which had stood on its plinth outside the Lubianka for thirty years as an inspiration to the resourceful men and women of the KGB, had been laid to rest in the Revolution's uncomfortable graveyard.

I circled the building, built in 1706 by the Rossia insurance company for whom Leonid's grandfather had once been a broker but headquarters of the Russian secret service in all its incarnations since 1802. I noted its many humanly encouraging features, and decided to go in. I'd seen John Simpson do it on television, why shouldn't I? I walked up the steps to the tall double doors and knocked politely, as if outside the headmaster's study. No one answered. John Simpson hadn't bothered to knock; I took hold of one of the handles, put my shoulder up against the panelling and pushed the door open.

A Bond analogy might seem to be called for but 'Joanna Trollope goes to the Kremlin' is more appropriate. A U2 pilot entering Soviet airspace for the first time probably would not have been more excited than I was. The Cold War had been going on for fifty years and I had spent most of my life under its tutelage. I even remembered its beginnings in odd bits and pieces: FDR at Yalta and then his death; Anna Pauker's brutal face on the front page of every newspaper when Romania turned Communist in 1947; my father coming into the restaurant where my mother and I were waiting for him with news of the invasion of Czechoslovakia in 1948. Now the war was nearly but not quite over and here I was kicking in the door of its last saloon.

The door opened into a sort of sentry box on either side of which was a wooden platform, a bit like an alcove, and on each platform, facing one another, stood a young soldier, rifle at the ready. They didn't greet me but they didn't point their rifles at me either. They knew everything was different now that Yeltsin was effectively in power and the KGB had a press office. But they were flustered, uncertain how to proceed. My excitement held.

A bell was rung and a middle-aged man in civilian clothes came to ask me my purpose. He wasn't especially friendly: it was nearly five o'clock, he said – closing time at the Lubianka these days. Grudgingly he agreed to call his colleague. 'Igor Prelin, Mr Prelin, he is efficient in this problem.' (The getting-to-see-the-archives problem.) Relieved and disappointed, I realized I wouldn't be spending the night in a cell.

Someone took me down a long sombre corridor smelling of furniture polish into a lecture theatre. Maybe it was Mr Prelin himself who escorted me: tall, handsome Mr Prelin in his geometrically patterned jersey. But it was an odd place to choose, since we sat in the auditorium chatting as though we were waiting for a lecture to start, while it was Prelin who really gave the lecture in his guarded sort of way.

He had nothing to say about Leonid except that someone else had been making inquiries about him. And maybe he only said that to wind me up and make sure that I didn't lose interest because, whatever else he did, Mr Prelin, like many of his colleagues, would soon be in the business of selling, leasing out or otherwise exploiting KGB archives. Hence, no doubt, the need for a KGB press office. The next time I met him I realized I'd put him on to a good thing.

In his more active days Mr Prelin, it turned out, had been stationed in Guinea-Bissau and Angola, and he was happy enough to talk about that; to tell me, indeed, that he'd been standing right next to Amilcar Cabral when he was shot while on a visit to Conakry and that he'd arranged for Agostino Neto to be flown out of Luanda for surgery in the USSR when Neto had cancer. Since Neto didn't recover from the surgery I wondered whether Mr Prelin was in some sense responsible for his – or Cabral's – death. (And if so, why was he boasting about it? Leonid would never have done that.) I didn't press the point but instead asked for the address of the Africa Institute (titular head, Anatoly Gromyko, son of the foreign minister who had always said no). 'I don't know,' Mr Prelin replied. 'I'm not a scientist. I'm a spy.'

4. Little Flower

My mother's uncle Motty stayed at the National Hotel when he went to Moscow for the fur auctions. My mother told me that and told me the hotel always kept the same room for him, which I used to think meant that no one was allowed to use it when Motty wasn't there. In those days the National looked out on the Alexandrisky Gardens and some of the rooms on the top floor had a view of the Kremlin, a privilege for which you had to pay a bit more. The Lux and the Metropole were the hotels where visiting Western communists were put up.

A cousin of Leonid's, an old lady called Reveka, remembered being taken by her mother to see Motty in his hotel sometime in the late 1920s. It was the first indication I had that some of Leonid's family and some of mine had in fact met. In the late 1920s Motty was a very prosperous fur dealer and lived in the States. Fruma, Reveka's mother, was very poor. Most of her bits and pieces – wedding presents mainly – had already gone to Torgsin, the state pawnshop, and she didn't know what to do next. Maybe Motty would help her. But maybe he wouldn't. If she had Reveka with her he might find it harder to refuse.

Always ready to charm and be charmed, Motty was immediately taken with the child and told his partner to come down straight away to see the *tsvetok* – the little flower – that Fruma had been hiding from them all these years. Reveka squirmed. 'I wasn't pretty,' she said. 'I had nice hair and a nice complexion, that's all.'

Motty asked after Leonid's sisters, Sonia and Sima, and then said, '*A vash glavny Eitingon*' – Your chief Eitingon – 'is he still a Chekist?'

'I don't know,' Fruma answered.

'That means he still is.'

'Then why ask?' she replied.

Motty took a hundred-dollar bill out of his pocket and gave it to Reveka, which embarrassed her even more. She didn't want the money and on the way home told her mother how angry with her she was for making her go to the hotel in the first place. 'You were just using me,' she said. 'You thought that if I came along you'd be more likely to get something from him.'

When they got home the hundred-dollar bill had gone. They turned out their pockets and turned them out again, and finally decided it must have been lost in the street as they walked back to their apartment. Some months later they moved to another flat. They were unpacking their things when suddenly, among the mess and the muddle, the banknote turned up. Reveka didn't remember how the money was spent, except that she got something she'd always wanted: a raspberry-coloured beret like the one Tatiana has in *Eugene Onegin*.

Anne Enright

Pillow

'Alison,' she said.

'Yes?'

'What is a homosexual?'

'It's a man who loves another man.'

'Yes,' she said. 'But what is it?'

'They are in love,' I said.

'But how?' she said. 'How are they in love?' And I thought I knew what she meant then. I said they put their things up each others' bottoms, though I used the word 'anus', to make it sound more biological.

'Ah,' she said and I tried to see what she was thinking. 'Thank you.'

But I didn't feel right about it, so when the next day Nancy said to me, 'What are you telling Li about gay sex for,' I felt awful already.

'She doesn't even know the other thing,' she said. 'She doesn't even know what *people* do.' She gave me a very hard time. She did not try to make me feel better at all. I think that is one of the things about Americans, when they decide to blame you for something, they really want you to know that you are to blame.

Nancy had requested me from the college accommodations office. She told me this when I arrived; that they liked 'an ethnic mix', so she had asked for someone Irish. I was a bit jet-lagged. I said I'd be Irish for her of a Tuesday, but could I have the rest of the week off? Actually, I couldn't believe this place, the size of it. When they said 'dorm' I expected rows of beds. I put my suitcase down and asked when there was hot water for a shower. Nancy didn't understand. She said that there never *wasn't* hot water – unless something was broken – there was hot water all the time.

9

Four bedrooms fed into the main living room. They each had a bunk bed with a desk built in underneath, and there were fancy pin lights on the underside of the bed to light the desk. I climbed the little ladder in all my clothes and lay down in the underglow. I was in college. I was in America. Fly me to the moon.

For weeks, I couldn't sit in the living room. The kitchen belonged to Li and Wambui. They put things on to marinade before they went to class: bowls of liver covered in honey and chilli, or fish turning grey in some strange sauce. Amazing food. They giggled in there like children and cooked like grown-ups. I didn't even know how to boil an egg. Nancy, wouldn't you know, got in takeaway.

I did want to go into the bathroom but Nancy showered three times a day in there. Vast amounts of water, then the sound of her humming and the low squirt, the slap or squelch of her 'products'. Little grunts, as well. I had to wait until everyone was asleep before I could take a crap. One night I stumbled out in a T-shirt and Nancy was sitting at the living room table. All the time we were talking she looked at my legs like she wanted to retch. I think it was the hair. I think she found it morally offensive. Nancy would rather have an abortion than a bikini line. Or so I said to Li, who looked at me and blinked a few times. Then, chomp!

'Alison.'

'Yes?'

'What is a bikini line?' Of course she knew what an abortion was, being mainland Chinese.

Nancy had a boyfriend, who was built like a brick shit house, and made no noise at all. They closed her bedroom door and disappeared. Complete silence. Afterwards, he would sit in the living room and look us over. Wambui stayed out in the hall talking on the phone all evening, which was one way of dealing with it. I just said the first thing that came into my head.

'God,' I said, coming out of the bathroom. 'Why does hair conditioner always look like sperm?'

The next morning the hair conditioner was gone. Bingo. I was good at that sort of thing, though I hadn't really had a lot of sex myself. I mean I had done it, and I liked it, but it also freaked me out. I shaved my head, for example. Though I had wanted to do that for a long time. But the next day I woke up and decided that today was the day to shave my head. So when the guy I'd slept with saw me across the dining hall, he nearly ducked. Physically. He flinched and checked the floor for a piece of cutlery he might have dropped. Anyway, I made him do it one more time, with my bald head, and then I didn't want to see him any more. But I liked the stubble. For a while, I looked pretty jaunty with my bristles and the little Muslim prayer cap I had bought in a thrift shop, embroidered black and gold.

I used Nancy's razor to shave my head. I'm pretty sure she noticed, because the next day she had a new electric gizmo and all the old plastic razors were in the bin. Neither of us said anything, but that kind of thing makes you feel dizzy, you could shoot yourself, actually shoot yourself through the head. Or you could just not give a damn. Like the fact that I know Li stole a pair of my knickers; plain cotton knickers, that I saw distinctly one evening being stuffed into her drawer.

'Shit,' said Nancy when I told her. 'No Shit!'

Neither of us had ever seen her underclothes. We said maybe she didn't have any, but Nancy discovered a pair of nylon socks tucked into a pair of plasticky shoes under her desk. They were see-through nylon, like pop socks but even shorter. Like ankle-high tights.

'Oh God don't touch them,' said Nancy. 'Oh what are we going to do about her?' she said. 'What are we going to do about the smell?'

It was pretty clear she didn't wash her clothes, because the week before she had asked me how the laundry machines worked; so we were looking at three months here. But the smell wasn't that bad – sort of dry and old and sexless.

'Oh my God,' said Nancy. 'Oh my God.'

We had gone into her room during Li's early morning class. Nancy wanted to get out of there, but Li never missed a class. She used words like 'catalepsy', and 'dramaturgy', which amazed me. She was from China and knew more English than I did. She was nineteen.

I opened one of the drawers in her desk and found it was full of tablets. Rows and rows of little plastic jars with Chinese labels. I tried an orange one, and a purple one. They were huge. They tasted of talcum.

'Come on,' said Nancy, who was holding the door handle and bobbing up and down like she wanted to pee. Nancy was at law school. If it didn't work out she would become a realtor. I had to ask her what a realtor was, and when she told me it was selling houses I felt pretty stupid, but not as stupid as she was for wanting to sell them.

The more I got to like her, the more she drove me mad. She said Wambui was a lesbian because she had a friend who slept over all the time. I just looked at her. Every time I got annoyed with Nancy, the word 'douche' came into my head. Like she had dirty and clean all mixed up. Douche douche douche! Instead, I said, 'You know, girls sleep with each other all over the world and no one says anything. All over the world, except here.'

Wambui's friend was called Brigid and I really liked her. She said she was taught by Irish nuns in Nigeria, then held out her hand for proof. 'Look at the scars.' She was funny, really deadpan. She told Nancy she should consider getting cornrows in her hair. Nancy was really interested and asked a load of questions. After she left, Brigid and Wambui laughed until they were hanging on to the furniture. Li got the joke, about half an hour too late – or some joke – and that set us off again. Li made a funny noise. I think she was uncomfortable laughing out loud.

But as my hair started to grow out I realized how really unhappy I was. I went to the college doctor and said I thought I had a lump in my breast; he felt both of them and asked me about contraception and gave me some sleeping pills. He told me to go to the counselling service and I did, but the woman there just thought everything I said was really funny. She said she loved my accent. She said the very fact that I was here meant that I was among the brightest, and that I should nurture my self-esteem.

But I didn't think I was among the brightest; I thought some of them were pretty thick actually. Apart from this guy from New York, who was massively clever in a dull sort of way. At mid-term I got my assessment essay back with a B despite the fact that 'you do not know what a paragraph is'. After that I stayed in more, and grew my hair.

At night I walked down to the lake. I stood with my back to the water and checked the lights of all the rooms I knew, to see who was in and where everyone was. It took me weeks to realize that they were all working. Actually working. They weren't having a good time somewhere that I didn't know about. There was no secret good time.

*

One night I woke up and saw Li standing in my bedroom with a pillow in her hands, or maybe she was clasping the pillow to her chest. It was Li and a pillow anyway, in the dark, and I had to check that I wasn't dreaming.

'Oh, Li', I said. And in my half-sleep the words came out all worn and fuzzy. Almost loving. Then she turned and walked out again.

Maybe she just wanted some company. It was the first night of the Christmas break, Nancy had gone home and Wambui had friends in Chicago. I didn't have the money to go anywhere and Li, I suppose, had even less. So it was just the two if us, feeling a little left behind.

The next day I said nothing. There was nothing I could possibly say. I felt a bit sorry for her, that's all. I wondered did she just want to sleep with me, like I told Nancy women do everywhere except here. Or did she actually want to *sleep* with me the way women actually do (especially here)? The thought of her skinny little bones gave me a sort of rush, but it wasn't really a pleasant one.

Meanwhile, she worked in her room as usual, and blew her nose as usual under the running tap in the bathroom, making me gag a little at the sound. Other times, she was so quiet I wanted to check if she had died.

We collided from time to time in the living room and she might throw a question at me: What did I think of advertising? or Was it true they give medicine to children here, to calm them down? or Was I shortsighted? Had I read Voltaire? After one particular silence she decided to show me a series of eye exercises they did in China, which meant that many people there 'did not need glasses'.(Oh yeah?) You had to rub your thumbs between your eyebrows and rotate your forefinger on particular points of the eyeball and around the socket, and when you were finished stare into the distance for a while. So we sat there, in an empty block in the middle of this deserted campus, while the rest of the Western world hung up fairy lights or went shopping, and we rubbed our eyeballs. Then we looked out the window.

Actually, I think it sort of worked.

She never knocked at my door, but I still found myself staying up all night and sleeping into the afternoon; I felt safer that way. When I staggered out on Christmas Day, she was working at the living room table. She got up really quickly and handed me a tiny package saying, 'Happy Christmas, Alison,' with a shy little duck and twist of her head. Inside was a little calender printed on a plastic card. There were two cutie-pie babies holding a ribbon with the year written on it. I said, 'Oh thank you, Li. Thank you,' and she seemed horribly pleased.

Later in the afternoon, I stole some late winter roses from a college flower bed and put them on the table along with a burnt chicken and a heated-up tin of sweetcorn. My life was too short to do potatoes. My life would always be too short to do potatoes. I said this to Li, who stared at her plate with a snake-like fascination. Does everyone do this? What does turkey taste like? Is it a sacrificial animal? I was worn out just listening to her. I tried to make her drink some wine and she finally took a glass, which made her giggle immediately. I drank and ranted on about advertising, which seemed to interest her, and nuclear power, ditto. She asked about Irish 'Catholicism' (with a lilting imprecision; I realized she'd never spoken the word before) and I put my head on the table, and said, 'Oh Li, oh Li, oh Li,' which we both seemed to find quite funny.

I'm not very good at drinking, I suppose. I'd only done it three or four times and I felt quite dizzy. Before I knew it, I was tackling her about the whole homosexuality thing. She did know about it – she must know – so why did she ask me? She said no, no, they have no such thing in China, they do not even have a word for homosexual in China. There must be a word for it, I said, it's nothing to do with culture, it's just a natural thing, but she laughed, like she was actually quite sophisticated and I was the simple one. No, she said. Really. Perhaps there was a word once, but not any more.

The phone in the hallway rang – my family wishing me a Happy Christmas. So I did all that 'Yes, you too, yes, you too' through brothers and sisters and aunts, shuffled at high speed on the long-distance line. Then I stood for a while listening to the dial tone. When I came back, Li had washed the dishes. She came into the living room and stood in front of me.

'Thank you for a lovely Christmas, Alison,' she said, with a little squirm. Then she walked past me, into her room.

*

They were sweet, nothing days. I managed to sleep through all the hours of daylight; the nights I spent reading or looking at the weather as it fell past the street lamp outside: a slight snow or drizzle, or just the night itself in a long yellow cone. This little slice of weather made me think that the air is really busy and there is an awful lot of it, and it was good to be inside and small and barely, just barely, existing. I felt almost flayed – peeled bare and true. It was so peaceful I jumped at the smallest sound: a plastic bag subsiding in the kitchen, my own breath.

It was a kind of spell, those endless night-days of sitting and pacing and breathing. At four in the morning, I might look at the street lamp and want to cry for the melancholy beauty of the light or the air fizzing about beneath it, or for the millions of street lamps and the millions of windows and all the drops of rain. Li was in there somewhere too, sleeping her Chinese sleep in those nylon pyjamas, not quite a Buddha but, still, my little plastic charm.

We met over her breakfast, which was my supper, and we murmured at each other like people who live together but have other business in hand. Everything was quite easy. When Nancy put her key in the door, I thought we were being burgled. I realized that I had missed New Year's Eve, somehow. And I was sad. Whatever had happened, it was all over now.

*

Nancy was in a complete rage. Something about her father's girlfriend and a dog, I think, or a car. Whatever. Her father's girlfriend was Superbitch, and so Nancy snapped at us all day and cried herself to sleep at night. We could hear her through the wall. Then, suddenly, I was in love with the massively clever but a bit dull guy from New York, completely obsessed. I talked and talked, and paced down to the lake and back again. I finally got him to call for some notes he wanted to borrow and, when he left, I shut the door behind him and slid down it on to the floor. 'Oh Li,' I said, laughing. 'Oh, Li.'

For some reason it became the roomies' joke. 'Oh, Li!' we said, 'Oh, Li,' when anything funny or desperate happened, like a burnt saucepan or peculiar-looking hair. It was better when she was there, but we said it sometimes when she wasn't. As for Li, she seemed flattered by the attention – she always made that silly, laughing sound – but it confused her, too.

One evening she announced, quite carefully, that Li was what we call a surname. Her given name, which came second in Chinese, was Chiao-Ping. But mostly Ping. Then she was silent. It seemed that she didn't want to do anything with this information, she just wanted to say it.

'Oh, Ping,' I said, after a moment's silence. 'Oh, Ping.' and we couldn't help it, we just dissolved, we just laughed and laughed until we were on the floor.

*

The next night I found myself struggling through a horrible dream. It was one of those dreams that soak right through you, a sickener. I think the guy from New York was in it, and he was absolutely evil. I fought to wake up and the dream lurched. My mother was there, warning me, I swear it. My mother was there saying, 'Wake up, wake up, darling,' though 'darling' was never her sort of word. So I did wake up, and my body was flailing on the bed. My head was stuck and there was something wrong with the darkness. I tried to breathe but it didn't work, somehow. I couldn't catch my breath. My hand connected with something, a face, and I pushed into it with all my strength. I pushed my fingers into the eyes.

Ping was trying to smother me. Finally. I suppose if it hadn't been a bunk bed I might have died, but, when I pushed, she overbalanced on the ladder and fell. I looked down and she was on the floor, scrabbling for the pillow. She grabbed it and looked up at me, then she said something in Chinese. It sounded really strange and vicious. I had never heard her speak Chinese before.

I might have left it. Isn't that funny? Like the razors and the knickers and Nancy crying all the time, I might have said nothing and just gone on, or dealt with it in some other, sidelong way. But the noise of Ping falling woke everyone and, the next thing, Nancy was knocking on the door, 'You OK in there?' and when she opened it Ping was still on the floor, and I was still looking down at her.

After that, everyone tried to make me feel guilty again. Ping was sent back to China (to where? to a camp?) and I had about three college counsellors, just in case I might want to sue. They all talked about racism. They sidled up to it. But I said it wasn't the fact that she was Chinese that mattered, it was the fact that she was insane. Besides, I couldn't tell them that I didn't care. I couldn't tell them what really happened to me, the weird thing, the real thing. Because, some time after my mother called me 'Darling' but before I pushed Ping off the ladder, I had the strangest feeling in my chest. It was a thing, it was me, it was my very self, fluttering in my chest and trying to get out of there, exultant, like it had been living in the wrong person and was finally going home.

Thomas Healy

I Never Asked for Nothing

Paul

I was ten when I first noticed Mary Martin, a glance on the street on a warm, sun-drenched day. Mary was on a bicycle, wheeling round and round and her skirt rode up and I tried to see her knickers. A sudden, mad attraction, and I could not take my eyes off her.

'Are you stupid or something?' I had stood in front of Mary's bike and she had braked and fallen off. 'What did you do that for?'

'I don't know.'

'Then you must be daft.' Mary had gained her feet. I wanted to run but I did not run and she split my lip with a punch, and she spat on me.

'What happened to you?'

'I got in a fight.'

'Who with?'

'Mick McCraw.'

'I thought that you were pals with Mick.'

'So did I.'

My mother sponged water on my face. 'Are you sure that it was Mick?'

'No,' I said, 'it was Mary Martin.'

My sister, Maggie, was ages with Mary. 'Were you after a feel?' she asked me.

'What would I want a feel at her for?'

'I think that you fancy her, that's how.'

'I don't.'

'You're blushing, Paul.'

'Fuck off, Maggie.'

It was around Christmas of that year when I spoke to Mary again. This was outside a ragstore at the top of the street where she had tried to sell a bundle of rags. 'But I'm a penny short,' she told me.

'What for?'

'It doesn't matter.'

'I've got a penny.'

'Have you?'

I fumbled for it in my shorts. They were a black, winter wool. 'You can give me it back sometime,' I said.

Mary screwed her face. She had white eyes and teeth and she was taller than me by a good head. 'I never asked you to give me it,' she said.

'I want to give you it.'

'Why?'

I was too embarrassed to look at her.

'Do you like me, Paul?'

'What if I did?'

'I've got a boyfriend.'

'What's his name?'

'Eddie,' she said. 'His name is Eddie Doyle.'

'Do I know him?'

'I don't think so.'

'You've had lots of boyfriends,' I said. 'So I've heard.'

'But this one's for real.'

'Is he?'

'Are you jealous?'

'What would I be jealous about?'

Mary pushed my head with the flat of her hand. 'Because I know you like me.'

She was in a dark trench coat. The collar was pulled up and it was belted at the middle. 'I think you're great,' I said.

'Do you?'

'I said I did.'

'I spat on you.'

'I let you spit on me.'

'Why was that?'

'I don't know.'

'Was it to get close to me?'

'It might have been.'

'Do you smoke, Paul?'

'No,' I said.

'I do.'

'I know.'

'I've smoked for years.'

'I've seen you smoking.'

'Have you seen me blowing smoke rings?'

'No.'

'Do you want to see?'

'I'd like to see.'

Mary lighted a cigarette and inhaled the smoke and she pursed her lips and pouted out about ten perfect smoke rings. 'I could blow them out all night,' she said.

'Is it hard to do, blow smoke rings?'

'No.' Mary leaned against the tenement, in her coat. 'It's dead easy when you know how.'

'Will you teach me how?'

'You don't smoke.'

'I can start.'

'If you want.' Mary handed me her cigarette. 'You draw in the smoke,' she said.

I tried too, but it caught in my throat and I was almost sick and feeling slightly dizzy. 'It can take a while,' she said, 'to learn how to smoke.'

'I don't know if I want to.'

'Do you feel OK?'

'I feel a bit dizzy.'

'How old are you, Paul?'

'Almost eleven.'

'I'm fourteen.'

'No you're not, you're thirteen.'

'How do you know I'm thirteen?'

'My sister,' I said. 'She told me.'

'But I'll soon be fourteen.'

'I wish that you were my sister.'

'To be near to me, do you mean?' Mary blew a few more smoke rings. 'You need to find a lassie your own age,' she said.

'I don't like lassies.'

'I thought that you liked me.'

'You're different.'

'Different?'

'You know what I mean.'

'Do you mean like special?'

'I think I love you.'

Mary pushed me again. Her hand in my hair, and I fell in on her and rested my head on her shoulder. The heat of her neck, and I had not thought that a neck could be so warm or that a girl could be so soft, and I could have stood like that all night, I think.

'Do you do that to all the lassies?'

'There's no other lassie.'

'Only me?'

'Only you.'

'You don't have another penny, do you?'

'I shouldn't have told you nothing.'

'Don't be silly, it's been dead nice.'

I yearned to touch her again, but I thought that she might laugh at me. 'You won't tell, will you, Mary?'

'Tell what?'

'I love you.'

'Aw, Paul,' she said. 'I wish that you were older.'

'Mary Martin's been put away,' Maggie told me. 'Have you not heard?'

'No.' I said. 'I've not heard a thing about her.'

'You used to fancy her.'

'So what?'

'Well, you won't see her again for a long time.'

'What did she do?'

'She jumped a guy, her and her boyfriend, Eddie, jumped a guy.'

'When was this?'

'Last week, I think,' Maggie said, 'up the town.'

'Mary took him inside an alley and Eddie almost killed him.'

'In the alley?'

'Where else?'

Mary was away from the Gorbals for the next couple of years and I tried to forget about her. I had my life on the street and my father was dead and it was only my mother and Maggie and me. It had been that way since I could remember, and I was beginning to be pretty tough, and when I turned teenage I chanced my hand at shopbreaking. My partner in this was my best pal, Mick McCraw. Mick was the youngest of five brothers, and he would go on to a big career in crime.

Even then it was on the cards that he would become big in crime.

Mick was a thin, dark-haired boy with a hooked nose. We were in the same class at school and he lived just round the corner.

For whatever reason he had little time for Mary, and he couldn't see what I saw in her.

'I feel like a boy.'

'You don't look like a boy.'

'My hair,' she said.

'It's short,' I said. 'That's nothing.'

'It's a big thing to me.'

'You still look good.' It was a winter's night and I thought I was seeing things, but it really was Mary standing on the street. 'When did you get out?' I asked.

'Two days ago.' She was in a duffel coat that had big, peg-like wooden buttons. 'Do you want to fuck me, Paul?'

I looked at the ground.

'You're all embarrassed.'

'I've not thought about it.'

'Fucking?'

'Come off it, Mary.'

'I bet you have.'

'No.'

'Would you like to?'

'I don't know.'

'Have you never been with a lassie?'

Her hair was sheared at the sides and back and I told her that I had not been with anyone.

'Come on,' she said, 'it's only me.'. And we went inside a close together.

'You'll know what to do the next time, when you get another lassie.'

'I don't want any other lassie.'

'But you will.'

We stood at the head of the close, one facing the other. 'I won't.' I said.

Mary shook her head, a smile. 'I go with men for money.'

I looked at her. 'I've got money.'

'Where did you get it?'

'I burgle places, me and Mick McCraw.'

'I wasn't asking you for money.'

'I know.'

'And I've got a boyfriend.'

'Eddie Doyle?'

'He's my man.' Mary stood defiantly in her duffel coat. Her eyes were blue or green or green and blue. 'A lassie needs a man,' she said.

'When does he get out?'

'In two or three weeks.'

'That soon?'

'I hope so.' Mary lit a cigarette. 'I think you're funny,' she said.

'Why is that?'

'The things you say.'

'I'm not a cheat,' I said.

'You don't need to give me money,' she said, drawing me back into the close. 'I never asked for nothing.'

The following day I told McCraw what had happened.

'You just got lucky,' he said. 'There's lots of guys have been up her.'

That night, McCraw and I got caught shopbreaking, and were remanded to a place named Larchgrove, where we spent the next two months.

Larchgrove was off of the Edinburgh Road, just outside Glasgow. It was built on a hill and shrouded in trees, and a gravelled driveway reached to it.

I had heard of the place, who hadn't? But it was still a surprise to be in there, and how clean and well-lighted it was.

We were neither of us scared at all, because we had each other.

In Larchgrove.

Where we were interviewed by a Mr Wilson. A few details. Wilson was tall and thin and he had bright blue eyes and you would need to watch your arse in this place. It was my immediate impression, how Wilson eyed you up.

I kept smiling to Mick and he to me, and Wilson took us for a shower.

There had to be five cubicles, but we were put inside one. That was OK with us, and we laughed together and laughed at Wilson, who stood outside, looking in.

That was the last I saw of Mick that first night, for after the shower we were split to separate dormitories.

It was no laugh then, in baggy pyjamas and bare feet, and the dormitory had beds banked out from both walls and you heard the groans and snores and grunts and whimpers.

This was the first, in the dormitory, that I was beginning to know what it was all about, that I was in captivity.

Larchgrove housed something like a hundred boys, aged from eleven to sixteen, seventeen. We were dressed in woollen jumpers and khaki shorts, and it was a contact time, for you met guys from all over Glasgow in that place. A sort of feeling-out, and it was inside Larchgove that McCraw began to build a name for violence.

A respected boy, when they spoke about him it was always *Mick* McCraw.

He had a couple of vicious fights and a boy got cut, and Mick began to swagger about as if he owned the place.

For myself, I saw no point in having guys scared of you. But that was Mick inside Larchgrove where, and what I thought was a peculiar thing, he palled about with much younger boys, and he was protective of them. Not for his boys the threat of rape, what sometimes happened in that place, in the toilets or late at night.

The time dragged on. I thought of Mary. It had been rotten luck to have got stuck in here when Eddie had been away.

When I got out he was back, and Mary had become a woman. Our age difference was at its most apparent then, and it was more that than Eddie that kept me from chasing her.

Eddie was a low-set thug with flat black hair and the darkest eyes you ever saw.

Again I met Mary on the street one night. She was in a white raincoat and her hair was long and full. 'I can't have two boyfriends,' she said. 'And Eddie's taking me to London.'

'When?'

'Soon,' she said. 'Tomorrow or the day after.'

'You're all done up,' I said.

'I'm seventeen.'

'I'll wait for you.'

'You might have a long wait.'

'I'll still wait.'

Mick

Paul's surname is McGrath. McCraw and McGrath. It has a ring, and we were neither of us soft touches. Unlike Eddie, who was only tough with women. Yet I think that Mary Martin loved Eddie.

'I should have killed him, you know,' Paul said.

'But she wanted to go with him.'

'I know.'

'He'll sort her out,' I said. 'Don't worry about that.'

'I don't want him to sort her out.'

'To get *even*.'

'I love her, Mick.'

Paul was never in a gang, but I had progressed to be the boss of one. It was the one sure way to get respect, and I needed that much more than most.

We had showers twice a week at school, and my eyes were fucking everywhere, and one day something happened between myself and a boy named Kevin.

I had followed Kevin inside his cubicle, where I felt his arse and he pretended not to notice. But he had noticed. I was thrilled with my own daring, that I could feel up a boy. Even if he had run out of that cubicle, it was my first move towards who I was and what I wanted. But he did not run out, and so I closed the curtain. I was tall and Kevin had to look up at me and it all happened quickly, for we were both hard.

It happens like that when you are fourteen and the next I knew I was down on Kevin. He came in seconds, inside my mouth; and I was holding on to his arse when the cubicle curtain was pulled back and I looked up at Paul McGrath.

When we were dressed and back in class I sneaked looks at Paul and wondered what he thought of me?

I was caught for a cocksucker on my first cock ever.

At lunchtime I tried to make a joke of it. 'That Kevin's got some arse on him.'

'I never noticed.'

'As tight as a drum,' I said.

'It's just another arse to me.'

'Nothing to Mary's, is that what you mean?'

'I don't fancy Kevin.'

'I know you don't.'

'He's a bit of a creep.'

'How about me?'

'You're still Mick.'

'It makes no difference?'

'Why should it?'

'I thought it might.'

'Then you were wrong.'

And that was that, with Paul.

It took time and a lot of patience before I finally got Kevin inside a house and on a bed and I had to slap his face to shut him up while I fucked him up the arse.

I was the odd man out, and I ran a gang.

Paul

I got into boxing through Mick McCraw. I think that he liked to see the boys. Mick never tried to box himself, but I was good at the sport and he was a big encouragement.

So life went on, without Mary. The boxing was a big part of it. Glasgow was changing, new, huge housing schemes rose up and, little by little, the Gorbals was moving away from itself.

My mother worked in school kitchens. and she would bring home food in glass jars for me and my sister.

Maggie thought the boxing was mad. 'You'll only get your nose bashed in.'

And, sure enough, I did. I got my nose broken in an amateur fight when I was fifteen, but I went on to stop the other guy. By then I was apprenticed to become a joiner. This was thought to be a big thing. that I would become a tradesman, but I was much more into boxing.

I began as a lightweight, and when I was in my twenties and at my best, I fought as a middleweight.

I had come out of my close and Mary Martin was just in front of me. I hadn't known that she was back in Glasgow.

'Your nose used to be straight,' she said.

'I took a punch.' The night was a wine light and it caught on her face and her hair was cut to shoulder length and it looked like copper. I told her I was a boxer now.

'Are you married?'

'No,' I said. 'I've been waiting.' We began to walk. 'They're knocking the whole place down,' she said. 'The Gorbals.'

'But we're here.'.

'I never thought I'd come back.'

'Why did you?'

To see you.'

'Come off it, Mary.' She was in a red coat and it was all the same magic, a sheer excitement, to be with her again.

'You still don't fancy me, do you?'

'More than ever.'

'It's been years.'

'I know.' I was taller than her now and she was looking up at me. Those wonderful eyes. Blue or green or green and blue. 'It's always been only you,' I told her.

'What if I told you I was married?'

'Are you?'

'No.' Mary smiled. She was without make-up, and had a pale, almost pure look. 'You must have plenty of girlfriends,' she said.

'Some,' I said.

Mary lit a cigarette. 'Are you still pals with Mick McCraw?'

'Still?' I asked. 'I've been pals with Mick all my life.'

'He's a gangster.'

'So I've heard.'

'I heard it down in London,' she said. 'A lot of the guys down there, they know about him.'

'I don't want to know about the guys in London.'

'You know about Mick?'

'I think so.'

'He fucks young boys.'

'So they say.'

She was in on the wall of the tenement, and it seemed to go with her that she was in on the wall of the tenement. 'I'm daft about you,' I told her.

'I'm just another lassie,' Mary said.

And she was a much smaller, lighter lassie than the one I

remembered. 'Not to me,' I said. 'You're not just another lassie to me.'

She smiled again.

'You must be fucking mad,' McCraw said, 'taking up with that Mary Martin.'

'I was always mad when it came to her.'

'Did she tell you what she was in London?'

'I've always wanted her,' I said.

I was in the habit of taking a drink with Mick, who was collecting from the owner of the pub that we frequented. 'That Eddie Doyle, he's doing time. Did she tell you that?'

'No,' I said. 'It's got nothing to do with me.'

Mick

My life in the gangs, I got a scar. I got back at the guy with a hammer. But I could have done without the scar and Paul could have done without his Mary. He never thought straight when it came to her.

I had never really fancied girls, but before Kevin I had been with two. In the backs of closes. I could have seen them fucking far enough, but I did not want to be suspected, to get the name for what I was.

So I tried to kid, when all the time I wanted to make love to boys. Inside Larchgrove I could have got a boy, but Paul was there and he had held me back. I had not wanted him to know, who would be the first to know, find out.

Larchgrove had been a terrible frustration, the chances all around me, and I would have killed someone had I been detained in there for much longer. But it was a turning point. When I got out I was finished with pretending, and not long after Paul caught me with Kevin.

Guilt? Not a bit, not then nor after, and in a way it was good that Paul had caught us, even if it was still awkward, the coming out, and I knew that I was talked about in the gangs, the gang boys.

Fuck them. They were too scared to say a thing, to even hint when I was there, and my brother's never mentioned it, my taste for cock, male arses.

I began to loiter in parks and public toilets when I was still at school.

Paul

Yes, well, let's just say that I was not without opposition in my romance with Mary.

In a receding Gorbals, Mary found an empty house and we moved in together. We were squatters, really, in a top-flat room and kitchen. But I had a roof, and I had her, and the next two years were wonderful. Then, when I was twenty, Eddie Doyle reappeared in Glasgow.

I saw him around and he would nod to me, but we did not speak. Not a word. There was nothing to say. Mary told me to forget him and I told her I wished I could. 'He doesn't even look at me,' she said.

'He looks at you OK,' I said.

'He means nothing to me any more.'

'But he used to mean a lot to you.'

I stopped Eddie on the street one day and told him to get out of Glasgow. 'I don't want to see you here tomorrow.'

Mary put up a Christmas tree against our kitchen window. It was a silver, fake one with little lights that blinked in and out, off and on. It meant a lot to me, that Christmas tree. My sweet girl. I was as much in love with her as I had ever been. How soft she was and the movement of her, and I can truly say that if I had loved her when I was a boy I loved her more when I was a man, and as much as any man has ever loved anyone.

You have the moon and stars at four o'clock in Glasgow in December. It was like that when I murdered Eddie Doyle.

Why did he come back? I don't know; I had come home and he was there and I took a hammer to him.

Mary was bleeding and battered. Her clothes were ripped. Eddie wore a leather jacket, Mary whimpered on the floor, and the house was wrecked. The hammer crashed into the top of his head and it stuck there, inside his head, and when he fell down he crawled a bit and then I kicked him.

Mick

Paul came to me, and I got rid of Eddie's corpse for him. It was no big deal, and I was miffed that he had murdered and I had not, when I was supposed to be the gangster.

McGrath was due for his first big-time fight about three weeks after Eddie. This was against a black American named Henry Jackson. When Jackson arrived in Glasgow, I watched him work out, and it was obvious that he was no pushover. Not even for a focused Paul, and Paul was far from focused.

There was no such thing as a gay scene then, not in Glasgow anyhow, and homosexual life was all undercover. There were some three pubs for the whole city so you got to know the faces. I was young, and I attracted older men. Some of them came on too strong, and I had to cut a man before I was left alone. Those guys valued their faces, and I was not to be pushed about, to be felt up in a toilet, not by some fifty-year-old when what I wanted was a boy of my own age, or younger.

I met David in a straight pub in Hope Street, across from the Central Station. This was a place I sometimes used before I hit the queer pitches. It was an October night, all dark and dreich, and I was standing at the bar when he came in and stood right next to me.

'Hello.'

'Hello,' I said.

'My name is David.'

He was about eighteen, an upmarket look – blue eyes and crisp gold hair – and an hour later we were in his flat, and I fell in love with him that night.

Paul

I was dropped inside the first minute of the first round in my fight with Jackson. My legs just went. I was more surprised than hurt and I got up, and in the end I won on points.

'You should see your face,' Mary said.

We were now in a house in a tenement in Govanhill.

'Is it sore?'

'It'll mend.'

She touched my cheek. 'Your eyes are full of stitches.'

I was feeling her back, and the smell of her, and we had not had sex since Eddie. Mary had not wanted it, and I had not tried to push her. 'Do you want to, Paul?' she asked me.

In bed with Mary, it was all worth it, and I would have killed ten men to keep her. The only lover I could ever love, even if she could not understand it. 'It's all a mystery to me,' she said.

I had one hand down between her legs, and I could feel my spunk come out of her, out of her hairy crack. My darling Mary. I had never questioned why I loved her. 'You'll never get away from me,' I said. 'There's nobody else will ever get you.'

Mick

Paul came through the Jackson fight but he was lucky. You could say that he wasn't himself at all that night. Maggie thought he'd lost.

'So did I,' I told her. 'And so did Jackson.'

'It's that bitch, Mary Martin,' Maggie said.

'Do you think?'

'I heard that he beat her up.'

Coming back from the fight in my car. Maggie and me and the guy at the wheel. A big-time gangster? I was at the head of the top mob in the city.

'Did he?'

'I don't know.'

'Have you heard anything about that other guy, that Eddie Doyle?' she asked. 'I heard that he was back in Glasgow.'

'I think that he went back to London.'

'You only think?'

'I don't think that he's still in Glasgow.'

'Did he see Mary?'

'What are you getting at?' I asked.

'I thought he might have tried to get her back.'

'And Paul was in the way?'

'Something like that.'

'What do you want me to tell you, Maggie?'

'That they're going to run away together, her and Eddie.'

'That won't happen,' I said.

Maggie mused. 'Then they might be stuck with each other.' she said.

In the gangland world I was known as Mick the One, and I had a sinister attraction: that I was the one, the single open homosexual in the Glasgow underworld. On the love front, things were good with me and David, and he sometimes cross-dressed, turning himself into a better-looking girl than Mary. How Mary was after Eddie, a drooped-eyed fright. It was a hell of a beating that he had given her.

Paul

McCraw's pub was a dive for hoodlums, like something out of a gangster movie. Mick the One. He was all of that, but you got used to it with Mick. He did not see what I saw in Mary; I did not see what he saw in boys, in David. But that was him.

In his pub, at the bar. I was still patched up from the Jackson fight. 'You should learn how to duck,' he said.

'It's more Mary's face that worries me.'

'She's a bit of a mess,' he said. 'I've heard.'

'She's got a drooped eyelid.'

'But you still love her.'

'I'd still love her if she had lost the eye and was wearing a patch.'

Mick laughed. 'I believe you would,' he said.

'Do you love David?'

He paused. 'It's something like you with Mary,' he said. 'Me and David.'

He had known David for only months, and I could not see how he could think that. Not that I was about to tell him. Mick was touchy when it came to sex, his boys. 'Don't you think he's beautiful?' he said.

'He's different.'

'I want to keep him,' Mick said. 'But it's hard to keep a boy like him.'

'I wouldn't know.'

'Believe me.'

'I've got enough trouble with Mary.'

'You will always have trouble with Mary,' he said.

'All I need is the fucking broomstick.'

'That's daft talk.'

'I don't think it's daft.'

'You're still the goods to me,' I said.

'Take a good look, Paul.'

'So, you've got a drooped eyelid.'

'I've got bumps on my forehead, too,' she said.

'I forgot about them.'

'But I never.'

'It would be good if you could.'

'I'm a woman, Paul,' she said. 'I liked the way I used to look.'

Mick

She was beginning to look like what she was, was Mary. Her drooped eyelid and battered brow, another woman would have been in hospital for a month. Whores are tough by necessity, and Paul might well have killed the only man that she had ever loved.

But enough of them, their problems; by March of that year I was having problems of my own, with David. It was a woman in a red coat who had done for John Dillinger, and I was beginning to wonder if it might be a boy who sometimes wore red lipstick who would do for me.

He was cheating, I was sure of it. Just little things. He was at university and he would tell me that he had to study and I would hear that he had been out. I put up with this because I loved him. What a power he had over me. Mick the One. Only I did not want to be a one, alone again. But you can't tell someone to love you.

I did not want to lose David, or had I already lost him?

'I'm sorry, Mick.'

'But I still love you.'

'That's your problem if you still love me.'

'Is that all you can say?'

'I don't want a scene,' he said.

'Can you tell me who he is?'

'It doesn't matter who he is.'

'I'd like to know.'

'You don't know him.'

'I thought that you loved me,' I said.

'I did,' he said. 'You know that.'

'But you love him more?'

'That's unfair.'

'I don't think so,' I said. 'I thought we had something.'

'We did,' he said. 'But it's over now.'

This was the first I had seen David for more than a week. He had simply disappeared, out of my life. Then a telephone call and we had arranged to meet in a queer pub in Hope Street.

He was in a light grey suit and looking every bit as lovely as I had ever seen him. His crisp gold hair and clear blue eyes. 'There is nothing lasts for ever, Mick,' he told me.

'Won't you reconsider?'

'It's over,' he said. 'I've told you.'

I had a driver and a car outside and I thought I should go. I should have gone. A bit of dignity. David did not want to know me. But I was madly in love and I could not go, leave him. It was something like Paul had been with Mary. The same mad, hopeless longing.

'What if I won't let you go?' I said.

'You can't keep me.'

'What went wrong, what do you think went wrong?' It was early evening and the pub was quiet, and I caught a young barman glance at us. 'Did I do something?'

'No,' he said. 'You know you didn't. It was time to move on, was all.'

'Not for me,' I said. 'Am I supposed to walk away now?'

'You'll find someone else,' he said.

'I don't want someone else.'

Paul

I visited Mick in prison. I went with Maggie. They were very close, her and Mick. They both loathed Mary.

Inside Barlinnie there were about a thousand other men, and Mick. 'I saw red,' Mick said, 'when he told me to find someone else.'

'I think that so did he,' Maggie said, 'after he had told you.'

And that was true, poor one-eyed David. A pint tumbler, the smashing glass, and Mick could expect something like five years for it.

We were seated at a round table and there were other round tables and other prisoners and other visitors and Mick in a blue prison-issue shirt and his big hooked nose and the scar on his cheek and he told Maggie, 'I should see a fucking head doctor.'

'But you won't.'

'But I should.'

'You're lucky not to be inside with him.'

'What?'

'I heard what you did to Mary.'

We were outside the prison, waiting for a taxi.

'Did you catch her with some other guy?'

'Don't be fucking daft,' I said, angry. 'There's never been anybody else.'

'What happened to her face?'

'She walked into a door.'

'Was it Eddie?'

'It wasn't me.'
I lost my next fight after Jackson.

Mick

I had been in prison for three weeks or four before they saw that there was no case against me, not one that would stand up anyhow. There had to have been ten people who could have gone as witnesses, but when it came to the crunch they were not prepared to go against me. I professed to have been elsewhere, so it was pretty much my word against David's, but it was a hollow victory.

Paul

Mick was with a new boyfriend, William, who was a barman in the pub where he had assaulted David.

'I've missed you,' Mary said.
    'Not nearly as much as I've missed you.'
    'Do you want to bet?'
    'No,' I said. 'But I want you out of here and back with me.'
    'I want to be back with you.'
    'You don't need to shoplift,' I said. 'You shouldn't be in here.'

When she got out Mary still went shoplifting. I could not get her out of it. She was part of a team of professional thieves, all women. Maggie got married and I stayed away because Mary was not invited.

Mick

Maggie married a professional guy, I think an accountant. Something like that. Paul would not go, but I went to her wedding.
    Mary was just out of jail, she had got thirty days for shop-

lifting, and I was done with William. A short romance, that one. But there were plenty of boys, and I could have my pick, more or less.

I was Mick the One, remember. I had been acquitted on two murder charges. The second one was a gangland shooting that had made front page, and it was a kick for the boys to go with me.

I have used the word 'queer'. The new in word was 'gay'. I don't know how it came to be, but there it was and I was now a gay man.

Paul

I had sometimes thought that every negro in America must have boxed at one time or another, like a fucking army, the black American middleweights. This was before the black British middleweights began to make an impact. The white guys, the Europeans, had until then been no problem to me in ring. The black Americans were all tough fighters and it was always a gamble, fighting them.

I had a run of wins and I got a crack at the European title.

The champion was a white Frenchman who had been beaten only once, the same as me, and interest in the fight was huge. The contract called for me to be in Paris a week before the fight, to help with the publicity.

Mick McCraw had arranged to come, and Maggie, but Mary would not leave Glasgow.

'Not even to see Paris?' I asked.

'You've got Mick and Maggie.'

'But I want you.'

'They don't want me.'

'That's their problem, if they don't want you.'

'They've been to all of your fights,' she said. 'It's only fair that they don't miss this one.'

'It's the big one, Mary.'

'I know it is.'

'I'll knock him out.'

'I hope so.'

'I will,' I said.

'I'll keep my fingers crossed,' she said.

'But you won't come?'

'No.'

I don't think I ever knew her. We had been to Greece and Spain on holiday, and I could write for ever about Greece and Spain. But I don't think I knew her.

She could not have my children.

'Next year,' she promised. 'We will have a baby next year, Paul.'

The European title deal changed everything.

'I love you, Paul.'

It was what she said on our last night, the night before I left for France.

The champion was named Arthur. The story went that he had been something of a street fighter. He had a wade-in style, and that suited me; the fight was over inside two minutes.

I was presented with a big gold belt, and McCraw was up inside the ring, and Maggie, and it was a wild, mad night.

'She told me that she loved me.'

'Women tell men anything.'

How would *you* know?'

Mick let that go. 'You want to start forgetting her; she's disappeared.'

We were in Mick's pub. There were the usual thugs and a couple of boys. I was beginning to drink heavily.

'You don't think you should look about and find another woman?' Mick said.

The house was the same, and Mary's clothes were there, a wardrobe full of them. When finally I realized that she had really left me, I smashed the house and broke up all the furniture. This disappearing trick of hers. There was no other man, I was sure of that. I could have coped much better had she died. And I sometimes wished that she had died, had been hit by a bus or something.

A clean break. Anything but fucking this.

I don't know. I was all at odds and leaning on the bottle.

Mick

I was shocked myself with Mary's disappearance, and she had a one-week start and had left no clue. I had initially thought that she had gone to London, but she could have as easily been in Manchester or Birmingham, or all the way abroad. There was no telling, and out with Paul, who fucking cared?

McGrath lost his European title in his next fight after Paris. Mary lost it for him.

Mick

In jail I had no compulsion to have sex; I could forget about sex in prison. The only confinement where I had considered sex had been Larchgrove. The khaki shorts. They did nothing to hide a hard-on, what I then had yet to touch, feel, suck or press against my face. I was never into taking it, and I am still a virgin that way.

Inside Larchgrove, I had been out of my head with lust. All-but-naked fucking boys. No wonder half of the screws were bent, those khaki shorts. I would go on to meet some of the Larchgrove screws in later life in queer pubs. They were pretty pathetic, really. Mr Wilson, he was not nearly as tall as I had thought, and he was badly frightened of me. The man I was, had become; and I had not been soft inside Larchgrove either. Wilson respected me, OK.

After Kevin I had an affair with another classmate at school. I was not in love with him or nothing, a physical thing, pure and simple. His name was Bobby, he was good at football, and all of the girls were after him. I had seen Bobby in the showers, and he was something. But I had not thought that he swung that way, so a casual admiration. A sort of boy next door who was always playing at football.

Bobby had had his football boots laced round his neck when

I had met him inside a park, near to a public toilet. He was very embarrassed, and we walked away from the toilet. 'I was playing football on the Green,' he said.

The Green was adjacent to the park, and it had lots of cinder-covered football pitches. 'You're always playing at football,' I said, 'but I never thought to meet you where I did.'

'Then it just goes to show you.' He knew about me, of course. We walked through the park to a place called the Rookery. This was something of a sunken garden, with stone paths between beds of shrubs and flowers. 'You never do know, do you?' he said.

'No,' I said, 'you never do.' This was late on a summer's night, and we were all alone and indeed I had not known, or suspected it, about Bobby. 'Will I wank you off, or what?'

'Here?'

'Sure. Why not? It's as good a place as any.'

'I suppose that it is,' Bobby said, and then he kissed me. On the mouth. It was a total, wonderful surprise. I had never been kissed that way before, on the lips. My thing with Kevin had been all suck and fuck, and I had been rough with him. Unlike now, with Bobby, who wriggled his tongue inside my mouth, and it was as strange to have a tongue in there as it had been to have a cock. But an equal delight, and there was more to kissing than I had thought, if I had thought about it at all, that is.

'We'll go inside the flowers,' I said.

Bobby had dropped his football boots; and he picked them up, and we climbed over the shrubs and flowers, towards trees, where we found a shaded, private place. 'An hour ago I was playing football,' he said.

'Fuck football.' We were on a grassy slope above the river Clyde, and I had his trousers down and his shirt was opened and I had my head against his chest. 'This is better than football.'

'Do you want to do it to me?'

'You know I do.'

'I thought you might.'

'I do,' I said, and Bobby turned over on the slope, in the grass, and I gripped his cock and my belly slapped against his arse, and slapped and slapped until we both exploded.

'You'll keep it secret?'

'You know I will.'

'I like girls, too,' he told me.

'Don't worry,' I said. 'What would I want to tell for?'

'I couldn't take it, if you told.'

'But I won't tell.'

'Not even to Paul McGrath?'

'No,' I said, 'not even to Paul.'

'He's your best pal.'

'He might be my best pal,' I said, 'but I don't tell him everything.'

I had a few more flings with Bobby, and there were other boys, too. I never told on a single one.

To a large degree I had avoided trouble with the law because of what I was, the people I had got to know, and to know about. A high-ranking cop and a leading lawyer, and there were several politicians. The first time I was up for murder, the judge was queer. I knew him and he knew me, only we were not supposed to know each other. It was the same with the cop, and the lawyers and the politicians. They were mostly married family men, and not even their close friends knew. But I did. The boys would say to one another, and it got back to me, Mick the One. I was a dangerous man, but a generous one, and it was worth their time to report to me.

I never used the information, but it was a worthwhile threat to have, that I could have used it. This other side of Glasgow. In the queer pubs. You got men as desperate, in their way, as a junkie looking for a fix. In turn, this led to suicides. There was a married dustman who topped himself to get out of a charge of indecency with another man. You got cases like that all the time, when we were few and criminal. It was all to my advantage for as in any sect of a secret few we had to help each other out. The judge and me. I helped a blackmailed lawyer. I would have helped the dustman, if I could, if he had come to me. We were all in the one boat, outlaws all, and if it could not save me time in jail,

I did less time than I should have done and would have done if I had not been homosexual.

Paul

One slamming punch when I was drunk was worth three months in prison. Barlinnie. I had broken some guy's jaw, it seemed, and what a fucking comedown. From European champion to doing time in prison. The sad part was that I didn't care, for I couldn't see how to live my life if Mary was not with me. Near the end of the three months I heard that McCraw was inside too. We did not meet inside Barlinnie. It is a huge place, like a locked-up town. But he was there, somewhere – all of the prison knew it – for about a week before they let me out.

Mick was facing another murder charge, his third.

Mick

I got seven years for manslaughter. This when I had a new boyfriend. His name was Kim. He was the first since David that I really wanted to be with.

Kim was a Londoner of mixed blood, half Indian.

He had had trouble at home and had run away to Blackpool. I had met him in a gay bar there, and the following day he had come back with me to Glasgow. But there were problems. Kim's age. He had turned eighteen, so he said, but he looked much younger. He looked about fourteen, if that.

We had been sleeping together when the police, about ten of them, burst in the door and arrested me. I could see the fear in Kim's brown eyes as I was hustled out, eyes I would see again.

Paul

Where Kim went to after Mick I do not know, but he did not stay in Glasgow.

I went to South Africa, where I stayed for eight years. I forget how many fights. They were strictly for the money. Towards the end of my eight-year stay, I got knocked out one night in Durban. I had been in boxing since I was fourteen, and that was the first that I had been stopped. This can happen to the best of fighters, one fight too many, and I was a lot of fights too many. The one knockout soon went to two, and inside eighteen months of that night in Durban the South African authorities withdrew my boxing licence.

South Africa had been barrels of wine and taking punches, paid-for women. I returned a pauper, a hefty tramp, and spent some time on the streets of London, where I should have died, but I made it back to Glasgow where, in the dead of winter, I found myself at my sister's door.

The house was a small bungalow. I wore a long black coat and had a bottle of wine in a pocket.

'Paul?' she asked.

'I think it's me.'

'Are you drunk?'

'I think so.'

'I don't know where the money went.'

'It's not important now, the money.'

'It was a lot of money.'

'I know,' Maggie said.

'But there's nobody going to give it back to you.'

We were in a small spare bedroom. 'You wonder where it all went wrong,' I said.

'The moment you saw Mary Martin, it all went wrong for you,' she said.

'We returned from Paris and she was gone.'

'Did you think that she might come back again?'

'I think I hoped she would come back again.'

'But she never did.'

'No,' I said, 'she never did.'

'You have.'

'I had no place else to go,' I told her.

The room was warm enough, with a bedside light, and there was a knock on the door and Mick McCraw. 'Maggie told me you were fat.'

'Where did you come from?'

'Maggie phoned me.'

'She didn't tell me that she was phoning you.'

'You should have come to me, Paul.'

'I couldn't find you.' I felt closer to Mick than I had to Maggie. 'The old pub's not there any more.'

'Maggie wants you out of here,' Mick said.

'I thought she might.'

'Come with me.'

'Have you got booze?'

'All that you can drink,' Mick said.

I had been sitting on the edge of the bed, but I stood up then. 'It's great to see you, Mick,' I said.

'She's in Australia,' he said. 'Did you know that?'

'No,' I said. 'But I'm not surprised. She has got to be someplace.'

Mick was in a dark suit and a cared-for look and you could smell his aftershave. 'But I don't know where in Australia,' he said.

'She'll be thirty-six, almost thirty-seven.'

'I know how old she is.'

'I wonder how she looks?'

'Come on,' Mick said, and he moved to the door. 'I've got a car outside.'

Mary

Eddie would not have killed me; the killing business is for men like Mick and Paul. It is winter time. We are all alone. We are waiting. We are always waiting. Twenty years ago, Paul had said he would wait for me, but he had been still at school and I had not believed him. It is winter time. It is quiet here.

Isobel Dixon

(I Want) Something to Show for It

I'm not the kind who treasures
love notes in the sand, laid bare
for the lobstered swimsuit mob

to stare at, for the tide to lick
away. I want a token,
solid, in my hand. Something

with staying power, not easily lost
or broken. Do you understand?
You murmur, puzzled by my greed,

'What is *it* that you want a thing
to show for, anyway?' You may
well ask. It's just a zero,

universal emptiness. It
brings forth nothing except need,
and the truth is, souvenirs

won't do the trick: no poseur
snaps, no neat, insipid
diaries, no sickly rock,

unusual pebbles, musty shells. I want
the shining cliffs, the posh hotel,
the whole shebang. The waiters

running across emerald lawns,
their heavy silver platters
raised in skilful hands. I want

the tacky postcard carousels,
the smugly clinking tills, the dumpy
women sweating at their counters

every summer, summer-long,
as well. I want their oily husbands
grinning now from ear to ear –

I am the sea come to swallow the pier.

Shaken from her Sleep

A girl wakes in the night. The room
is trembling and at first she thinks
it's just her anxiousness, a dream,
the heat – her boyfriend's T-shirt clinging
damply to her skin. He's gone,
left on the train, just yesterday,
called up for Basics. (Now, in camp,
he's polishing his boots and trying
not to cry.) The cloth still smells of him.

She goes out on the balcony
to breathe, to stop the midnight quake,
but finds it waiting for her
in the humid dark. A coming
storm, steel banks of clouds advancing,
thundering? But no, the drought's
not broken yet. The streets are dry
and she can see Orion's Belt,
the jewelled sword poised in the sky

above the town, the plain. Can he see
it too, where he is – hair shorn, close
to his skull, that handsome head,
caressed and loved, laid in her lap?
Leaning on the rail, she gulps
in air, to drown the ache, and feels
the metal shiver in her grip.
Through the trees, down at the crossing,
she now spies the cause: a convoy,

giant tortoises, lumbering, down
the main street, to the church.
Will the spire shake too as they pass,
head for the town hall and the park
where the angel stands, raising
her sword above the lost sons' names?
Soft summer nights, he'd steal the roses
planted in their memory, for her,
without a thought. But now the world
is real, though she can't make sense
of those distant wars and this night's
visitation, how they fit, or not.
In these small hours they loom immense,
slow, clumsy creatures hiding keen,
ferocious cleverness. But in
the sunshine of Commando Day
they'll seem much tamer, as the children
clamber over the displays and fathers

marvel at design, 'in spite
of sanctions', talk of threat calmed
by this show of powerful
defence. But now she lies down, hopes
her heart's mad drum will let her sleep
again. Disturbed, she's not sure what
she fears the most: what's outside
all she knows; or that their love,
her silence, and this little, peaceful
town, are small, efficient levers
in some terrible machine.

Jenny Diski

Strangers On A Train

'Imagine you're de Tocqueville. What do you think of us Americans?'

Imagine you're making a train reservation by phone in England. Imagine being asked such a question. I was back in the stevedore's building calling the 1–800 number for Amtrak reservations to find a train to take me from Savannah to Phoenix. Not impossible, but not quite straightforwardly possible either. I had to take a train for two hours from Savannah to Jacksonville, where I would pick up the Sunset Limited which ran only three days a week from Orlando, Florida, to Los Angeles, California, passing through Jacksonville on the way. The Jacksonville connection was leisurely. I would arrive at Jacksonville at midday, and there would be a ten-hour layover before the Sunset Limited arrived at 10.06 p.m. It would reach Tucson, Arizona – as close as I could get to Phoenix by train – forty-eight hours later. I had to stay in Savannah for three days after I disembarked, until Saturday morning, and would get to Tucson at ten o'clock the following Monday night. There had once been a train connection between Tucson and Phoenix, but no longer, so Amtrak bussed passengers to Phoenix. I'd arrive there at just past midnight on Tuesday morning, the reservation clerk at the call centre in Chicago explained, and then explained it all again so that this time I could pay proper attention and write down the labyrinthine arrangements instead of just letting my mind wander through the sound of the mythic places and suggested vastness of time and space of my proposed journey.

'So you're from England, by the sound of it? Have you got a minute? I guess you're travelling around. I'm curious. Imagine you're de Tocqueville. What do you think of us Americans?'

His name was Mike. He told people about the train schedules

and took their credit card reservations. He also wondered what Europeans thought about Americans. He was well placed to find out. But I explained that I hadn't been travelling, and that I'd just come off a freighter and was in Tampa dock.

'Wow!'

Now he was really excited. He had a penchant for sea travel. In fact, he was currently reading Conrad: *Typhoon*. So had I on the ship. What did I think of Conrad? How was the sea journey? And Americans? I must have been to the States before. We talked about the language differences between English and American. The formality I found in American speech that lived so strangely with the vivid slang. A magical combination of ease and discomfort. That actually was how I found Americans. We talked about the smallness of England, the oddness for me of being able to take a train that took three full days to get from one side of the country to the other. He said he hadn't realized.

'Really, less than a day to get from top to bottom? Jeez, that must really make a difference to how you think about the world.'

We talked about the sea again, and he said he'd just read *The Perfect Storm*. I'd seen a documentary based on the book just before I left England, and I'd videoed it. I promised to send it to him when I got home though he would have to get it transferred to the US standard. He gave me his address and we said our goodbyes. My train booking had taken half an hour or more and after three and a half weeks of small talk I'd talked with some passion and thought about things that seemed quite important, to a stranger called Mike somewhere in Chicago.

I spent three days in the sweaty, mad heat of Savannah adjusting to living on solid ground. My hotel ('The Magnolia Place Inn, located in the heart of Savannah's historic district . . . Built in 1878 . . . each room is uniquely furnished with English antiques, period prints and porcelains from around the world . . . As featured in *Southern Living*.') encapsulated the fabled gentility of the South. It was elegant, self-consciously beautiful and old world to a tiresome degree. Mint tea was served in the lounge ('parlour') at five every afternoon, the beds were four-posters, the owners distantly charming and the bedrooms and public spaces were non-smoking. Much of what I have to describe in this book is predicated on the fact that I smoke. Cigarettes and my desire to smoke them formed the humming rails of my train of thought as I travelled. What I did, who I spoke to, what I had to say, was very often directly related to my wish to smoke. Some travellers have a goal, a mystery they want to unravel, a place they want to reach, a mental task they want to perform, a world they want to describe, but I had none of these. For the most part, cigarettes dictated my actions. Where the difficulty of smoking is so prevalent – is, indeed, a moral force – nicotine addiction and the pleasure of lighting up turned out to be as good a way as any other of finding a relation to a place and its people.

I have smoked since I was fourteen. I sat in front of a mirror in my bedroom practising, just as I worked at kohling and silvering my eyes and posing naked and enticing to my reflection in preparation for future public performances. Much of the time of the fourteen-year-old is spent in front of the mirror. Life must be rehearsed. At my boarding school, there was a boiler house by the organic vegetable beds. It was warm in winter and secluded in summer and the perfect venue for smoking breaks between lessons if the weather precluded a trip to the neighbouring unmown field where sex as well as smoking could occur uninterrupted. I smoked Black Russian – black papered, gold tipped – and sometimes Abdullahs, Turkish and oval. A packet cost a week's pocket money but it was important, if one had to perform one's most sophisticated activity in the ignominy of a boiler house, to do so with style. At that time, style seemed to me mostly black and gold or oval and exotic-smelling. I toyed with the idea of a cigarette holder, but it was one more thing to hide in my knickers, and I decided that such extended glamour would have to wait. The following year, a coffee bar opened in the town. It was, of course, off-limits. They served espresso and cappuccino in glass cups, which at the time seemed very dangerous to the adult world. There was also a jukebox. It played Ray Charles' 'I Can't Stop Loving You', Roy Orbison's 'Crying', the Everley Brothers' 'Cathy's Clown', Dave Brubeck's 'Take Five'. I sat there with my kohl eyes, my jeans and oversized black sweater, smoking (was there for a brief period a small pipe?) and idly stirring the froth on my cappuccino, wrote poems in a notebook, and waited for a kind word from the first love of my life, Tub (who wasn't, though he had crooked teeth which were so moving they made my heart stop), a junior reporter on the local paper. He called me Nej, reversing me, reasonably enough since I was in turmoil over him. He sort of let me be his girlfriend, though he was careful to remain remote and dismissive. I existed for those occasional moments of encouragement he allowed me, when he would smile suddenly and briefly directly at me, or turn at the door after he got up without a word to leave, and mutter, 'Are you coming?' I could spend several hours at night, lying in bed remembering and reliving the quality of that moment, of the bare acknowledgement that he wanted me, actually me, it had been only me he had been speaking to. Or at any rate, he didn't not want me. Hours would pass as I savoured his tone of voice, the fleeting warmth of inclusion, the inescapable fact (if I thought very hard about it) that he didn't want to leave without me that made up for being ignored entirely for the rest of the time we were together. All the disdain, the apparent absence of my existence for most of the time we spent in each other's company, the endless periods of waiting in the coffee bar which often ended (after all) with him not showing up before I had to get back to school, the terrible moments when I couldn't get to the coffee bar at all and he might be there and waiting for me; all that, the majority of the time, anguish, agony, shrank to fleeting nothing beside the memory of his momentary encouragements. 'Are you coming?' They were real, the rest was reserve, resistance, a game of reticence that boys played for reasons that were not then obvious. And no moment was more treasured, unwrapped in the dark night of the dormitory to gleam hope at me, than the times when, after taking one for himself, he took a second cigarette from my pack of five and lit it before putting it between my lips. And Roy sang 'Only the Lonely'.

So . . . smoking. Later, when I was twenty, I spent five months in St Pancras Hospital, North Wing, the psychiatric unit. Cigarettes were no longer an accessory, they were an addiction and a constant source of concern, since I had only the ten shillings a week that was doled out by the hospital to patients without income as pocket money. Not nearly enough to keep me in smokes in a world where smoking was a way of passing the time.

The Mystery Man had been admitted by the police when he had been found wandering and confused around King's Cross. He had lost his memory. He didn't know his name, where he had come from, nothing whatever about his life. He was a blank sheet in his forties. I became his first friend. We played poker for cigarettes. His inability to remember caused explosions of rage from time to time, but mostly he was extraordinarily gentle, a man who listened intently to whatever one had to say, whose interest in other people was as much a learning process for him who had had no life that he could recall. We talked a lot, he wondered who he might be, and we imagined a variety of lives for him. It was a game in which he would accept or reject my suggestions according to whether he fancied the idea or not. In reality he was not at all eager to find out who he was, although having no access to his past made him bang his head against the walls sometimes. We considered the possibility, the likelihood, that he had a wife, certainly a family somewhere who knew him, and the idea was intolerable, like a narrowing of vision from a full panorama to a single ray of light that led only where it led. He preferred the more fantastical versions of himself: he was a spy, a master criminal, a private eye, a lost prince from far away. Probably these stories I told him about himself appealed to him because they were likely to be the furthest from the truth. Eventually the police discovered his name and that he had been missing for a week or so before he had been picked up. He was a builder from somewhere up north. He had a wife, and a daughter of nineteen. He had left his house one morning with the rent money and had disappeared. The police and his doctor thought he might have been mugged and the money stolen, or he had spent the rent money – he played the horses, apparently – and then lost his memory in an attempt to deal with his guilt. John (we'd been calling him John, but it turned out to be his name) told me all this after he came back from seeing the doctor. None of it meant anything to him. The story was as strange as any we had invented. His wife and daughter were coming to London in a day or two, and he would be meeting them, as far as he was concerned, for the first time. He was terrified, actually sweating at the prospect. I could quite see why.

'We've been married for twenty years. What if I don't like her?'

I could see the enormity of it. Much more shocking than being a spy or arch-criminal. To be an everyday person, a family man with qualities and failings, a husband, a father, to have an intimate history with others, to be an ordinary person with a past, was terrible. To have to find out that past, all in a rush, to come to terms with it, not over forty years but in a matter of days, was frightening beyond belief. And my friend, John, was going to turn out to be someone, to have a life of his own, and I, for a while the first and most important person in his life, the co-inventor of him, would become just a moment in his passing life, a part of an episode of forgetting that he would probably want to forget. He was scared and so was I. I felt as unconnected with my life as he was. We were outlaws together. Uncluttered and new. I was as unhinged from my past as he was. His Jenny was just a few weeks old and without a history. The present in the safety of the hospital was far preferable to both of us than any ongoing truth.

At first he refused to meet his wife and daughter without me being present, but, of course, that was vetoed by his doctor.

'What if I don't like them?' he said, haunted by the invisible past, threatened by the future.

How much I wished he wouldn't like them. But at the same time I could see the awfulness of that. Of discovering say that he had had a life of unhappiness to which he had to return, and of realizing that the intensity of our friendship of a few weeks in a hospital with no past and no future was unsustainable. The doctor told him he was living a pipe dream, that not only did he have a past but so did I, and that real life would scupper us. Living in a brand new present wasn't an option. I was difficult and needy; he wouldn't be able to cope. He refused to acknowledge this. We would manage. We had a special relation to each other. Old wounds wouldn't apply. The point was that we hadn't hurt each other, and without a past there was no reason why we should. If he didn't like his family, he told me, he wouldn't go back, and he and I would find a flat and live together, though in what relation we didn't specify. And what if he did like his family? That was simple: he would adopt me and I would go and live with them. I found it unbearable that he could even think it possible that he would like them. I knew our time was over. I stayed in my bed in the ward, refusing to see him, leaving him alone, the evening before his wife and daughter were due to arrive. My past, at least, had caught up with me.

When they left, he came to tell me about them. Nothing had come back to him during the meeting, but he liked both of them, an intelligent daughter of my age and a wife he found attractive and good company. He thought he might have had a good marriage. He couldn't imagine he had walked out. He must have been mugged. He was saying goodbye to me, although several meetings were planned and he wouldn't be going home for a while. There was no more talk about adopting me, and though he spent most of his time with me when his new family weren't around, I could feel him separating. He talked about what they had told him of his life, as if trying to fit himself into it. It was an ordinary life, but clearly full of affection. He liked the idea of it more and more.

'But why did you run away from it?' I asked.

He shook his head. 'No, I'm sure I must have been mugged.'

I gave him up to his life. But we went on playing poker and smoking together until his wife came with a suitcase to take him home. John introduced me to her. She seemed very nice.

Smoking is a love that has never gone wrong, never seen sense. I trust cigarettes. Thirty-seven years after I first practised smoking in front of my bedroom mirror, I sat on the veranda overlooking a lush garden in Savannah late into the singing, sweaty night, smoking and waiting for Saturday, when I would start travelling again. I woke, washed and left my elegant bedroom to take breakfast on the front porch so that I could smoke while I drank my coffee and watch the joggers: alone, isolated behind earphones, alone but connected by mobiles, with dogs, with babies in buggies, with lovers or encouraging companions, young, old, fat, thin, black, white, running – puffing or effortlessly – round and round the outside of Forsthye Park across the road. Walking slowly, each step taking account of the saturating heat, I crossed the garden squares surrounded by Gothic mansions, past live oak trees dripping with Spanish Moss to Shriner's bookshop to buy Faulkner to take with me to Clary's diner – 'Smoking section, please' – for gazpacho or a salt beef sandwich. Then I'd walk, to the river or just through the squares. Never very far and always slowly. Watch people, take in place names and proud plaques on the older houses claiming not their inhabitants but their age as their fame, stop at a café (non-smoking) for mint tea, sit in a square on an unoccupied bench so I could have a cigarette and read or look at the squirrels – the city is overrun with them. One bench declares that it is in the place of the bench that Tom Hanks sat on in *Forrest Gump*; the actual bench has been taken away back to Hollywood by the studio. Still tourists come to stare and click their cameras at the substitute. It's a fake bench, but it's a fake bench in the right place. Back at the hotel I'd have a shower and then take my tea from the lounge out to the front porch again to smoke and watch the late afternoon joggers doing their programmed circuits round the sultry park, whose mile-long periphery seemed to be its main civic purpose. I returned to the back veranda on the first floor to watch the light die and my cigarette begin to glow as I drew on it in the dark. One, two, three days. All stillness, all alone in a strange city, not lonely for a second. Never alone with a cigarette in my hand.

And if I thought about anything at all, I wondered with a heat inspired lassitude what I was doing in this far off Southern city, waiting, pausing between a sea voyage and a train journey, neither of which I had any reason to do other than the theoretical wish to he moving through grand empty spaces.

*

A gangly young man queued behind me to have the conductor collect his ticket and board the train at Savannah station.

'Are you familiar with Jacksonville?' he asked me nervously, as we sat next to each other in our allocated seats and he noticed from my ticket that I was connecting to the Sunset Limited. 'What will you do all that time?'

'Wait. There must be something to do in Jacksonville.'

He didn't look convinced. His name was Troy and he was

taking the Sunset Limited to Sanderson, Texas, from where he had a six-hour drive to the small town where he lived and worked as a teacher. He'd spent a long weekend in Savannah, having read *Midnight in the Garden of Good and Evil* a story of gay love and death in the mannered South. It was his first weekend away from home on his own. It was a real adventure, a breaking-away, an acknowledgement (though he didn't say so explicitly) of his own sexuality. He had wandered about the old city and spent hours sitting in Madison Square looking at the house where the drama of the book took place. He had even knocked on the door, but no one had answered. He had cruised the gay bars and perhaps made contact with other gay men, but somehow it seemed unlikely. I got the feeling it was quite enough just for now that he had come to this sinful city alone. He was in his mid-twenties. Troy would come to Savannah again, he said, now that he knew he could. The town where he lived was where he had grown up. His father had been a teacher in the same infants' school and still lived locally, widowed and retired. Troy had had to travel a long way to come out, and he was filled with surprise at himself. Even so, ten hours in Jacksonville on his own alarmed him.

'Well, we'll find something to do,' I comforted, half promising to stick with him.

'It's supposed to be a dangerous city.'

'Why?'

He shrugged, uneasy and awkward.

'Oh, you know . . .'

Jacksonville station was a utilitarian box: a few seats, a Coke machine and not much else, except a stationmaster who rather proudly told us there was nothing nearby. It was miles away from the city. So what did people with ten hours on their hands do? He shrugged. There was The Jacksonville Landing, a riverside shopping development, and a bus left for it every fifteen minutes. The answer to what to do in Jacksonville for ten hours was a mall.

'Hold on, I'm gonna hang out with you guys,' a husky woman's twang behind us said.

Bet stepped on the remains of her cigarette with the toe of her black cowboy boot and joined us at the bus stop. We had been adopted by a small, delicately thin woman in her early sixties, neatly packaged in tight jeans, a white poplin shirt with a black string tie at the collar and a smart black jacket. Her face was scored with lines, well lived-in but with a recollected prettiness emphasized by big blue eyes starkly outlined with kohl and fringed with spiky mascaraed lashes. Her thin lips were lipsticked pink and her cheeks rouged. Her curly, reddish light brown dyed hair was caught in a small ponytail at the nape of her neck. She had a swagger, a consciously boyish way about her that jostled with her physically frail appearance.

The three of us sat on the bus with three or four other people heading into town. During the twenty minute trip the bus stopped several times to pick up passengers, passing through obviously black suburbs on the way into the centre of Jacksonville. By the time we were nearing the mall, it was almost full and we were the only white people on the bus. I noticed this vaguely, but it seemed no odder than being on a bus going through Brixton. Troy and Bet, however, had become silent and I could feel the tension. Our travelling companions were the usual range of passengers: old, middle-aged, young, working people, noisy teenagers, the usual urban busload, with us as tourists. When we arrived at The Landing, Bet let out a deep sigh of relief. Troy nodded and said, 'Yeah.' There were beads of sweat on his forehead from more than the heat.

'Jeez,' Bet said, releasing her pent up breath. She was sweaty too.

'What?' I asked.

'That was pretty scary.'

'Why?'

'I don't care to be outnumbered like that. In a strange city.'

'Me too,' said Troy.

'But what was so scary?' I insisted, as we walked towards the entrance to the mall.

'We were the only whites on that bus. This is a black city. People like us . . . white and strangers . . . it's not safe.' Bet spoke in an undertone.

No one, as far as I could tell, had given us a second look on the bus. But it wasn't what people did that represented the threat, it was the idea of being a stranger, of being in a white minority, that made Bet and Troy deeply uneasy. Blackness was dangerous. We didn't look substantially richer than most of the people on the bus, so the danger from a black majority would have had to be our whiteness and their hatred. It was a historical fear. And hysterical. Neither of them lived in inner cities. Troy came from small-town Texas, and Bet lived in and kept to the suburban outskirts of Albuquerque. In their America a bus full of black people was a rumour, a story they'd heard about an America in which they did not and were pleased not to live. Nightmare in Jacksonville was a bad dream come true. We might have been travelling on a bus full of aliens or retributive ghouls, those creatures from movies which represent the fear of being over-whelmed by otherness, so strangely dangerous, so dangerously strange was the situation for them. It was probably the fact of the city that frightened my companions as much as the racial ratio. Neither had ever been to New York; neither would have contemplated it. America might look vast on the map, but for many people it's as small as their local town, beyond which is an uncharted wilderness inhabited by monsters. Once we'd left the street and entered the air-conditioned, security-policed mall, Bet and Troy relaxed. The shops, restaurants and ambience were familiar or versions of the familiar, and peopled by a much higher proportion of whites. Even so, the danger lurked outside.

'We've got to make sure and catch the bus back to the station before dark. If we get separated, we'll meet at the entrance at five p.m. OK?' Bet told Troy, who, delighted to find himself under the protection of this tough matron, nodded vigorously and checked his watch.

'I need a beer,' Bet announced.

There was a piazza outside by the river, with cobbles, a plashing fountain and half a dozen places to eat. We settled on the least crowded and found a smoking table. Troy didn't smoke, but he was happy to go along with the requirements of his two older women companions. Bet downed a bottle of beer fast and ordered a second. I sipped mine, more intent on nicotine. Troy ordered Southern fried chicken and fries and tucked in.

'So where you all going?' Bet asked.

Troy retold his story, wide-eyed in surprise at himself for his achievement.

Bet concurred. 'Good for *you*.'

I explained that I was from London, had just been on a freighter and fancied taking the slow route across the continent to see my friends in Phoenix.

Troy was amazed. 'On your own?'

I said that I was writing about the freighter trip for a British newspaper and that I liked travelling alone. He shook his head in admiration.

Bet approved. 'I'm a train freak. I travel the trains whenever I can. I write about them for local newspapers.'

We were bonded. Her parents were both children of Irish immigrants, and she had been a wages clerk in a local government office in Albuquerque for twenty-five years. Now she and her husband were retired on a small pension and living in the same house they had bought thirty-odd years ago. Before that he had been in the army, and she an army wife, travelling the world but living always in the America of the base.

'What was the boat journey like?' Bet asked.

I told them about how I'd set off with the idea of writing about nothing happening for three weeks while I crossed the Atlantic, only to find tragedy caught up with people anywhere.

Bet nodded grimly. She took a long drag on her cigarette.

So was Bet writing about this train trip, I asked.

'No, this is a different kind of trip. I was in South Carolina for a funeral. I figured I'd take the train back to give myself time to recover.' Her mouth turned hard as she spoke. 'I guess one of the reasons I was so upset by that bus ride was because of what happened.'

Bet had a brother who lived in a small town in South Carolina. When he was young, he'd thought about becoming a monk, but as Bet said that wouldn't have worked out; he was too keen on girls. Either in spite of or because of that, he had never married. He was in his late fifties and owned the town hardware store. He lived alone. 'Drank some,' Bet said. 'But he minded his own business and ran the store.' He sounded like a sad, ageing and lonely man. One night, a week or so before, he'd closed the shop, had a drink in a bar, and was walking home on his own when he'd been shot several times in the back by three kids.

'*Black*,' she said in a stage whisper, after a quick glance at the nearby tables. 'The youngest was thirteen. When the police picked them up they said they had nothing special against him, they just wanted to know what it felt like to kill someone. They didn't even know him. He wasn't anyone to them. They wanted to kill someone and it happened to be my brother. They killed a perfect stranger for kicks. My brother. We weren't that close, but he was my baby brother. I buried him two days ago. It makes me so mad. What are kids like now? What the hell's going on in this country?'

The nightmare of America, although still somewhere else, was closer to Bet than I had imagined. Troy looked aghast.

'My God, you read about these things, but . . .'
The house from *Midnight in the Garden of Good and Evil*, that he'd stared at with such fascination, was as close as he had come to the nightmare. Now he was right here, almost at the centre of the drama; he could reach out and touch it, and it wasn't just a story set in the past.

'Oh my God . . .'
Bet shrugged and drank down her beer. Her hand shook as she lit another cigarette.

'I want to forget it. But that bus ride . . . it got to me again . . .'
It didn't seem appropriate to point out that three black killers in a small town in South Carolina had nothing to do with a busload of people going about their business in Jacksonville. It didn't even seem decent.

'I'm going to look round the shops,' Troy said.
'You want to shop?' Bet asked me.
'Not really.'
We sat on while Troy went back into the mall.
'You think he's . . . you know?'
'Gay? Certainly. Sounds like it's difficult being gay where he comes from.'

'Jesus, small towns. I bet his father doesn't know. This must be the first time he's been open about it even to himself. I don't have anything against them, so long as they keep it among themselves. Well, good for him for getting out. He's such a scared little kid. It must have been a real effort.'

Troy came back and reported on the shops. There wasn't much, but he'd got talking to a guy at the ice-cream stand. He thought maybe he'd go back and talk some more. He checked his watch nervously.

'You won't leave till agreed. Without me?'

'Absolutely not.'

'We'll come and drag you away, kiddo.'

Troy beamed happily and returned to the mall.

'Ah,' crooned Bet. 'I feel just like his mother watching him go on his first date.'

There were hours still to kill. Bet and I walked down to the riverside.

'What's the river?' I asked.

'The Jacksonville,' she told me, as we watched the boats ply up and down. It was wide and flat, a busy river with new developments on both banks. The water was a weird rust-red.

'Let's go for a boat ride,' I suggested. There was a small ferry going back and forth, just a little boat with a sunshade and seats for about a dozen people. The heat, once we had left the air-conditioned restaurant, was exhausting. 'It'll be cooler.'

Bet and I stayed on the ferry for a couple of hours, going from one side to the other, paying the $2 fare on each turn. Every so often we got off so that Bet could get another beer.

'You don't drink?' she asked me as I got a Diet Coke.

'Not much,' I apologized.

'Well, I *do*. I drink a lot.'

The afternoon on the river was quite blissful, catching the breeze on the water, going backwards and forwards to nowhere. Bet and I congratulated each other on having found a perfect way to spend our layover.

'What's the river called?' I asked the captain of our ship on one of our crossings.

'This is the St John's.'

'The Jacksonville?' I turned to Bet.

'Hell, I don't know what the damn river's called. I was just trying to be helpful.'

We giggled a lot, though we talked about nothing much. Bet was catching the Sunset Limited as far as El Paso.

'My hero's picking me up and driving me home. There's no connection to Albuquerque.'

'Your hero?'

'That's my husband, Bob. My hero. Because he is my hero.'

It sounded fine to me.

'He didn't go to the funeral with you?'

'He had to stay home with Joe.'

'Joe?'

'Our youngest. He can't be left alone. He's brain damaged.'

Joe was in his late twenties and had just qualified as a policeman when he was in a car wreck which left him in a coma for eight weeks and damaged him enough to be completely dependent on Bet and her hero, who were just reaching retirement age.

'He's a sweetie. Got a mental age of a kid. Can't remember anything from one day to the next. Hell, one moment to the next. He's got to be watched all the time. He's always trying to do things he can't do, and then he gets mad because he remembers he can't do what he used to do. But he's so loving. And funny. A real joker. He's a joy. Our other kids are all grown and have families of their own, but we've still got our baby.'

Only the words were sentimental. She spoke sharply in the face of a permanent tragedy. She lived with Joe as he was now. I liked Bet's toughness, though I wondered how deep it went.

Back at Jacksonville station we still had hours to kill. We sat on a bench in the open on the platform, where Bet and I could smoke, next to a huge black woman in her mid-twenties with a voice so loud you felt it in your solar plexus. It was the only place to sit, and at first I felt Bet's uneasiness; she was on her guard at the excessiveness of the woman. She was sprawled lazily on the bench, her great thighs comfortably separated, monitoring the comings and goings of her two tiny children – a boy of six and a girl of three or four – who ran in and out of the station. When they had been out of sight for some internally judged time limit, she would call out their names, and although they were behind a glass wall and closed door at the other side of the station, they came running. She never turned to look at them, her antenna was so highly tuned, she knew exactly when the kids needed to be recalled before they got on anyone's nerves. The children returned instantly and amiably to their mother and hung around her knees for a while being groomed, hair raked, mouths wiped, while she smoked and warned them not to get themselves dirty, before they went off again, both they and their mother reassured.

'And don't you go bothering people, you hear?'

They were dressed smartly, quite formally, while she wore a voluminous red tracksuit and trainers ground down by the weight they carried. The two children were obedient but never frightened or cowed by her great voice and monumental presence.

Bet relaxed and she, Troy and I were entertained during our wait watching the way the family worked together,

'Hey, they're great kids,' Bet said to the woman.

'They better had be,' the woman boomed in mock ferocity. 'Or they'll catch it.'

But her pride in the compliment and her smile suggested that they didn't need to catch it often, and whatever they caught wasn't anything compared to the love they received. Bet seemed quite at ease now with the woman who though black, young, loud and outsized, and perhaps somewhat strange and potentially dangerous at first sight, exhibited what to Bet was a proper understanding of social control and correct public behaviour when it came to her children. They were never going to grow up to be disaffected, morally blank wanton killers. We introduced ourselves. Her name was Gail, she was on her way from Virginia Beach, where she lived with her husband, to stay with a girlfriend in Los Angeles. She was exhausted, having had the same ten-hour layover as us but with the added responsibility of keeping two small children entertained. She had spent the afternoon with them at the movies, window-shopping and buying food and drink for the train journey, which was going to be the full three days. She had got back to the station an hour or so before we arrived hoping she had worn the kids out enough for them to fall asleep. She could have dropped off at the snap of a finger, but the kids had hours of energy left in them. Like Troy, they were travelling coach, which meant sitting all three nights in reclining seats which were comfortable by airline standards, but still seats in a public coach. Bet and I had sleeping compartments. Travelling by train is cheap if you don't want a bed and a space to yourself for the night. If you do, the price rises steeply, well beyond the means of a working family with better things to spend their money on than a bed on a train. My enjoyment of the day in Jacksonville with my new friends had been predicated on the knowledge that when the train came I'd have a bed and a door to close. But I was delighted by the way the layover had turned out. Bet and Troy were people I would never have come across travelling any other way, nor by spending time in one place in a hotel, not even staying with friends. I was intrigued by Bet's contradictions and her bearing, and moved by Troy and his lone efforts to be who he was. I could only imagine the pressure against that in his Texas town, and how hiding himself, even to himself, must have made it fearfully difficult to make any kind of break.

A train passed through without stopping, hooting from a distance to warn anyone off the track which was flush with the platform. Troy watched it come and go.

'When we were kids we used to hang out at the station. They put pennies on the rail when a train was due. Flattened them like pancakes. You ever done that?'

I hadn't. Trains had never been so accessible in the middle of London, and the platforms were always raised. It was an all-American tradition.

'I never managed to do it,' Troy said. 'I always got too scared at the last minute.'

Bet and I gave each other a maternal glance at this confirmation of Troy's timidity.

'Well, there's another train due before ours comes,' I said. 'Do it now.'

Troy looked alarmed and shook his head.

'It's OK, I was only kidding.'

But Troy became silent and intent. The loudspeaker announced the imminent arrival of the next train, which would be slowing but wasn't stopping, so we should keep clear of the track. Gail told us how she had missed the train this morning because her husband had overslept and she'd made him drive them hell for leather to the next station in time to catch it.

'Or he sure as hell would have caught *something*. But we got there cos he was scared as a kitten,' she bellowed, laughing with every inch of her body so the bench and all of us shimmied in the failing light. It was quite dark by now. Suddenly, Troy got up and took a few steps forward. Then he stopped dead.

'You OK?' Bet called. Usually when he went off to the lavatory or to get a drink he would tell us where he was going. But he didn't answer, just kept standing. In the distance we heard the incoming train whistle. It seemed to startle Troy, who began to walk towards the track without looking back.

'My God, what's he doing?' I asked, quite amused at the intensity in his walk.

The train whistled again, it was much closer now. Troy put a hand in his pocket.

'You know what? He's going to flatten a penny,' Bet gasped.

The three of us watched in silent admiration as he bent down and put something directly on the nearest rail, stepping back just in time before the train arrived. Then, as the train slowed, he turned round to look at us with a look of perfect satisfaction on his face. Bet, Gail and I cheered, whooped and clapped Troy's achievement. The other people on the platform and in the station looked alarmed at the rowdiness. After the train had passed through, Troy collected his penny from the track and held it aloft as he came back to the bench. He held it out for me. It was now an elongated oval with distorted markings, and bright as the proverbial new penny from the buffing up it had received from the train's wheels. It was as thin as a sliver of ginger. I was as proud as anything of Troy.

'Wonderful. Well done.'

'Isn't that great?'

'Yeah, you did it.'

He smiled hugely.

'Wow, I was really scared. It was just like being a kid again, my heart was in my mouth walking to the track. But this time I was determined to do it. It's to celebrate my weekend. Here,' he said, pushing the penny towards me. 'It's for you.'

'But don't you want it as a souvenir?'

'No, you keep it. It'll remind you of your day in Jacksonville with Bet and me.'

I was getting sucked in. America was rolling over on its back and waving its legs in the air, offering me its soft sentimental underbelly to rub. And of course like some stray cat that I was determined to resist, which I had not the slightest intention of taking in, I was overcome by its charms, quite won over in spite of my objections to its shameless methods. The Jacksonville Penny rests proudly above the corkboard in my study, a monument to what a person can do when they make their moment come, and a reminder that, every now and then and in the right circumstances, I really do like people.

*

I had better come clean and admit that the right circumstance, the essential circumstance, is strangeness. On the whole I'd rather have been Jane Goodall. Well, not Jane Goodall exactly, but a version of me who spent my life in a forest befriending and observing a troop of chimpanzees. In lieu of that I became a writer, which is not so very different, except that the forest and the chimps have to be imagined and the discomforts are far fewer. I was reprimanded once by someone who said that she suspected people like that preferred animals to people. I said I could confirm her suspicions, which were certainly true in my case. At the very least, given a choice between a human family and a troop of chimps, I'd take the chimps. I quite understood her air of disapproval; I disapprove of myself, but it does seem to be an inescapable fact.

I have not, so far, given excessive rein to my delight in animals. I have three cats, which were accumulated somewhat reluctantly at my daughter's entreaties rather than planned as the beginnings of a home menagerie. I try to keep control of my more questionable desires. Now the daughter has left home and the cats apparently are mine because, according to her, it was I who wanted them all along. She may well be right.

Sometimes, when one of the cats is sitting on my lap, I have one of those rare experiences of existing completely in the present moment, of apprehending the reality of now with a blinding clarity and of being part of something extraordinary. I find myself astonished that a creature of another species, utterly different from me, honours me with its presence by sitting on me and allowing me to stroke it. This mundane domestic moment is as enormous, I realize, as making contact across a universe with another intelligence. This creature with its own and other consciousness and I with mine can sit in silence and enjoy each other's presence. It becomes remarkable. I smooth the cat's fur, feeling its muscles beneath the loose skin, and trace the structure of its skeleton, backbone, shoulder blade and skull with my massaging fingers, while he sits and purrs with the pleasure of physical contact, encouraging my exploring hands by pressing his head and body against them, turning his face this way and that to receive extra attention here or there. This is a perfectly everyday scene but sometimes it takes my breath away that another living creature has allowed me into its life.

But then I wonder at my wondering. Not that it isn't marvellous and extraordinary that a cat chooses to keep company with me, but it occurs to me that I might be just as amazed by the company of other human beings who choose to make contact with me across the chasm of separate individual consciousness. Rationally, both cats and people have a built-in need for making contact, but that doesn't make the fact of connection less extraordinary. Yet when I try to transfer the state of awareness to contact with my own kind I fail. I can't apply my sense of miraculous contact to people. It's a flaw, perhaps like being colour-blind, or the spatial deficiency that prevents me from transferring the information on two dimensional maps into actual geography. What I experience most with other people is my estrangement from them, the distance of a mutually unique separation that words or touch never quite bridge. Unlike cats, people interfere with my apprehension of reality, they muddy how I can know myself, confuse my understanding of how I am, which is predicated on solitude, on the simplicity of being alone. People complexify things; they place their glass of beer on the table and break up my view of the horizon by including themselves in the landscape. A cat might walk across the table with impunity; a lover putting his beer glass in front of me announces his place in my existence and ruptures my uninterrupted vision of perfect nothing.

My problem, if that is how it should be termed, and it probably should, is that I am never lonely on my own, but I am often lonely when in company. Alone, I might experience all kinds of discomfort but hardly ever the kind of discomfort that I feel would be improved by company. The discomfort arrives when I'm with other people, and then the urge to find a remedy is strong. The best and most effective remedy I know for such discomfort is to get alone again. The problem is that being alone isn't a problem. The idea that someone I am with feels he or she knows me throws me into a fretful anxiety about what and who they think they know, and my sense of what I know of myself is threatened. That is a perfectly proper human adventure but I have no wish for such adventures. So familiarity is difficult, while strangeness is comparatively easy. One day on the freighter, the reticent Roz commented on the ease with which I got on with the crew.

'You seem to be able to talk to everyone. And they want to talk to you. You have a way with people.'

I didn't say: Only in the company of strangers who are guaranteed to disappear back into their own lives. There was no call for such an intimate admission.

Gerard Fanning

Prayers at the Coal Quay

The spine of the *Leinster*
pipes its basso continuo,
its triple note linear fugue,

and with flexed sirens
turns in its own length
prompting a slight recoil

where lazy barques nuzzle hulls,
windsurfers crouch in the swell
and all the walkers in their stride

pause and check the midday bell.
In this sweet communion
within earshot of the next drowning,

mailboats yawn or come about,
taking stock of wind and light,
and like us, list to port

at exact extremes of home,
dreaming a world of meridians,
purlins for Cancer and Capricorn.

Ludwig, Ruth & I

Gathered on your veranda we drink and talk
About the neighbours in a found land. You brought
Susanna Moodie's clarity, settled in Victoria's air
But never spoke of that albino shack at Cape Spear.
Its charcoal heart on your landing now
Beseeches the children to come home safe and sound.

In this street of maple quarter lots
Built for the plain man in the early 1990s,
Your next door neighbour
Has summoned the municipal inspector
To translate a template of rods and perches,
To admonish the laburnum when it over reaches,
So that in another time and far from home
When we unspool the fences, language alone
Might lasso the blond interior or confuse
The world we live in with the words we use.

Teepee at Bow Lake

Teepee at Bow Lake, Medicine Hat, Alberta
July 10, the man looking towards Eden
Has his mind set on the spiralling cost
Of his film set, soon to be called, *Heaven's Gate*.

Everything in Its Place

I glance down the windy canyons
where all the metals flow
and an American Indian

shinnies up a column of steel
retrieving core samples from far below.
Settling the rods

he follows his pit-helmet's gaze
and in a moment or so,
a beam comes floating towards him

making so easily
it barely ruffles the undertow.
He might be one of the high-steeled Iroquois

composing a mute store
while pursuing the hint of snow
found only in his forebear's air.

I stare through double glazing,
hugging my indoor vertigo,
and he taps for sweet air

as though in baby semaphore
a silent major chord could show
that melody we all revere.

Paterfamilias

We were completing the last bank of the dam,
When he appeared and waved down
to my sister playing tennis on the strand.
Driving from the heat of Stephen's Green
he came to define our here and now
though his swaddled Vaseline gave off that acrid fear
also known to Sargeant Troy and Paul Revere.

Strolling to the water, he made to cross over
and though he had five thousand days in store,
he was assembling the route of departure.

If he should lay down his little bundle
like a goalpost or an umpire's chair,
perhaps he could strike out in a coy freestyle,
making it up as he went along, like Stonehouse.

Menzies' Field

The first sun of the year
clips the spongy red trunks
of the red woods,
as I sniff the Pacific air,
that Menzies,

ship surgeon on the Vancouver expedition,
quaffed two hundred years ago.
St Patrick's eve,
give or take a decade,
the ground is like a trampoline,

I am up to my neck in resin
and my goitre throat
stinks of gum,
recording last year's triumphs
like the painted cemeteries

of Audubon.
Even the smallest flight
is here preserved,
though the wing beat
and the throat song,

are less revered.
As I play your new year tape,
sweet nothings from the Grateful Dead,
I hear that Menzies,
as if to fend off scurvy,

told his ancestors
to turn their backs on the sea
and when they knelt down
with my wicked uncles,
they grew an island of barley.

Character in Search of an Author

Past the wide boulevard of ships and sheds,
dry docks, cranes, riggers, marine railways
there is a serpentine, salt-caked house
where bramble, fuchsia,
honeysuckle and heavy vine
have crept out of my control.

Should my heart give out
and I am left on this porch to watch,
this will all slide into wilderness
and as I lay aside my espadrilles,
the panicked wren fleeing a patch of salal
is there to remind me that I know
the date of my birth, but don't yet know
the date of my death, and never shall.

Bill Duncan

Nightwalk

The nightwalk taking you from a world of impossible sleep, far from the tower, into the darkness beyond the housing scheme, through the perimeter blackness of remembered fields, tracks and burns. Further, over forgotten paths into woods, moors and low hills unknown. Hour after hour through dark landscapes, the city now a distant blur. The rhythm of breath and limbs, the drag of feet in the gravel of a dried-up stream, the slickness of dew on grass, the pull and struggle of mud. The slow rise, the catch of breath, then your heart beating evenly on a remembered contour as darkness falls into half-light above a valley recalled from a lifetime ago: rocks, heather and lochan unchanged but you altered beyond all imagining as the morning pulled you back into another world. In the early chill you listened to your heart, watching your breath smoking silver, rising like a ghost in the stillness. Your city now miles away, like a place from a dream or still to be known, its light and darkness an indecipherable code, forgotten or unknowable. Once you walked, trackless and timeless, only the rhythm of breathing and moving, the repetition like an enchantment; everything you knew left far behind, vanishing. Then the first light behind your shoulder made you turn towards the trembling paleness, the low cloud above the river tinted with the slow stealth of dawn. Waiting for the dome of the sun to burn into the sky, you imagined a far city below the horizon, undiscovered and unknown, its existence rumoured in the secret glow that pulsed its flickering energies into the morning; the quiet background hum of its terrible possibilities of murder, destruction and love. That day you stood silent and still, listening for an echo from that world you would never see, in those minutes before the grinding dazzle of the sun as your gaze settled on your own city, strange and familiar, to the East.

Some nights you could walk for ever under the moon, new and perfect, rising then tracking, across the winter sky from horizon to horizon, you wandering further into the mysterious spaces beyond memory and loss then the sudden thrill of the smell and touch of her, alive in the darkness, imagination quickening into clarity and recall, the past more real than life. Night passed again into morning with the dawn spreading like a slow stain and drawing you back into a world where you were alone and lost. Some nightwalks you wandered, far and blind, on the lines of a secret map: a bridge then a river, the touch of damp in the air, the sudden smell of sea, the sharpness of pinewood and the light breaking over the strangeness of a beach remembered from a June morning or from a dream of a distant summer. The red glow of the trunks of the Scots pines, flawless green swaying in the breeze from the sea, a smiling girl dressed in white, moving slow and quiet, the beach golden through the forest The same shore under cold stars at midnight or the same pinewood as dusk fades into the darkness of a January night, decades later.

The rhythm of past and future becoming now as you emptied of memory in the moments when the path, like an invisible force, led you into the unknown coordinates of night, as if the places themselves were seeking you, as you moved in a trance through the forgotten hours. The slow drone of a car engine and a line of trees flashed in the stillness, dreamed or remembered, vanishing then reappearing then returning, into the silence of the world. The scent of resin on the wind and a path took you to a stream trickling through a wood, the winter constellations burning above the river in the Orion months, The Hunter slowly looming above the trees, wheeling across the sky, Canis Major and Canis Minor following in the hours after as Orion climbed higher. The water's voice stilled in the freezing radiance of January as you remembered telling her the names of the winter stars, forgotten, until they rushed back to you in that moment: the white brilliance of Rigel and the perfection of Sirius, brightest of all the stars. The coldness of her skin and the soft give of her lips, fresh and new as you buried your face in the dark fragrance of her hair these years past when Orion rose in the South and the river spoke a different language. Beside your feet a pool stopped shimmering and reflecting, a dull translucence forming at its edges, opaque white lines etching the curves of its outline as the water sealed under a skin of ice, trapped in the clench of winter. A frost whispered across the surface and your stroking fingertips glued to the burning cold.

Nights when sleep would never come without walking, when you would smell the past in the wind and dream of memory. Rising, you would gaze from the tower across the river, the lights of a night train flickering across the rail bridge, beyond hearing, beyond sight, into the darkness of other fields, other cities, other lives. That first night, now distant, when you wandered beyond the tower, past the houses on the edge, walking into the furthest darknesses that you never truly left. Time vanished in the blur of your rhythm and movement and in the calm of the world you walked. The language of a stream, its voice flowing and endless, the panic of a deer as you startled the secret of its world, the flurry of a nightbird, its call echoing far into the emptiness. Nights when you would sit for moments or hours and fade into a wood, then your senses would open, nervous and quick under the razor clarity of a winter sky. Like an animal, still and calm, innocent and without history.

A year of your life given to the nightwalks: a year of the sleeplessness of remembering walking into a landscape that spoke for ever of the past. A clear day and the slender white tower of the lighthouse visible at the furthest edge of the headland. A lifetime ago, the slow sweep of its flash burning through your childhood nights. Its light still drawing you back through the darkness, through the decades: a walk through the trees, taller now, over the dunes that had crept nearer the sea. You as a child, you with a lover, then you with children now unrecognizable strangers, with their own narratives and distant lives, lost to you. Years alone and the nightwalk took you to the deserted space between land and sea where the lighthouse, now in ruin, once pulsed its lonely message through time. Hours of walking on the edge of sleep and the lighthouse faded into a haar; sound and vision muffled in a slow drift of fog from the sea. Exhausted, you sat beneath the tower and dreamed or imagined the days of wreckers before the light, and the tales you had listened to in boyhood times. The crackle of their bonfire signalling the shore, the distressed ship lured by the promise of the false beacon to the hidden fangs of reef, the calls of the distressed mariners kindly answered from the beach, their relief then the shock: the grinding scrape, the whine and splinter of timber, heard through mist. The familiar ceremony of panic, confusion, cries and prayers in an unknown tongue then the boiling sea and the waiting of the villagers for the tide. Spars of blond Dutch timber, a crate of oranges, fuel for a year's heat, a cask of brandy. Sometimes the clothes of the dead warming a family for years. The chill rain and the lighthouse, blind these two decades, towering above you in the grey of the morning. Searching the lighthouse that day, you saw the work that time and people had done: the great lens hauled from its mounting and shattered, the beauty of its prism smashed in a thousand fragments, each facet throwing back at you the shock of your own pain and age, reflected in a thousand faces as you circled the ruined light. A trapped seabird flapped against the cracked window, a flurry of panic as you approached to gather its whiteness in your cupped hands, launching it into the sudden freedom of the dunes.

Sometimes the nightwalk tempted you back into the dangers you had loved in your youth, once choosing to walk the rail bridge that spanned the river for miles. You walked uncertain but thrilled, your path the narrow platform, a half-metre wide, at the side of the tracks: the surface stained with oil and grime, studded with the cast-iron pattern remembered underfoot and stamped on your memory from childhood. Minutes of walking then the low threatening rumble and the advancing clatter: the mounting rhythm shuddering through your feet as the train approached on your side of the tracks. You were surprised but glad of the recesses, at intervals, packed with oil drums, pickaxes, shovels, tar and paint tins, but with enough space for you to stand, teeth clenched and eyes tight as tons of hurtling iron shook your bones in its sudden deafening rush. Then the thrum of vibrating tracks and the high soprano whine. The judder of the train rumbling into the distance, its trace vanishing into the silence of night but still the race of your heart.

*

Night turned to morning as you stopped on the road bridge, miles downriver, its footpath bringing you home. Mounting the spiral staircase that took you to the openness of the observation platform, approaching the far end where the desperate would climb on to the barrier in their pain and loss, feet unsteady on the bevel of the handrail before the lurch and the plunge into space; the whirling horizon and the river hurtling upwards. Your fists clenched the handrail, cold as bone as you gazed across at the great sandbank looming out of the dimness, the early light tinting, the sands a pink glow against the sky turning purple to lilac, the low moan of the first seals rolling on to the bank as it rose like a great beast itself above the retreating waters. To the West, the old rail bridge where, hours before, you had shivered in risk and fear. The bridge now slowly forming, solid and black, against the dark of the hills beyond the river and the slow gold of the reed beds in the risen sun fighting the greenness of the nearer hills. The call of a bird, liquid and pure, in the innocence of the morning. To the East, the lighthouse, tall and pale as it had always been. The beauty of the new day an ache in your being as you gazed at a landscape scarred by the pain of memory.

The last time you walked the road bridge the far nightwalks ended. Deep in winter, returning from the beach with its pine forest and dunes, the strange space where the long green-grey curves of the Scots pine needles blew among the sand, ghosted by the shorewinds. Shells: razor, scallop and artemis, dry and white, lay among the depths of years of needles under the shade of the trees. Walking from the beach through the darkness of the woods you entered a zone of memory: you as a boy running breathless through the light and shadow, feet slowing and sinking in the effort of the deep sand at the edge of the pines, then the steepness of the rise to the crown of the dune and the pause as your heart caught. Blood pulsing at the thrill of the first sight of the shore: the perfection of the sand, smooth then patterned at the edge of an endless sea. The hurtling tumble over the dune, the far sweep of sand, dry then moist then wet, and the thrill of the cold dazzle of spray at the sea's edge. Returning years later with your own children, then years later alone. Leaving the forest that night you hurried as you heard the wind rise and felt the sift of snow through the trees as the snowclouds gathered, you still hours from the tower. Halfway across the road bridge the blizzard came sudden and quiet with its whiteout, your city fading and vanishing in a swirling blindness seething between the river and the sky. Then the shock when the wind stilled and the snow cleared, your city further away than before the storm, its light gleaming now, shocking in its distance. You nearer the beach you had left, then your fall and the blind walk back towards the shore. Returning to the tower that morning you slept for a day.

Nearer home you walked the quiet of city streets: rain slowly drizzling a fine mist across the muffled yellow of the street light, your ear tuning to the nervous electric hum, the pavements gleaming wet after a heavy shower, reflecting the trembling red and green neon of the 24-hour store in the rush of a sudden flurry of wind. Once you walked in the early morning darkness and the smallest bird, its quick flicker and pulse the only life in a freezing world, fluttered across your path, a visitant from some other place. Your companion for a mile; appearing, vanishing, reappearing. Sometimes the streets falling silent for an hour then the sudden blur of sound: a distant car approaching, voices, a door slammed and the click of footsteps hurrying. You watching from the darkness, unknown and invisible as she passed, her face echoing another's.

Beyond the nightwalks: the unaccustomed peace of day but still the call of woods, lochs, beaches, hills, trees and moors through years and you returning to the place where forest and shore meet, under the greying sky. A big bird circles the gloom twice then leaves, its call fading into the slow dusk of other evenings, other birds, this beach, other beaches. The waves breathe a memory of other waves, the birds flash and turn like a changing current, dark to light, dark to light, an unreadable chaos of signs. The shore darkens then fades, every rush of waves blurring the imprint of birds, erasing your footprints a minute old. Everything stills except the beat of the sea. The first snow

flickers from the twilight, touching your skin, reading your face like blind fingertips, trying to remember something lost. Picked from the shore a ring of bone, white and cold, sleeves your finger
   delicate grain
      porous as memory

Nick Laird

Firmhand the Queried

1

I remember poncing a fag off some guy at the bar,
then downing the dregs of my last pint of stout,
spotting the wink of the head of the state,
then pinkie rings denting my flesh epaulettes,

waking alone on the floor of the gents
with the unshakeable sense that the room was afloat,
bracing myself with the sink and hand dryer,
then eying the blur swimming up through the mirror,

which seemed vaguely familiar, and I remember
being dimly aware I was late for somewhere.

2

A slow and dry-mouthed stretch of night:
the heating's sad machinery sleeptalks
its poem through the firedoors' artillery,
paper cuts, windsor knots, artificial light,

an Anglepoise so annoyed the cords in its neck
tilt at full stretch as it poses and tuts like
a gull on the deck, that, and the daily weight
of being unable to swim, idling the plank

of the corridor, and diving beneath the desk
when someone tried to give me work.

3

But, flexing the strut of my glossy umbrella,
I scarcely remember snapping the throat
of a cormorant caught in the dragnet, though their
similar colour – shrink-wrapped street – and angular

shape – knocked-over ink – brought it back
to the poems shipwrecked on Manila
that fight over deadlines, tiepins, doubloons,
and a map on a beermat that might just disclose

a reef offroute to planes and ships, where the natives refuse
to keep off the grass and wear garlands of pea-green paperclips.

4

I was whistling the secret last note of its anthem
as my pen bloomed through Armani and onto my shirt.
I stagewhispered help before faking a swoon,
and left the cctv a last grainy shot of a door, swinging shut.

I leapt astern in a harbourtown famed for its spice
and honey-thick silks, and there I was showing the locals
that to stand on a chair completely changes your view,
when I fell off and came to in this bar. I don't know you

but should you have questions, drink late at the establishment
down at the river. It will feel both new and oddly familiar.

The Last Saturday in Ulster

Behind her radiator
the leather purse is caring
for the old denominations:
liverspots of giant pennies,
fifty pences thick as lenses.

A Pentecostal home outside Armagh:
antimacassars, oxygen masks,
Martha glancing towards the screen
as if checking delay and departure.

An Orange march in Antrim
will see me late arriving:
and standing out at Aldegrove
an English girl might well believe
that time is how you spend your love.

Undriven cattle graze the long acre.
Pheasants fidget and flit between townlands.
The coins were warm as new eggs
in the nest of her priestly-cool hands.

Maggie Graham

Precious Little

Marie

The sky would turn pink at night, steelworks sunsets. Something to do with smelting or cooling; something that made loud bangs anyway. I never asked; it was all to do with men. Men marching past the window in shifts every day; men in bunnets and heavy boots, with piece boxes and tea and sugar tins tucked in their pockets or in canvas bags slung across their chests; men on bikes but hardly ever in cars. I suppose the bosses had cars, I wouldn't know; I never saw a boss.

My father worked there, off and on. In between times he signed on at the labour exchange and claimed National Assistance. Kind words – exchange, assist. He never exchanged his labour, but they assisted him in his drinking career.

He dragged me up there with him one morning. It must have been a school holiday. He was arguing with a man behind the counter, a man wearing a suit with a clean white shirt and a tie. I liked the man; he reminded me of the daddies in books, daddies who spent their evenings by the fireside with slippers and the wireless on. I thought, when I'm big I'll marry a man who wears a suit every day, not just on Saturday nights.

My father didn't like the man. My father was shouting and swearing at the man. Then my father lifted me up on the counter, half turned me round to face the man.

Have you had your fucking breakfast? he asked the man.

The man nodded.

My father said, Well, she fucking husnie.

I didn't cry; that would have suited him.

My poor wee lassie.

I drummed my heels against the counter, fast, faster, loud, louder until he couldn't hear what the man was saying.

He grabbed hold of my legs, That's enough.

I stopped, and then I spoke.

That's a lie, I did so; I had Rice Krispies.

I watched the flush rise up from his throat as the all the men in the queue behind us laughed, spluttering and choking on their roll-ups. I jumped down, jooked past him, out the door and away home; I knew my way.

The man must have given him something, for he didn't come home till late. He'd been spending time and money in the bar with all the other sad bastards seeking sanctuary, on the run from responsibilities and the threat of hard labour in the iron and steel inferno down the road.

I hurried up the stairs when I heard him coming staggering down the brae, belting out his rendition of the Glenn Campbell classic, 'Like a Nine Stone Cowboy'.

Helluva man, my father.

I must have been about seven or eight when I found out what else he did instead of working.

The pipes had frozen in the school, so they sent us home. We went to my house first, and I knocked and knocked at the door but nobody answered. We went along to Kathleen's, but there was no answer there either. I wanted to go up to the town, but we had Peter with us. He was only five, and we weren't allowed to take him that far. I was cold and scared that we'd be left out all day. Then we heard noises from inside the house, so Kathleen knocked again. Her mother came to the door wearing her dressing gown, with her hair down.

She said, Wait there, and went away in.

I keeked round the door and saw a black and blue striped jacket, just like my father's, hanging over the chair. She came back with her purse and gave Kathleen money.

Go and get sweeties for the three of you, and mind you hold his hand tight.

She shut the door, and we trailed along to the wee shop. Peter threw a fit because he wanted a Mars Bar and a Lucky Bag, but we didn't have enough money. The woman behind the counter checked him and gave him just the Lucky Bag but he swore and kicked at Kathleen's legs all the way home; I wanted to slap him.

Poor Kathleen.

I didn't ask her why her mother was in her dressing gown, when she'd had her clothes on in the morning.

When we got to my house my father was at the window, waving me in. I left Kathleen dragging Peter along the road, kicking and swearing.

Ya fucking bastards.

I ran up the path, dying to get away from them.

I asked my father, Where were you? I was knocking for ages.

He was clearing out the fire, something he usually did early in the morning. My mother was in bed, that would be the Mogadon.

He said, I haven't been out, darlin. I must've been in the toilet; I didnie hear you.

But that was a lie, because he was wearing his black shoes, not his slippers, and his jacket was lying on the chair where he'd flung it down in a hurry. Same jacket, different chair.

Years later when they shut down the steelworks and all the men were redundant, he faked casualty status.

Aye, we're all on scrap heap now.

Kathleen

I've never understood how my mother and Marie's mother could be pals. I mean, Anne didn't go to the pub or the bingo, but they would for their messages together, and they would sit and drink tea in the afternoons when we were at school. And before Anne took to her bed, they would have a go at decorating and doing the gardens. My mother had no option; there was no man in our house, although sometimes uncle Matt would do electrical repairs and stuff like that.

One time they sent way for a twin pack of bathroom wallpaper from the catalogue. It was one of those cheap deals where you didn't get to choose, you had to take what they sent you. Oh my God, they sent us green trailing vines and horrible big orange poppies. The vines weren't that bad but Marie's mum took them, and we were left with the poppies.

They put the paper up themselves; it took them all bloody week. My mother thought her bathroom was lovely and bright till our Michael screamed the place down when she tried to get him into the bath. He was scared that the big flowers would lean down and suck him up. I know what he meant; every time I went in there it felt like a bloody horror movie.

Marie was the same. She said it was creepy, imagining the vines wrapping themselves round her throat and strangling her, and them finding her naked and blue in the face with her eyes bulging out of her head. But that was Marie, a right drama queen.

I liked their bathroom; it always smelt nice. Anne couldn't afford good perfume, and she wouldn't wear the cheap stuff, but she always had nice soap and Nivea cream. I used to open the wee blue tin and sneak some on the tip of my finger every time I went in there. I would smell the soft cleanness of it, then stroke it on somewhere secret, like my stomach under my jumper, or the inside of my thigh. The scent would stay on my hand for a while, and every now and again I would sniff my fingers.

I went out and bought some when I got my first pay packet. No, my mother took the first one and gave me pocket money, and then she was pissed all weekend. That was the last time I worked for her drink money. The next week I paid her digs, told her if she didn't like it I would move out, although Christ knows where I thought I would go.

Big Joe never did anything about the house, except take care of Marie after her mother got bad. The day she fell on broken glass in the play park and cut her leg, there was blood everywhere and she was screaming blue murder. I raced round to get him, and he ran with her in his arms all the way up the hill to the doctor's surgery. I wandered home like a wee lost soul, worrying that Marie would get her leg cut off and have to get a wooden one like Mr McGrath that had been in the war.

I was standing at the window when I saw them coming back. Marie's leg was all bandaged; I bet she still has the scar.

I said to my mother, They didn't take Marie away to the hospital.

She stood behind me, watching them pass by, big Joe still carrying Marie like a baby. She laid her hands on my shoulders.

I heard her whisper, Ah God.

I tilted my face back to look up at her; she had tears in her eyes.

I said, What's the matter?

She turned away.

Nothing; I've just got a wee touch of the cold, that's all. C'mon and you can help me to peg the washing out; your wee pal won't be coming out to play for a while.

Marie

My mother stopped sleeping with my father and she stopped taking care of me. Then he started bringing folk back to the house when the pubs closed; Kathleen's mother was one of them.

Lying in bed listening to him, all drunk and cheery.

I've brought some folk back to see you, Anne.

Hush, Joe, you'll waken the wean.

Kathleen's mother singing 'Your Cheatin Heart'.

Trying to fall asleep before he came peeking round the door with one of his cronies.

She's a right wee stoatir, is she no?

Aye Joe, she's a wee beauty, right enough.

Feeling his hot boozy breath on my face when he kissed my cheek, God bless, beautiful.

Waiting for them all to leave. Waiting for the shouting to start.

You bastard.

Now Anne. Now don't, Anne.

Her calling upstairs, Marie, go and get the police. Tell them your father's assaulting your mother.

Getting up and running out into the street in my slippers with a coat over my nightie. Looking up at Kathleen's window, hoping that she was all right. Knocking on the door of the police house where Constable McLean lived with his wife and his safely sleeping children.

Telling him, My daddy's hitting my mummy.

Hating the pitying look on Mrs McLean's face as she sat me next to the fire to wait, while her husband put on his jacket and boots. Going back out into the dark, feeling the gentle clasp of the big policeman's hand in mine.

Wanting to say to him, Please don't take me back there.

Going back and lying with the covers over my head.

I want him charged; he's nothing but an animal.

She sleeps with a seven-year-old lassie.

Maybe if Constable McLean had arrested the pair of them that would have ended it, but all he ever did was talk.

Finally falling asleep, but always wakening up with her beside me.

I love you, precious girl.

I love you too, Mummy.

Too scared to say aloud what I screamed inside, Go away. Go back to your own bed. I'm only a wee girl. Go and sleep with my daddy, like you're supposed to. Make everything the way it was before. Make everything all right again. Stop making me tell lies.

She kept her pills in an old battered school desk beside her chair: bottles of uppers, downers and sleeping pills. Even as a wee girl I knew all the names. Valium, Librium, Dexedrine, Mandrax. I would chant them inside my head as I bounced my ball off the side of the house.

Val-ee-um . . . *bounce* . . .

Lib-ree-um . . . *bounce* . . .

Dex-eh-dreen . . . *bounce* . . .

Man drax . . . *bounce* . . . *bounce* . . .

I knew that the names were a secret. And I knew that they made her all the different ways she was. I didn't like the ones that made her stay in bed all day, especially in the winter. One morning when I tried to waken her, she opened her eyes, looked at me and said, What the hell is there to get up for?

Me.

I went back downstairs and found a cardigan to wear over

my pyjamas but I was still cold, so I got my coat and put that on too. Then I sat waiting by the grey ashes in the fireplace for Kathleen to come. When I opened the door she looked at me in my weird rig-out.

Why are you not ready for school?

I said, Just tell the teacher I'm not well.

But what's wrong with you?

She knew, but she never said. Just like I never said, Your mother was in my house drunk last night. I looked at her, all nice and cosy in her coat and gloves, with her breakfast inside her. A wee lassie worth getting up in the morning for.

Never mind, I said, and shut the door in her face.

I looked out of the window and saw her running back along to her own house. She went in and came back out with her mother. I was scared that I would get into trouble, that Mrs Boyle would shout at me. I hid behind the curtain and watched her kiss Kathleen goodbye at the gate. She knocked on the window.

It's all right, Marie. Open the door, hen.

I let her in. And then she was moving about doing everything all at once. She had the kettle on and an egg in a pot on the cooker, and she was clearing out the fire.

She said, Is your mother sleeping?

Yes. I tried to waken her, but she says there's nothing to get up for.

She was on her knees, twisting newspapers for the fire. She looked up at me. She didn't mean that, Marie, she's just not very well.

When the fire was blazing she sat me down in front of it with my breakfast. Then she went upstairs, and when she came back I heard her sigh.

She said, You're a big girl, Marie, why did you not put your clothes on?

I sucked on a toast crust and said, There was nothing ironed. And I don't know how to iron.

Well, we'll sort that in two ticks of a lamb's tail.

She was already pulling things out of the sideboard where my mother shoved all the wrinkled clothes. She ironed my green trousers and my favourite jumper with the ballet dancer on the front. She even ironed my vest and pants. Then she handed me the warm smooth pile, with a pair of rolled-up socks on top.

I said, But what about my school things?

She said, I'll do your school things for tomorrow. I think you've maybe caught a wee chill, Marie. Your daddy'll write a note for you to take tomorrow; you should be better by then.

She did all the ironing, even my dad's working shirts. She'd switched on the radio, and as she ironed she sang and jived about. I was doing a wee wiggly bop in the chair when I remembered Michael. I pictured him all alone, crying for his Mum.

I said, Mrs Boyle, who's watching Michael?

She said, Michael stayed at his Auntie Becky's last night. Did you think I'd left him all by himself? I would never do that, Marie. Now, I need to write a list of things to get at the shops. Where does your mum keep her pen and paper?

In here, I said, opening the desk.

Her eyes widened when she saw the pills and all the other stuff my mother bought from the chemist: packets of pick-you-up pills and boxes of headache powders. She picked up a writing pad and uncovered all the bars of chocolate, dozens of them, another secret I wasn't to touch.

Here, she said, you can choose one, seeing you're not very well.

I said, They're my mum's. I'm not allowed to have them.

I'll sort it out with your mum, she said. Go on, take one.

I chose a Fry's Cream, and then I picked up another one and held it out to her.

This one's for you, I said.

She reached out and touched my hair.

Thank you, Marie.

When my father came home from work she spoke to him in the kitchen. I heard them.

But Rita, what can I do?

You'll bloody need to do something, Joe; that wean could have been deid.

Kathleen

Looking back, you wouldn't know who to blame. I could go all the way back and blame Mick Boyle the Bastard for leaving us in the first place. But I let him know what I thought of him the last time I saw him, and it didn't make a blind bit of difference. That night we were at the Labour Club with Bruce's mum and dad. It wasn't my idea of a night out, but Moira and Jim were bloody good to us, giving us the deposit for the flat and everything. And my mother was always desperate to baby-sit. So, to please Bruce I went along, even though we were too young for that place and it bored me to tears.

I was watching all these older couples dancing foxtrots and quicksteps, wondering what Marie was doing. She was back with Tam the Bam by that time, going back and forward to gigs in that old van of his. I worried that he would get stoned out of his head, crash the thing and kill her. To be honest, for a long time I couldn't see what she saw in him, especially after the way he acted when she was pregnant. He was nothing but a skinny wee dope head. Still, I supposed it was better than sitting in with her mother every night, or in the Labour Club, come to that.

I talked Bruce into going to a gig once, when they played the town hall. Marie looked beautiful that night. She had on one of her handmade dresses, all rainbow patterns, and her hair was braided in lots of plaits with wee coloured ribbons. She'd been standing next to me, listening to Tam singing 'Light My Fire', but then she disappeared. Tam finished, and then he said, We have a guest vocalist with us tonight. Please put your hands together for Marie Devlin.

And there she was, up there on the stage in front of everyone, singing 'Do Right Woman'.

I couldn't believe it; she hadn't said a word to me. Tam and wee Neil Gibson were backing her, and she was absolutely bloody brilliant. I knew then what she saw in Tam. When she finished I clapped and roared and jumped about like a loony. She just stood there, smiling down at me, playing with the ribbons in her hair.

We had to go then. Bruce was uncomfortable because people

kept offering him joints. Dead straight was Bruce; but that was why I married him.

Anyway, that Saturday night I was back in the Labour Club, watching folk birling about to old tunes. Big Joe was there, but I kidded on I didn't see him. Bruce and his dad were up at the bar getting the drinks, when Bruce's mum reached across and touched my arm.

Kathleen, pet, she said, is that not your father over there?

I looked over to where she was pointing. It was him all right, I knew him straight away. He was dancing with some woman. And the next thing I knew I was up on my feet and heading straight for them. Bruce had seen me, I heard him calling out.

No, Kathleen. Kathleen, don't.

I wasn't listening. When I got to them the woman was smiling up at him. You're one of the Boyle boys, aren't you? Which one are you?

And he answered her.

Me? I'm Mick. A'm the cunt wi the two wives and the eight weans.

I shoved the woman out of my way and stood facing him. Is that right *Mick*? Is that who you are, *Mick*? Well I'm the eldest of your eight fucking weans. And do you know the life me and my brothers have had because of you, you bastard? He just smiled.

Well, well. Wee Kathleen. Still as beautiful as ever.

I went mental, took at dive at him, slapped him right across the face. All he did was turn his face away.

Go on darlin; take another shot if it makes you feel better.

By then I was sobbing.

You bastard. Fifteen years and not as much as a fucking birthday card. I hate you. I hate you. How could you do it?

Bruce pulled me away, took me outside to where his mother was standing holding my coat and bag. His dad was still inside, apologizing to the committee. I never went back there; I'm probably banned for life. Moira was affronted; she couldn't look at me. She was walking up and down, looking up the road.

Where's that taxi? Bruce, where's that taxi got to?

Then somebody behind me said, Are you OK, Kathleen?

I turned round. Big Joe was standing there. I rounded on him. You? Who are you kiddin? You're as much to fucking . . .

But then I remembered Marie, singing in a rainbow dress with ribbons in her hair, and I shut up. The taxi came, and as it drove away, I looked back and saw them standing together, Big Joe Devlin and Mick Boyle the Bastard.

I've always wondered what they said.

Marie

I was her bridesmaid. We wore pastel-coloured dresses with matching coats, hers pink, mine blue. I've still got the photo. There we are: Bruce and his pal Ronnie, in suits and Ben Sherman shirts, and me and Kathleen in our cheap rig-outs from Grafton's. That morning we'd gone to the hairdressers, and left mortified, under lacquered curls braided with artificial blossoms.

Who took the picture? Michael. That's right, her wee brothers were waiting outside the register office, along with all the lassies from the mill.

You can't tell we're pregnant. Silly lassies, trusting our bodies and our futures to daft boys. Tam told me that it would be OK; he'd use the withdrawal method. Actually, what he said was, It's cool, I'll get off at Paisley. Paisley, the last train stop before the big city. I never liked Paisley, that's where the hospital was.

And there was me, scared to go to the doctor's for the pill in case he told my mother. I had to go anyway, for a pregnancy test. The doctor, who barely looked at me, was the same one that had been fucking up my mother's mind for years, the same one who'd stitched up my leg while my father held me tight, the same one they sent for that morning.

And I didn't even like sex. But then I knew damn all about it.

Years later, at a women's health workshop, a woman with a shaggy perm and a tie-dyed T-shirt told me the truth about the phallacy, as she called it, of the vaginal orgasm. Would it have mattered if I'd known that, when I lay down in the back of Tam's van? No. Nothing would have helped. Because I was looking for love, you see. And I picked a wee guy with a clapped-out van, a guitar his mother was paying up, and a pocketful of spliffs.

Kathleen was the only one who knew I was pregnant. I told Tam that night, after Bruce had driven her away to a honeymoon in Girvan. We were parked in a lane off the Largs road. When I told him he laid his head on the steering wheel.

For fuck's sake, Marie.

I jumped out, and walked away through the dark, tearing paper roses out of my hair.

A fortnight later I started to bleed, and I bled so much, and the pain was so bad they sent for the doctor. His sheathed fingers poked and probed, then he went away. I listened to low voices on the landing.

Miscarriage. Haemorrhage.

My mother appeared at my bedside.

You'll need to go to the hospital.

An ambulance came and they carried me out, past my father with tears on his face.

Oh, my wee lassie.

Past Michael, standing in the hall with the football pools money clutched tight in his fist, freckles standing out against his wee pale face.

Hiya Marie.

Past the neighbours,

Oh my.

My baby's body soaked into hospital sheets. A wee nurse exposed me and stood staring.

Do you think I'm supposed to keep this for Doctor to see?

Doctor arrived wearing a pinstripe suit and a flower in his buttonhole.

Spontaneous abortion.

Thinking, *I did not.*

They wheeled me along to an operating theatre. A man in a mask loomed over me.

Just a little prick, my dear.

They sent me home the next day. My father wept sentimental tears, and my mother upped her Valium. Kathleen visited. She sat with her arms folded over her stomach, saying little. One day I met Tam in the street. He took my hand.

I'm sorry, Marie. I'm so sorry.

No one else had said it. So, nothing really changed, except that Kathleen had her baby. I held her the day she was born.

Hello, precious girl.

Kathleen

The night I met Bruce, I'd been with Brian. It was the night I lost my virginity. Losing your virginity. Always makes me think you should be down on your hands and knees looking underneath the bed for it, so you can dust it off and shove it back up. That'd be handy.

Brian had been chatting me up all night in the pub. I was there with Marie; it was the night she met Tam. I'd watched him eyeing her up, but I never thought she'd be interested. I mean he was nothing to look at. Brian was dead handsome, still is. Same sexy eyes, long black lashes. I love to look at them when he's lying beside me.

He'd asked us back to a party at his mate's house. Marie said she had to get home. I knew she was hoping that Tam would make a move, and he did. Poor Marie. But she was only eighteen, and look at the life she'd had. She didn't even have any new clothes; all her wages went on keeping that house. She didn't know I knew that. Christ, it was like she was the one with no father. I think she had a loan of something of mine that night.

When she started hanging about with the band she trailed out her mother's old sewing machine and made her own clothes: wee bright-coloured frocks out of old curtains and lengths from the remnant shop, and floaty embroidered tops she wore with her jeans. And she hennaed her hair and plaited it with ribbons, years before anybody else did. She'd a style all her own; folk used to turn and look at her in the street. She was beautiful.

Anyway, that night I left her sitting with Tam and I went away with Brian. I was dead chuffed, all the lassies were daft about him, but he wanted me. There was a crowd of us, all back at that wee guy's place. What the hell was his name? I should know; he was in our class at school. We had a couple of drinks, listened to records. They were all smoking dope but I was too much of a big feartie for that. It was the same with the drink then, never touched anything stronger than beer.

Brian was kissing me, and I didn't want him to stop, but it was embarrassing with those other folk there. He took me through to the bedroom, we lay down, and . . . funny, you hear all that stuff about the first time being rotten, but it wasn't. His hands . . . He made me come with his fingers before he came into me. I don't know why I let him. I'd been out with other boys, did all that winching up against the trees in the park, but I never let them, I was always too scared, scared of what they would say about me, scared of falling pregnant. With Brian I didn't care, he was . . . is . . . God, Kathleen, you'll burn in hell.

About a month after that, Brian was gone and I was lying in a bed and breakfast in Largs with Bruce. He was worried about blood on the sheets, but there was none.

Who took your virginity? he said.

I wanted to laugh, he sounded like a complete prick.

I nearly said, Oh, Brian Cochran fucked off with it in the back pocket of his jeans, that night, the night I met you.

I didn't, though. I baffled him with science, said it was the Tampax.

But that first night Brian and me lay there for a while, cuddling and whispering.

He smiled and said, So, what do you think of my eyelashes?

I near died laughing.

He fell asleep, and I lay, just watching him. But I couldn't stay; I had a Saturday shift at seven. I got dressed, kissed Brian. He opened his beautiful eyes, said Baby, and went back to sleep. I started to walk home, all loved up, dying to see him again.

A couple of years later, I was sitting here in the kitchen with my mother. She was nursing Laura.

I asked her, Mum, why did you marry my father?

She took the bottle out the wean's mouth, and put her up on her shoulder to wind her. She looked at me as if I was daft.

I was expecting, she said.

I said, OK, but why did you go with him in the first place?

She kept on patting Laura's wee back.

Well, she said, he was a good-lookin fella and he had a nice smile, and he was a terrific dancer.

I laughed. She got all offended.

I don't know what you're laughing at. That's how most women get caught. They think a pretty face'll be enough.

I knew she wasn't just talking about Mick. And I was every bit as daft as her. She went for a nice smile and a birl about the dance floor, and I fell for long eyelashes and tricky fingers. I think she knows, but she's never said anything

Anyway, that night I was about halfway along the main street when a car drew up and a voice said, It's a bit late to be out by yourself. Do you want a lift?

I was ready to tell whoever it was to fuck off, but then he rolled down the window and I recognized him. Bruce. He'd lived round the corner from us for years, until they moved to one of the bought houses at the back of the park. He drove taxis for his dad.

I said, No, you're all right; I haven't got any money.

He smiled. I said a lift, not a taxi. C'mon, jump in; I've got to go round the scheme anyway.

So I let Bruce drive me home that night, and after that he kept turning up outside my work, until I let him take me out. Brian called me baby one more time before he fucked off to London; leaving me thinking he was away for good. I was ages before I showed Bruce how to make me come, but by then he would've done anything for me, even take somebody else's wean.

I've remembered his name. The wee guy that had the party. Tommy Dempsey. I wonder what happened to him.

Sean O'Reilly

A Fire in Hell

Yvonne was wearing her green linen dress. As she came towards him through the restaurant, with that stride of hers that had always seemed too long, she threw back her head, smiling so broadly that he had been forced to lower his eyes. She knew it would embarrass him when she took his head between her hands and kissed his hair. She was laughing, pretending she couldn't have cared less about the looks of the people at the other tables. He had not expected her to behave like this but he realized now that he had witnessed this tactic before. As soon as she had sat down, she lit a cigarette and blew the smoke into his face.

'So . . . talk to me. I'm all ears,' she said in a dramatic whisper.

As she leaned towards him, the dress fell loose across the top of her breasts. Her eyes, blue and large and too far apart in his opinion, had the moist sheen of delighted defiance. She stared giddily at his mouth until she forced him to smile and then she sat back in the chair and fanned her arrogant gaze around the room.

'I haven't had a night out in ages.'

She had trouble understanding the waiter's accent, a short bald man from Cork in a bow tie. They ordered wine and curries cooked in coconut milk. Yvonne lit the candle on the table before the man could find the matches in his pocket. There were statues of Indian deities in each corner of the restaurant; golden giants with raised jewelled arms and sleeping. He told her he didn't like them but she said that she thought they were right for the place and then seemed to forget all about it. The other tables had filled up and people were talking very loudly, he thought, with flushed faces, amazed faces and unredeemable faces. Above their heads the spicy smoke curled and unwound like dirty silk.

'There's so many people about,' Yvonne said, glancing

towards the window. The excitement in her voice troubled him and he told himself that 'tactic' was too strong a word, that she was genuinely happy and couldn't hide it. She had a right to enjoy herself like anybody else; even he couldn't manage a smile without feeling guilty. Strangers passed in the summer evening, in a rich yellow light that made their shadows stretch far away behind them.

She laughed suddenly: 'I bet you, you've been having a great time. And there's me thinking . . .'

'What?'

'Never mind.' She threw back her head, grinning.

The first sign, he thought, the sarcasm starting to show through. Cracks in the facade. She could never take anything that he did seriously. She put up with him without ever really trying to understand what was bothering him. 'My bloody head,' he would shout at her, 'my eyes, my tongue, my body, you name it.' But she would look at him as though she had already decided that he was just making excuses, that the apathy could be turned on and off.

He had come down to Dublin a month before, with a man he knew who was driving down with some racing pigeons. At the time, he had no clear plan to stay longer than a few days, in a hostel maybe, but the two of them had started drinking and a week went by and then one morning he found himself moving into a bedsit in Stoneybatter, an old shabby part of the city that sloped steeply down to the Liffey with Viking street names. Some days, he thought he was near to grasping why he had come, why he had left his wife and child without an explanation in Derry. He would try to sit still, concentrate his mind, like a hunter or a sniper with a long wait. To his disgust, he would always feel these approaches turn to nothing, a shadow on the empty road or the wind in the trees, and the dullness would settle back on the world, and the silence, and the repulsive sense that only on his knees in prayer was there any possibility of escape.

'I need space,' he had told her on the phone one night. 'Time to think just. That's all.'

'You'd think you'd be sick of that by now. I'm coming down.

Whether you like it or not. I'll stay with our Caroline's friend in Glasnevin. Do you want me to bring your Bible?' she had joked.

A pain had gone through him at hearing her mock him, an intense sordid pain in the depths of him, worse than anything he had ever known, even stripped and battered in a room where it was too bright to see your own hands protecting your face.

'Cahal,' he heard her say, 'don't just sit there and stare out that window, I'm warning you. I've had enough of that the last year.'

He turned and faced his wife. She swept the hair from her eyes and raised her eyebrows. Her nostrils were noticeably large, like two fat black teardrops.

'OK?'

He nodded. 'How's Charlotte?'

'She's not sleeping. She lies in with me.'

There was his daughter now, summoned up before him, her pale face on the pillow on his side of the bed. The sheets around her waist and her hands joined under her chin. She was moving her lips as she gazed through the darkness at the curtained window inflamed by the street light outside. A lone voice at the waterlogged corner would break out into a brief spasm of song long after the street doors were locked and the dogs had howled out their news.

'She's all right, Cahal. Don't worry about her. She talks away, making up wee stories. The other week there she said we had got her name wrong. So I asked her what it should have been but she put her finger on her lips and said she wasn't allowed to tell. She's all right.'

He probed the compassion in his wife's eyes for something he couldn't name. Was compassion the right word? Was that the only feeling he aroused in people in these days? Once, men much older had followed him out into the hills and lain beside him in ditches and abandoned cottages.

'Tell me about the letter,' she said. 'I have to be honest; I didn't understand most of it.'

He shrugged and tried to laugh. 'Neither did I. Forget about it.'

'Did you go and talk to a priest?

He shook his head. 'Forget about it.'

Pushing a trolley across the burgundy carpet, the waiter arrived with their food. Cahal wondered at the resentment he felt towards his wife as she pushed back her fringe and savoured the smells and colours of the different dishes. She was only too keen to keep the conversation on her level, afraid of losing control. There was so much he would never be able to explain to her. She lacked the patience to listen to anything that threatened her. Over her freckled shoulder he caught sight of the statues again; the strong and elegant arms were raised, outspread in some kind of dance, the golden palms lifted up, but it was hard to know what they were trying to say.

While they ate, they talked mainly about Charlotte and events in Derry. Her father was sick and a man they both knew well was in hospital after he had thrown himself off the top of a new multi-storey car park. Yvonne also told him that some men had called one night and took their time believing that he wasn't in. 'So you haven't missed anything,' she said. 'Other than me of course.' She laughed and leaned across the table towards him so that he could see down the front of her dress. Chewing a mouthful of food, she pouted playfully at the same time. Then she pushed out a sulking bottom lip. 'What's wrong my love? Aren't you pleased to see me?'

They burst out laughing together. Cahal refilled their glasses from the dripping bottle in the ice bucket; the wine was cold, sweet and cold.

'I haven't had a night out in ages,' she said again. 'Waiting on the phone to ring. Waiting on my husband to come back. Back in from the desert. Some desert though,' she added, with another nod towards the window. 'The weeping and wailing is deafening. Tell me the low-down then.'

'I don't do much.' He shrugged. 'A lot of walking mainly.'

He meant what he said. During the day he wandered the tracks in Phoenix Park, hoping to see the deer come out the trees to feed or a zebra or camel through the fence of the zoo. Lying on the grass one afternoon, he thought he heard the roar of a lion but he couldn't be sure. Or he would sit on the high steps outside the house and watch the people collect at the bus stop.

There were faces from all over the world in the area, and voices that made him try to imagine Africa or Spain or Russia and forget that he hadn't spoken to anyone that day or the last. The local drunks sometimes climbed up the steps and joined him; together they saw the cranes swinging their arms across the city like gigantic weathervanes driven round and round by secret winds. The sun cut the city up into a maze of shadow and light.

At night, he found himself drawn towards the city. He walked alongside the empty river, past the bridges with their three green eyes. The crowds in the centre attracted him more than he was able to admit. He would try to have a pint in the pubs but he felt uncomfortable and pitiable amid the crowds of youngsters drinking in packs so he would take to the streets again or a late café. It was a city of young people, of youthful moods of wild enthusiasm and desolation and violence. As the bars closed he would find a place to watch the drunken crowds as they swarmed unsteadily through the streets – dancing, screaming, exhilarated and weeping, madly determined and concussed, screaming, mesmerized, vomiting with rage and lust – like a delirious sect that preached a gospel he had never heard before.

Only the night before, he had ventured into a local bar and fell into conversation with a character by the name of Fada. He decided to tell Yvonne about him.

'He's a kind of street poet. You ask him for a poem, Yeats or Pearse or somebody, and he recites it for you. Then you give him some money. He does it well. He puts his heart into it. He makes a fortune from the tourists. He told me he was in a mental hospital and he passed the time learning off everything by heart. There's a lifetime of stories in him – mad ones, over the top ones – but they're probably all true. So we had a few drinks anyway.'

'Did you talk to him?' Yvonne asked abruptly.

'How do you mean?' Something about the question or the way she asked it annoyed him. He frowned at her and she turned away. 'Do you want me to shut up?'

'Go on,' she said, dropping her fork on the table. She lit another cigarette.

'I will. We had a few drinks and then he took me along to this party.'

'A party?'

'Exactly. In some house. Every room was crowded. Most of them were on drugs probably, the eyes bulging out of their heads like they'd just been dug up out of the grave. I was still just talking to this fella Fada for a while and then – I don't know if he took something, or it was the drink, or it was just him himself – he stands up in the room and starts ranting at people, talking away in all these different voices, men's and women's voices, some of them in Gaelic as well. I didn't know what to do. It was funny one minute, then mad stuff the next, ugly stuff.'

'Ugly? Like what?' Yvonne merely glanced at him out of the corner of her eye.

'It's hard to describe. Imagine somebody in a trance, somebody possessed. But some of it was ugly, really ugly. He was shaking. It went on for about half an hour anyway and then I decided to get him out of there. I pushed him out the front door and started walking with him then making him run, to calm him down. He was running all over the street, banging into everything, talking to everything, the street bins, parked cars, scaring the hell out of anyone going by. But he got it all out of him in the end and then he's silent for a while and then he asks me what he had been saying. That's when I noticed he was crying. There was this fear in his eyes. He was terrified, complete panic. We were sitting down by the river by this point. It was dawn. The light was all pinks and reds and the water was like milk. And Fada's asleep beside me. It was the first time everything wasn't dead, like the skin wasn't falling off everything. Like I was saying in that letter about . . .'

The words died on his tongue as if they knew they weren't wanted. Yvonne was dragging hard on the cigarette. Her face was agitated, trembling.

'He sounds like a head case.'

The words seemed to cost her an unbearable effort.

'It's just somebody I met. Yvonne, listen, it was the first time since I got out that I felt—'

'You got out a year ago,' she screamed at him above the noise of the restaurant.

The scream came as a shock to him but he didn't allow it to

show, fixing his eyes threateningly on her. After a moment, the conversations around them were resumed with greater energy.

Yvonne fought him back with her own stare but then relented for no apparent reason. She spoke quietly: 'What do you want me to say? I've come down here to see you and you're sitting there going on about some head case.'

His wife was crying, crying proudly, refusing to wipe the tears from her face.

'I'm not here for another wee visit, you know,' she went on. 'I had five years of wee visits, remember? I'm a dab hand at wee visits. So how are you getting on, Cahal? How's the form? You bearing up? How are all the other hard men doing this weather?'

'Stop it.'

'Make me,' she sneered, and he saw a milky tear drop from her chin and land in her food. 'What do you expect me to do? Pat you on the back and tell you to keep on with . . . What is it you're bloody doing down here anyway? Thinking? What's that, Cahal? What's thinking Cahal? I don't have a clue what you're talking about, you see. Or maybe I'm just stupid. This isn't the bloody road to Damascus. You can't hang about in your wee bedsit, reading your Bible, and wait to be hit by the bolt of lightning. You just get on with it. Like everybody else. That's how you change. Not by digging a big hole and jumping in.'

'It takes time. Change takes time.'

'Does it really?' She laughed bitterly. She wiped her nose and face with the back of her hand. 'I know all about change, you see, Cahal. I saw my man into jail and come out a ghost. Then I saw him sit in the house for a year looking out the window like an old woman. And I tried not to push him. And then he vanished on me, and I'm left with the memory of another ghost. And now he's sitting here telling me about the great laugh he's having with the lunatics. That's change for you. Do you think you're the only one?'

'You're lucky. I don't even have any memories left,' he told her angrily, stabbing at his chest with his finger. 'Maybe I wore them out. I don't have a memory, I don't have any feelings. I'm dead. I don't have anything . . . bloody nothing.'

Yvonne gave him a long look of repugnance, of shocking

disappointment, and mouthed his words quietly back to him: 'Bloody nothing.'

She got up and walked towards the toilets in her green dress, striding through the restaurant like she was on her way down a busy street. A few amused faces were looking in his direction. A waitress flapped a fresh white cloth in the air and he watched it float down and settle perfectly across a table. The languid shapes of smoke and steam drifted towards him. The dreaming gilded statues somehow seemed less awkward now, as though what they had been trying to say had now become serenely obvious. A woman at the next table dabbed at her forehead with a napkin. Beyond the window, three girls were jammed into a telephone box, Spanish he guessed, with their skin like warm crushed sand, their heavy heads of dark hair. The three of them were laughing. Yvonne would come back and say what? Was it the time for ultimatums?

But even as he considered these questions, he felt them moving away from him, fading uselessly away. Words and questions: love, home, daughter, wife, freedom – nothing stayed in the mind for long. A fire in hell, that's all life was. A fire that burned and burned to no avail, consuming nothing. And why now was he thinking about the view from his cell window, the bullet distance from the gravel to the scrubland to the fence, and the restless sky above, emptying and filling and breaking and streaming to no avail? On fine days he used to stand with his back to the window between 2 p.m. and 3.30 p.m. and watch his shadow move across the floor. Prison took away your shadow. The overhead lights burned it up. The day he got out his shadow was waiting for him, like a stain he had left on the wall. The truth about a thing is the shadow it casts; he said these words to himself and wondered where they had come from and whether he believed them and the girls across the street were holding on to each other they were laughing so hard.

Yvonne was away a long time. She sat down again, checked his face once and then lit another cigarette. It was immediately clear that she was granting him the time until her last drag to speak. His heart jumped at the bloody graze her lips made on the filter. Her face was drained, a looseness about the skin. He smelled perfume off her, probably in her cleavage, he thought, the fine white hair between her breasts.

He told her that he hadn't meant what he said.

'What do you think I'm doing here, Cahal? Do you have any idea at all? Do you? Look at me.'

Her eyes wouldn't let go of him.

'What's thought when it costs you everything you love?' She stubbed out the cigarette at the edge of her plate, spraying the smoke out from between her thin tensed lips. Cahal bowed his head.

'Say hello to the devil from me. I'll give your daughter a kiss.'

He left the restaurant long after she had gone, long enough to be sure she would have given up waiting for him, in case the idea had come to her on the street that she couldn't let him away so lightly, that she had more to say. He looked around and set off down a quiet side street of mainly shuttered shops. He had no desire to go back to his room. The night seemed barely present, a half-hearted shadow across the city, measly and futile. Yet the air was heavy and soiled with the smell of the rancid green pulp of the river. He spat to clear his throat and smirked to himself when it landed on the bonnet of a car; he imagined the driver stepping out of the darkness, an insult, a threat and then beating the man's head against the curb while his wife stood screaming on the other side of the street and . . .

He hurried his step to leave this image behind and soon he was on the busier streets lined with big creamy globes of light and surveillance cameras. He watched the drunken squalls of people outside the pubs and asked himself if the grinding ache he was feeling was envy or pity. Or nothing at all. Fada would be somewhere on the town that night, amid the many and the smoke and the sweat and the shadows, talking, talking from out of that fraught emaciated face and startled eyes.

Seeing those debauched terror-stricken eyes again, Cahal suddenly became afraid; he stopped dead in the street as though somebody was behind him. What am I doing here? he asked himself. Any attempt to answer would bring the buildings down around him, a merciless laughter echoing in the dust. He did not dare to mouth the name of his wife for fear that he would inflict this horror on to her. Why had he pushed her away? What had got into him?

Summoning all his strength, like those moments before a beating, he forced his mind to concentrate on some small detail of the street – the lobster-coloured brickwork under his feet, the graffiti on a shutter which read Give Freely, a plastic bag of rubbish twisted around a telephone wire overhead, an empty beach vista in a travel shop window – anything to get him through those moments where he was about to convince himself that he was possessed by evil. In a kebab shop window, in the shadowless white light, a couple were feeding themselves and staring towards him, but it was impossible to tell if their expression of squalid poignancy was a response to him shaking on the street, his hands trapped in his trouser pockets.

He ran for a while. At the entrance to an alley, he turned off the street. He put the palms of his hands against the wall, struggling with his breath. It had been years since he had had a run. At the far end of the alley, a small light showed part of a greenish fire escape. The feeling that he was going to throw up slowly began to pass. There was a pile of rubbish bags near him; he listened first for rats before he pulled down his zip and spread his legs. One palm still took his weight against the wall. His cock felt small, a poky limp stump, but he took great pleasure in pushing the piss out of him, the fine stream of it hitting the wall and bursting, the steam rising into his face. Then he heard a sound like a small groan. He reeled around, spraying piss, and saw a dark figure. It was a woman, tall, dressed in black, long-haired, leaning against the wall. Her face was in shadow but she seemed to be looking upwards. In an anguished voice, she said, Please don't stop, please. No words would come to his mouth in reply. Please, she said again. He looked down at her thighs, naked and white where she had pulled up the front of her dress. Dumbfounded, he turned back to the wall. The effort to piss again brought sweat out on his forehead. As the urine spread around his feet, he heard her groaning, and the groaning become louder, wilder, until she cried out in ecstatic pain. Then there was silence. He had nothing left in his bladder. He heard her straightening her clothes but he remained still. He was about to speak when her hands touched his hips and turned him around. She was kneeling under him. Her tongue licked the wet tip of his cock, once, twice, and then she took his cock into her mouth. He shut his eyes and gave himself over to the long powerful draws, the danger of the teeth. His cock was hard now, pushing against the roof of her mouth. The suction drew all of him into her mouth, every heartbeat and every thought in his head, leaving the darkness empty, purified, slowly emptying even of him. It wasn't long before he was ready and he came deep at the back of her throat, with a loud groan. She must have pushed him back against the wall for he slid to the ground. He felt he was pouring like a jet of black piss through the dark. He was dizzy and formless. He didn't want to open his eyes. Gradually, he began to tell himself that he was lying in his own piss in an alley. Opening one eye, he saw the fire escape at the end of the alley; in the other direction, the floodlit street was as empty as the golden palms of the gods. She had gone. His limp cock lay out across his trousers. He let his eyes close up again.

Jamie Jackson

Night of the Brown Cow

He was in his chair when I went round. I could see him through the net curtain. I knocked and waited and he called me in. There he was, hunched up, the television on, an afternoon soap playing. He turned his head slightly to see who it was, then turned back to the TV. Oh he hadn't changed much, his cocked head like a little eager bird, his small ears, still the beard. Though that was white now, not ginger.

He sat and watched the TV so I sat down and took the place in. It was the same wallpaper, same carpet, same furniture. By his arm a gold box of cigarettes, Bensons. It wouldn't have surprised me to see the three-legged cat sat curled by his feet. But it wasn't there.

After a while I became conscious of the rich smell of my perfume and I wanted to laugh. How it stood out in here, he must be able to smell it.

Then I said, 'Hello Bobbie. How are you?'

He turned as if he didn't see me, then grunted. Then went back to the TV.

I managed a smile. 'D'you fancy a cup of tea?'

He grunted again and I got up and walked to the back where the kitchen was and looked for the tea stuff. 'Not got any milk, Bobbie?' I called. 'OK, then, I'll just go and buy some.'

Out I went, up the street, round the corner, and then down again. The shop was still there, but I couldn't decide whether it was the same owner. I mean, he looked old enough, but then everyone round here did. I bought a litre of milk and ten Bensons and went back to the house. I didn't knock this time, I walked straight in.

The kettle boiled and I poured the water, waited, then pulled the tea bags out and left them on the side.

'Here you go.' I put the cup on the arm of his chair and sat back down.

He grunted something.

'Sorry?' I said.

'Three sugars.'

Yeah, I nodded. Three sugars.

He took a sip, then put it down, not taking his eyes off the TV. I drank some tea. Then he said, 'That your car outside?'

'Yeah. You like it?'

'German,' he grunted.

I took the box of Bensons out and put one in my mouth and got up and moved over for his lighter, which was by his arm. I picked it up and lit my fag, then looked down at him. He was staring past me at the soap opera.

'You want one?'

He had to look now and a greeting of kind formed in his eyes before he clutched the cigarette off me, and I went and sat down.

I thought it was time to get into it.

'How've you been then, Bobbie?'

He grunted.

'You know, I never realized how much colder it was up here. I mean, I'm only sixty miles away, but what a difference it makes, especially this time of year.'

He looked like he was going to say something. He said, 'Sssh.' And re-glued his eyes to the screen.

'Work's never brought me here, you see. Manchester mainly. Wigan, Blackpool, Southport.' I knew what I was saying and wanted to see how he'd react.

'It's not so cold,' he said.

'Maybe not to y—'

'You should know that,' he said.

I smiled but he'd turned again. 'Well I did. Do. I must've forgotten.'

He didn't say anything.

'Look,' I said. 'I've brought you something.'

I pulled it out from my coat and offered him it.

He turned, then sneered. 'What are you wearing?'

'What, my perfume?'

'That as well. That coat. I'm surprised you feel the cold in *that*.' It was like it cost him something to speak.

I did laugh now. He was right, in a way. A white fur coat, here, in this town, in this house.

He wasn't laughing though. 'What's that you're holding?'

I knew he wasn't going to like it. 'A present.'

He dragged the words out. 'A present.'

'Yeah.' I laughed, but more for myself.

He took some puffs on the Benson.

'My latest CD.'

He sneered again, then turned back to the TV.

I drank some more tea, then said, 'Shall I put it on?'

'Do what you like. It's finished.'

He was talking about the soap. I looked for the stereo; all I saw was a record player.

'No CD player Bobbie?'

He brought another cigarette out from the box. I had the lighter. For a moment I thought he was going to go without, but I knew better. He looked at me and motioned his head and I stood up and handed it to him.

'No CD player Bobbie?' I repeated.

He lit the Benson and looked at me and hissed, 'No fucking CD player.'

I sat back down and looked at the CD where it lay on the sofa. The picture of me, pushing forty, in leopard-skin fur, too-red lipstick. My latest collection, *Cat on a Northern Town Roof*. Big in Manchester and not much place else.

'I can't play it then,' I said quietly.

He smoked some more, then picked up the remote control and flicked through the channels. He did it twice, then turned the sound off and put the remote down and looked at me.

'What d'you want?' he spat.

I smiled again, thinly. 'I thought you'd never ask...' He waited. 'Well, you know, I wanted to see you. Know how you are. It's been a long time.'

He made a little laugh at that.

I said, 'Nineteen years, Bob.'

'Bobbie. Twenty-one years.'

It surprised me, this acknowledgement, but then a shiver ran through me. It was like he'd been expecting me, all this time. Like he'd not moved from the chair since I'd last seen him.

'Yeah, I suppose you're right.' I repeated the figure softly to myself.

''So . . . how've you been?''

He sneered.

'That's good to hear,' I said, then immediately regretted it. But he didn't react. 'I just . . . I thought you might want to see me after all this time. That's all.'

He nodded, he didn't look at me.

Well, he was how I expected. But I'd come here to do what I'd decided so I got on with it.

'D'you know what happened to me? When I moved down there. Well, in a way you were right. I had it rough. Everyone bullshitting me and trying to get me to sleep with them or do dodgy gigs for no money. But I met this guy, see. Met him, funnily enough at the dodgiest gig I did. I was desperate for money, was even considering stripping. Something stupid like that. But then I met Mike. What he was doing there that night, God knows. But we got talking. I thought it was the usual patter, but it wasn't. Luckiest night of my life. Well, apart from—'

He got up then, and I noticed his leg for the first time. I'd clean forgotten it! It was false, the left one. He'd fallen from a balcony while on holiday, drunk. How he'd survived God only knew. It was one of the stories he told me, when I first met him. How he'd made me laugh then. Fifty-two years old and bright as a button. Full of scorn and laughing. His little head cocked to one side as we sat at the bar and he tore anything and everything apart. Made me see the truth behind the lie. Or as he liked to say, 'The lie behind the truth.'

He hobbled to the back by the sink and reached for the cupboard. It was difficult for him but he managed to bring the bottle down and grab some glasses and stay on his feet.

Back he came with the kit, hobbling along, eyes staring ahead. He reached his chair and fell into it, passing the bottle and glasses into one hand. He puffed a little, then laid the glasses on the arm, unscrewed the vodka and poured.

He held a glass out without looking at me, then picked his up and drank.

'No ice,' he grunted.

'That's fine,' I said.

It was too early for me, but I drank. He drained his glass down and poured some more, then brought it back up to his mouth. I clutched on to mine and sipped. I lit another Benson.

'I have to keep mine by me,' he said.

I looked up. 'Eh?'

'My fags. Otherwise he robs them.'

I looked at the gold box. Then said, 'Who?'

'Him. Eric. My son.' He drained his glass and poured some more.

I got hold of what he was saying. 'He steals from you then? Your son.'

'Oh yes. All the time.'

'Dear me,' I said, quietly.

'You're right,' he grunted. '*Dear me.* I can't get around you see. Not really. So he takes advantage like, the little bastard.'

'Great.'

He looked at me then. 'You're right. Again. *Great.*'

I offered him a Benson and he nodded so I stood up and passed it over. I was waiting for the booze to kick in and so was he.

'How old's your son?'

I sat down.

'Seventeen.'

I looked at Bobbie then. He was now at least seventy, seventy-one. That was a long time to be him, I thought. Still, it was probably a long time to be anyone.

'Are you married?' I blurted out.

'Fucking joking, aren't you,' he hissed. He drained his glass and offered me a top-up. Then he poured himself some more. He drank, then picked up the Benson I'd given him and leaned over for a light, but I still had to stand up to reach him. As it flamed I saw his bird-eyes looking up at me, smeared with glee.

'So, you really made it then.'

The scorn was there.

'Not really. Well. You know.'

He grunted, then leaned forward and picked his crutch up, examined it, then put it down on the other side of him.

'I've seen you on the TV.'

I couldn't deny it.

'Pat Kane, eh.' He made the little laughing sound again. An echo from the years. 'Your idea or,' he worked a sneer up, 'Mike?'

I giggled. I had to. How right he was. And what else did I expect?

'That's right. Pat Kane. I wanted to use Elsie Tanner or Diana Dors or—'

'What about Cass?'

He stared, waiting.

'Doesn't sound right.'

'It was all right for us. Wasn't it?'

'Yeah. But that was here.' I laughed. 'Down there . . .'

'Down there,' he hissed. 'Manchester.'

The vodka warmed me, so I told him softly, 'That's right, Manchester.'

'How much do you earn exactly?' His eyes glittered and I wondered how I'd forgotten them. Then, I wondered why it was all, all of it, so familiar. 'Well?'

I stood up and offered him my glass. 'Enough, Bobbie. Look at the car.'

He poured. 'Enough, eh? For Manchester. Pat Kane!'

I sat back down. 'Listen, I don't know what your problem is. All right?'

His eyes glittered, he stuck his tongue out.

'Ooh-ooh, "I don't know what your problem is,"' he mimicked. 'How right you are. You talking to yourself?'

He shuddered a little then and pulled his dressing gown closer. 'Well Cassie,' he said. '*One* of us made it. Eh?'

'Look. I came here to say hello and be friendly and to say sorry that this is the first time. In so long. At least I'm here.'

He tried a grin. 'You know you're right.' He examined each word as it came. 'How right you are.'

'At least I came,' I repeated.

He nodded, then finished his drink and picked up the bottle.

'But enough of this; I fancy a small drink more. Go to the corner shop will you. Quarter bottle.'

I shook my head and smiled.

'What d'you mean?' he hissed.

'Look, Bobbie.'

I did it then. I reached inside my fur and pulled out a bottle. And his eyes glittered and he grunted, 'Smirnoff.'

I poured us both a large drink and said, 'When was the last time you played?'

The eyes, the ears, the beard now white.

'This morning,' he said. 'Every morning.' He drank. 'Every fucking morning.'

I couldn't believe it. 'You're joking.'

The door opened and two lads came in. They paused, and for a moment everything was quiet.

Then the first one said, 'All right, Dad,' and looked at me.

'Cassie,' I said. 'You must be Eric.' He was tall and lanky and well dressed.

'Nice to meet you.' The second lad was looking at me like he recognized me. Either that or it was my cleavage.

Again there was a moment of wavering, everyone unsure. Then the two of them disappeared upstairs.

I looked at Bobbie.

'That's my boy,' he said. Then laughed. 'Dirt, words. Put 'em together. What else?'

'Breath,' I said, and we managed a good laugh.

Something seemed to settle down in his eyes then and he made an effort. 'Listen, I may be a bit drunk now, but . . .' Then he stopped and looked down into his glass and a sly look came to his mouth. 'In fact . . .' He put his glass down and with much wheezing slowly struggled to his feet. I watched and wanted to help. But there was no way, not Bobbie.

Up he got and I handed him the crutch. He gazed at me and swayed. 'Cass and Bobbie, "The Horseshoes". What a fucker. Did you dream that up or what?'

I shook my head, feeling relief for the first time.

He grunted, then started up the stairs. I watched him slowly disappearing and wondered if it was still the same up there. It had to be, I knew that. But I wondered whether that would seem all too familiar as well.

I heard him overhead. The same bedroom then. When he'd bought this place I could never believe it. To buy your own home! All cash. All paid up. I thought that was great.

I got up and poured some more vodka and drank it. Bobbie, I thought. He used to spend money to insulate himself from the stuff. I realized that now. It had no power if he got rid of it quick. He could defy it then. And when he bought this place it was a sure sign. To me, anyway.

Bobbie. The fiddler. Cass and Bobbie. I loved it. Seventeen-year-old and local celebrity. How we played together! My parents didn't like it. Who would? Who did? Apart from the people who came. How strange we were, to us, to them. In this town. God I must've been messed up. I knew it as well, at the time, as it was happening. Still, look at me now.

I supped some more and felt another wave of relief. There was a sound and I looked up, at the staircase. Clump clump. Clump clump. Bobbie was coming back.

I saw the foot and ankle of one leg and then the crutch. I saw knee and thigh and more of the crutch. Then I saw all of the good leg and the stump of the bad one. He'd taken the false leg off. The leg had a black stocking on it and the stump had a cut-off black stocking on it, replete with garter. And the stockings were attached to a blue suspender belt and he was naked underneath the red leather skirt he was now wearing. I saw a shrivelled ball and the tiny eye of a penis. And his face was rouged and the lipstick he'd selected was worse than mine on the CD cover.

Down he came. Now I was grateful for the vodka. Either the stuff we'd drunk had gone to his head more than I'd noticed, or he had a supply up there because he was gone. He slipped once, but you could tell he'd done the stairs many times before in this state. He let out a slow belch and flopped down in his chair and looked at me.

All I could think of saying was, 'Jesus Bob, your son,' then immediately felt how old it sounded.

From under the cushion of his chair he pulled out a ginger

wig. It was long like a doll's and he put it on. I should've laughed I know, but I couldn't.

He started in: 'You know what?'

He waited and I drank some more, not taking my eyes off him.

'Go on then,' I said.

'You know what? I can never understand . . .' He picked his glass up from where it lay on the arm of the chair and drained it. Except it was empty. 'Eric!' he yelled. 'ERIC! YOU BEEN AT MY VODKA YOU LITTLE BASTARD!' Then he looked at me and burst out laughing. 'He'd rob the piss from your penis if he could.' He pulled the flap of the skirt up and showed me. 'That's right. Even from mine. But it's all right, you don't have to worry, do you?'

'Why's that then Bob?'

'Because you haven't got one, have you? A prick, I mean. A prick Pat. Pat's prick. Maybe that's what we should've called ourselves, "Pat's Prick". That would've got 'em. Pat. Patty. Pat Pat! Pat Kane. Jesus, was your friend, *Mike*, taking the piss when he thought that up?' And he burst out laughing again, the sound I knew well.

'The Horse fucking shoes. Eh? What d'you think? I've still got it. Haven't I? Oh Pat. Say I have. Oh Pat Patty Pat. Say I have.' He started wailing then, but he wasn't crying, not yet. He cocked a bird-eye at me. 'Go on then. Go get it.'

He adjusted the wig and pulled the skirt down and stuck his glass out and though he never needed it, I poured some. He threw it back into his head and closed his eyes a little. 'But it is nice, isn't it? Oh but it is. What is a lady to do?' He opened them. 'Go on then, go get it.'

'What?'

'My fiddle of course. Get the fucking fiddle and then we can all get fiddling.'

I stood up and headed for the stairs.

He said, 'No, you silly cow,' and burst with the laugh again.

'You what!' I reared up.

'My fiddle. You daft cow, Pat. Get it?!' He was beside himself now, he nearly slipped off the chair, but he recovered. 'My fiddle, cow-Patsy. It's there, underneath. Where you've been sat all the time!'

I reached underneath and felt for it and pulled it out. It looked like the same one of course, but I couldn't be sure. I handed it to him. 'Now what we're going to do, you and I, is a performance. Oh yes. For old times sake. OK.'

What else could I do? But I was drunk enough anyway, and well without the outfit and this, the reunion would never have been complete.

'Remember at the Brown Cow. The first time, eh?'

I nodded and giggled. 'Sure I do, Bob.'

'I turned up with me fiddle, like this, and that was nearly that, wasn't it? There nearly never was a Cass and Bobbie. Nearly never "The Horseshoes".' He hiccuped and scratched out some sour notes. 'And what a shame that would've been, eh? Where would the two of us be, now? If it wasn't for that.'

He tried to get to his feet but he must've forgotten that his leg was off and he only had the stump. Because he couldn't do it and he fell back into the chair.

I laughed. Maybe it was nervousness, maybe it was the vodka. It was probably, though, because it was funny. Only that. I mean, it was sad as well, the whole thing. Sad and funny, it just depended.

'Come on,' he was saying. 'Come on. It's not the same if we're not standing.'

'Bobbie, you can't stand, can you sweetheart. Not without your leg on.'

'I know that, you daft cow, how drunk d'you think I am? But it's the Brown Cow. Remember?'

Oh yeah, I remembered that. Turning up for the gig dressed like that was one thing, but taking his leg off near the end of the show, pissed up, was another. People didn't like it. Me, I didn't mind. It was just Bob, you know. I'd seen him in worse states. But I didn't mind. He was good to me, and good for me. He helped me to grow up, become a woman, learn to cope. Adjust. And you know, I couldn't blame the crowd that night. A man dressed like a bird they could just about handle. But seeing his stump with stocking and suspenders and his bare arse. Well.

There was no way. He nearly got the shit kicked out of him, falling around all over the stage with that thing out on display. They couldn't handle that. That wasn't why they were there. They just wanted to drink and forget. Not have to face something like that. Glasses were thrown and there's him laughing and bawling and there's me telling them all to fuck off. Bastards. My parents as well. When they found out, Jesus.

'Come on then, get us up on me feet.'

I stood up and wobbled a little myself, then grabbed him up and we both started laughing.

'How the hell you going to stand?'

'I'll lean. That's what I'll fucking do, I'll lean. Take me over.'

He meant to the wall by the TV, which was still on though the sound was down. He was panting and I was close enough to smell breath and age. Up this close his skin was mottled red beneath the white whiskers and I felt a little sick, I have to say.

So we moved over there and we must've looked quite a state. I got him to the wall and in trying to prop him up, lean him against it, I had to slam him hard. But he just giggled, eyes glittering.

'Go on then,' he said. 'Pass me the fucking fiddle.'

I left him and took the steps over to the chair where the old instrument was laid. And of course it happened: he slid slowly, like in a cartoon or something, down to the floor, and somehow the suspender snapped and the stocking came off his stump, and he looked so small now, down there.

'Get us up then.' He giggled.

'OK Bob. OK.'

He was shrivelled but still heavy, deadweight almost, but I did it. There he was facing me, close, and slowly he brought his hand up.

'You're not drinking no more.'

'You daft cow. Fiddle.'

I shook my head and had to laugh and handed it to him.

'For one night and one night only, "The Horseshoes",' he said, then belched. 'Are you ready,' he said. 'Well are you?'

I nodded and stepped back.

He started fiddling wildly and I wondered what the hell he

was playing. What a noise it was, but gradually it started to ease down and a low bass sound that was a melody started to form and it affected me. He always could play it like it was part of him, like it was the way he breathed, how he managed to do the deal with himself each day. His eyes glittered and his foot stomped as he leaned there against the wall, the mute TV playing alongside. And then I recognized the tune, the one we always closed the show with. Or, like the night of the Brown Cow, tried to.

I looked at him and grinned and started belting out in my rough, Pat Kane voice,

'God save our gracious Queen
Long live our noble Queen
God save our Queen'

And there Bobbie was, fiddling away like a madman, I could feel the smoke and beer of those nights years ago, people whooping and calling, charmed by the strange energy coming from the stage.

And I came back in, right as his virtuoso arm faded the solo back to the low bass,

'Send her victorious
Happy and glorious
Long to reign over us
God save the Queen'

We were making quite a noise, but it had to be a good sound, didn't it? I mean we were enjoying ourselves after all. And he still looked kind of good in the skirt and the wig, especially without the leg – for some reason it was all the better.

'Dad. DAD!'

I turned and there he was, the son, with his friend.

'DAD!'

But Bobbie didn't stop, it egged him on.

'DAD! FOR FUCK'S SAKE!'

I looked at him and his friend, who was trying not to laugh.

'Fuck's sake!' Eric said.

But it got me mad. I loved that bloke in my own way, I had to. So I said, 'Oh come on, Eric! He's your dad. Without him you wouldn't be here. You understand me. You're his son. Don't tell me you haven't seen it before.'

He looked at me yelling at him over his dad's fiddling.

'Of course I've seen it before, you slag,' he hissed. 'And I know who you are and what you did to him. It's still fucking embarrassing and it's got fuck all to do with you!'

I smiled slowly, then winked at his friend, who was taking Bobbie and my breasts in with some trouble.

The fiddling stopped and Bobbie yelled, 'Of course he's seen it all before.' His eyes glittered. 'He knows all about me and you and the Brown fucking Cow. Who doesn't round here!'

He dropped the fiddle and bow to the floor.

'What he doesn't know is that's the last fucking time I play that piece of shit, that's for sure! Right, son. And he doesn't know why, either!'

He waited and we watched.

Then he started in again. 'I'll tell you what he doesn't realize, what no one does. I'm dying. FUCKING DYING!'

It was a sharp blow. I was surprised how much it got me.

I moved towards him. 'What's wrong with you, Bobbie? Oh Bob, why didn't you tell me?'

'Eh!' he yelled. 'You what?'

'What's wrong with you, sweetheart? You should've told me.'

His eyes raged now, he could hardly believe it. 'Wrong with me? Fucking wrong with me? There's nothing wrong with me, you daft cow. I'm not ill. Fuck's sake. It's my age, can't you see? I'm dying. Fucking dying. DO YOU UNDERSTAND THAT? My age. I'm old! It's old fucking age!'

He closed his eyes and then opened them and looked and hissed, 'Can no fucker understand that?'

Lavinia Greenlaw

Pollen

Dear Zed

How can you send me bloody flowers? It may be twenty years, but have you completely forgotten? That morning we walked home after our night in the corn field I wasn't crying with joy, you know. While you skipped along the path singing, I know I should have felt like a princess for apparently making you so happy, our first time and all that, but I could hardly fight my way past all that cow parsley or whatever it was. I could hardly breathe.

No, I won't have lunch with you. I know what I need to know about your career, the lovely wife, the no-doubt beautiful children and I'm glad for you, but no. Besides which, it's bloody summer and all I want to do is stay sealed inside my flat, my office or my car. I don't want you to meet Adam, ever, but do you know, if I told him I was going to have lunch with a man who broke my bloody heart twenty years ago in the space of just six months, whose face won't stop popping up in the papers, whose trumpet playing won't stop spilling out of speakers, whose name still makes me blush, he would help me choose what to wear and send me off with a kiss. He's taking me to Iceland for the weekend, and I can't bloody wait.

Lilies, for God's sake – grown-up flowers. Do you know how vicious they are? Apart from looking entirely unreal. Try looking inside one. I did, till the sneezing got too much. The petals are far too perfect and then there are those huge stamens, quite obscene, plastered with bright orange sticky grains of pollen. Pure poison for someone like me.

So flourish and prosper and all that, but no lunch, no. You make me feel old, Zed.

Flora

Dear Flora

You didn't sneeze or wheeze as long as we lay in the corn. Have you not found another cure by now?

Zed

So it's Zacharius, the great conciliator!

You never would say what Zed stood for. After you'd gone, I thought it must have been an affectation, and that your real name must be Colin or Gary or Brian (which was my favourite) but back then I wanted to believe everything about you was beautiful and true. I have tried. I've tried beeswax, homeopathy and prayer. So no more flowers, especially not two bunches in the same day. This time my assistant Sophie asked what the occasion was and everyone thinks I'm pregnant or something. At my age. So I wish you hadn't sent the English country garden. Our reception area now looks like a cross between a funeral parlour and a wedding marquee. I have to take a client to lunch, and my eyes feel as if someone's poked them with stinging nettles so I can't get my lenses in.

Flora

Dear Flora

When did you get lenses? I loved your glasses. What else is new?

Zed

Dear Zeppelin

Yes, as in a lead balloon. My glasses, that you now claim to have found so alluring, steam up in cold weather, get streaked with rain and slip down my sweaty nose in summer. They sit between me and the world. Why do you think I hid them from you at first?

Do you know what else happened that night? I had my glasses in my jacket pocket and we rolled on them. When you left me at the top of the hill, to get to your band practice, I couldn't see a thing. I ran to catch a bus, only it wasn't. It was a bus shelter. I could just make out a grey-green shape down by the station, the same colour as the local bus, and I ran. When I got near enough to see what it was, I also saw a queue of people staring at me so I had to keep running, to pretend that was all I was doing, a girl in a stained dress with a love bite on her neck and straw in her hair, out on a bloody jog.

Orchids in a box, like diamonds. Now they think it's a lover. Stop.

> Flora

Dear Flora

What a charming story. Why did you not tell me before? I remember your dress, your hair (my bite). You were beautiful. Those people must have thought the corn field had gathered itself up and run. I felt like a god emerging from a grove of oaks with the loveliest maiden. Such heat.

> Zed

Dear Zeus

What will you 'remember' next? A thunderbolt? I was no nymph and there's nothing charming about hay fever or short sight. When I got to my lunch meeting, the maître d' had to guide me to the table while I mopped my eyes and blew my snotty nose. I had to ask that client to order for me and as for when it came to finding the loo . . . I'm tired of being thought of as vague or aloof, of flagging down taxis that aren't for hire, of falling over roadworks and into potholes, and since you've been away, this city has become nothing but.

> Flora

Dear Flora

Goddess of the garden. How was Iceland? Could you breathe? We make our own atmosphere. Still here.

> Zed

Dear Zeno

Iceland was heavenly. Your persistent little pot of violets is causing more scandal, not least because I have kept it in the office, sort of, I mean outside the window. Go home.

> Flora

Dear Flora

I'm home. I spent the morning lying under a plane tree watching it let go of fluffy wads of blossom that floated slowly away. If you had been there, your poor body would have erupted. Is there really no pleasure in it?
        Zed

Dear Zola

When I was a child, I used to think that seeds caught under my skin, behind my eyes and in my nose and lungs, and that I was about to burst into flower. No pleasure. I am tired, blonde (to hide the grey) and almost forty years old. I love my husband and I have a life in which I can breathe. You have told me nothing, just sent me a garden because you wanted to. Nothing for twenty years and then, of all things, flowers. This is not about me, though, is it?
        Flora

Dear, Dear Flora

If you want to know, why not lunch? I'm back next week.
        Zed

Dear Zee

Isn't that what they must call you over there? The herbs and evergreens have proved harmless, so thank you. The box sits well on my window sill and Sophie waters them without being asked. She fusses over them, picking and polishing, and peering over my shoulder. I have never been so interesting.
        Flora

Dear Flora

I asked you to lunch again. Please. The chillis are decorative rather than culinary.
        Zed

Dear Zeuxis

Indeed. I was hardly going to rip them off the stem and chew. OK, lunch.
        Flora

Dear only Flora

Next week, I am going to show you a photo of my wife. I fell in love with her because she looked like you, long brown hair, pale skin, weak eyes. Is that so bad? In our ten years together, I have watched her lines deepen and her features set. She has white hairs now among the dark and cuts it to just below her ears. She is more and more beautiful, as if becoming clear, whereas I have only softened and blurred. Through her, though, I have followed you. I still know you. So we can have lunch, no?

Zed

Dear Zed

Just Zed. Let us lay our loved ones on the table like gauntlets. They can defend our honour while we eat. We don't actually know each other at all so God knows we'll need them.

I am curious, but not in need, and there is no room left on the window sill so the orange tree has gone out in Reception. It's a silly glass atrium, full of trees and running water, light and sky, but you would never for one moment think yourself outside. I rather like it. So there! We will meet only indoors, with air-conditioning, and don't bring your bloody trumpet.

Flora

Dear Flora

The flowers are because I wanted you to do more than remember, to feel. I have never felt as much since. Better than this pigeon post alone and better, yes, than turning up again too soon. Last night, when I played, I felt like the west wind, as if I could fly across half the earth and reach you. Tomorrow, I will. Can you hear me?

Zed

Dear Zephyr

First of all, I was late. I didn't have my eyes in and couldn't find a cab, and was trying to figure out bus times when some kid asked his mum, 'Why's that woman sniffing the timetable?' I felt shabby and mad. Then, on the bus, some show-off adolescent asked why I was wearing sunglasses. 'You used to be a film star or something?' 'No, a spy.' I don't know why I said it. He looked lost. 'Anyone I'd have heard of?' 'No, a spy. A famous spy.' I think he actually believed me because then he asked, 'What was your name then?' And I was ahead: 'Code name you mean? Hope.' 'Hope?' 'Blind Hope.' He didn't laugh, just sat there, turning this over in his mind, finally coming up with, 'How can you be a spy if you can't see?' I batted it right back. 'How can I be a spy if I am famous?'

Are you laughing? I thought it would amuse you. I wanted, I don't know, to arrive at the restaurant with something to amuse you. In our six months together, I hardly dared speak. Just watched you and wanted you and listened and thought if I say something that assumes anything, it won't be true. Because we never formally declared ourselves as an item, just fell into place after the corn field. We neither began nor ended. Not properly. Zed Starr and Flora Hope are . . . what?

I found the restaurant. Not what I expected one of those Soho doorways to lead to. One minute you're standing among puddles of God-knows-what, and the next it's all beech and white leather and halogen lights. There were lovely young things in businesslike aprons and black trousers buzzing around carrying vast plates of next to nothing, and trays of lurid drinks. I couldn't help but peer and nearly knocked one lot flying.

That was when you turned round. I already knew it was you, by your back. I had got out my glasses so as to find you, and you're right, you are a bit blurred, round the middle anyway, and in the folds of your neck, but your shoulders are the same. Winged. That was a joke. It was shocking though, to me, that I should know you from behind at five yards through my cracked old glasses after all this time. The same sleepiness and tension. I thought you might have your eyes closed or your fists clenched, or both.

So. I was there and I saw you and moved forward at the same time as another waiter dashed past. Crash. I was down on my knees, saying sorry and picking up bits of plate and food while scrabbling around for my glasses when you saw me, didn't you? I know because I caught you in the mirror, not in great detail I have to admit but I know the look: bored and even a little disgusted. I am of that age when a man's face empties as he meets my eyes. So.

So Zed, I turned tail. Go home, love the lovely wife, cover her in flowers. Sophie, by the way, has resigned. She says she is moving back to the country. I had no idea she was that sort. I can't guarantee that the window sill garden will survive her absence but while it's still here I will enjoy it. I will keep the windows closed and sit and look, and when it all yellows and dies I'll just turn back to my desk again. Just like that.

Flora

Dear Flora

I was late, too. Even later. You didn't see me in the restaurant, I wasn't there, but I saw you, running from the doorway and into a cab. You are softer and fairer, but I know how you move, how you hold your head and push away your hair and wipe your eyes, how your mouth is always a little open, as if to let out those flowers. It was you, wasn't it?

Zed

Patrick Clinton

The Party

Go softly, without a sound
Slip through the curtain
Out of the living room and into the garden
Before anyone notices you're not around.

Outside and alone
The garden is once again your own.
No one ventures outside in the dark,
        while the party's in full swing.
The music, the conversation and the dancing

Keeps everyone occupied, so that when you return
It's as if you'd never gone,
And in a sense this is true,
Since the company always possesses a part of you.

And after the living room lights are switched off
And everyone has gone home,
Stay for a while and observe
How quiet the whole house has become.

Fiona Ritchie Walker

Cragside

We pretend its normal, picnicking
to National Trust standards,
pies and peaches, plus
a plastic-backed rug

but when the other tables
are deserted, we send the kids
scuttling to find pine cones,
twigs, anything that will burn.

When the warden catches us
by the car boot, stashing
sticks by the picnic box,
I want to scream

this is the real countryside,
no money, and a dead fire
when we get home.

The Price of Gutted Herring

She found it while searching for traffic news,
risking taking her eyes off the road
to drift between stations, would remember
the next morning that somewhere
between Five Lane Ends and Old Man's Bottom
Newcastle waned and Scotland conquered again.

A cheery voice told of upturned hay loads in Carmyllie,
broken lights in Bearsden and a main road closed
in Kirkintilloch, while she was heading to Catton
and Corbridge and queues on the Western Bypass

but for now, she was pulled in where the signal was strong,
head in hands, listening to the price of gutted herring
and catches unloaded everywhere north and west of there

on cobbled harbours glistening with fish scales,
where men with mobile phones and lilting voices
bid and bid again for cod and mackerel

and all the spoils of the sea that she remembered
miles inland, licking salt tears from fingers,
starting up the engine, trying to keep tuned in until
the voice faded and Radio Newcastle took over again.

Douglas A. Martin

You Stripped Bare

I was trying to wash you away, walk you off in the lowering night lights. The restaurants would get brighter and warmer the longer I'd walk. I knew I wasn't going to be walking over later to bed down with you. This I knew. I stayed at home as long as I could, until I felt the need to get out for a walk, to get some air.

I would look over my shoulder. I knew I'd seen his face before, one night or another on this very street. It was helping me linger over being out.

I thought when you were away in that other city that you might just realize how much you needed to speak to me, that you might feel like you still needed to see me, knock on my little wood door, how much this touch would bring this night to a quicker close.

You'd show up like you'd never really left, but you'd be now somehow even brighter, in all your blues and purples.

My hand could go out to your soft hat of lilacs, but it doesn't. We aren't supposed to be touching.

For a time, I think it doesn't matter. I think I've found your dark twin, this bachelor, in the one restaurant open late. I circle even in the rain, stand at the end of the street, hoping to see him leaving work or walking by in the night.

Instead there's the driver from the limo service, who backs up a white stretch for me to get in. He's between clients, after a wedding party, or allowed to use the car whenever he wants, between his calls, however he chooses between his drives. Nights like these in the rain may be the only reason he took the job, to have some better-looking excuse for circling the blocks.

The driver motions with his head, dry inside, the tinted

window he rolls down, recedes back inside behind, back against the headrest. There's all this room, the love gasoline. There has already been once or twice, in the front there beside him, while he held a white Kleenex over me, jerking up and down over the road swiftly, tightly holding on with one hand while saying how much he wished I had a place where I could fuck him, where he could let me fuck him, since I said I liked to fuck.

I am still wishing there was no need for a retreat so steadily from you. At the end of a night, I used to walk over to you.

You drape open your jacket, inviting me out to dinner.

I'm ready to go. Just let me lock up against your solid chest and all these weeks that have gone unspoken. We won't mention it, the way my knees are still nice and hoping. We won't bring up yet the subject of upstairs and bed. I finished dressing and descended. I met you down on the street. You wanted to know how I'd been keeping myself, what I'd been up to, and I didn't say. I wouldn't admit the man in the lot where cars are left parked behind that fence all night, how he unzipped after he followed me, tracked behind, over into a corner the concrete had made. Too afraid of being arrested, he brought nothing to completion.

There was this and nothing more.

There is you with your stories of dances and movies, plays and wherever you wanted to go. It's up to you, none of my business how you've taken to spending your time now, looking for better material with which to potentially mate. I tell the men in the car lot, no. No. I have nowhere for us to go, nowhere to take them. I listen to their wistful maybe some other times, their low whistles, their catcalls, their no problems.

You and I still aren't touching. Night after night there is this probability, this attempt at resistance, as the clock strokes its hands around later and later, and in a restaurant up the street, where you and I retreat, to catch back up, there are these words that can be so easily misconstrued as meaning whatever I'd like them to, to saying there can still be an even later for us. I may read too much into every little detail.

I try to be more spare with my wishful thinking.

It can be only the grasping at straws of your hair.

I catch a look in the eye of the bachelor I've decided will stand in for you. He might be more tender, more absorbing. I think he might be ready for me, to take me, after you're done. He keeps me busy looking for him, hunting him out in occupation. One night he follows me up the street around the corner from the restaurant he works in, acts as if he's gone out to smoke, to take a break for a cigarette.

I turned the corner up the street. He followed me with his cigarette in his hand and then mouth. His sweater was green, in that dark light, your twin almost, the focus of something like a soft moss, near a sea you loved.

The engaged couples come for the weekend to my neighbourhood, for the new restaurants on all the old corners, while your dark twin paces himself picking up dishes at the cluttered tables.

You are undoubtably thinking how good it was to be free, how unaccountable you felt as you crossed water on a train over a bridge. You'd send a postcard, want to see me whenever you got back.

In your best man's voice, you'd accuse me of thinking you were bull-like that night.

Swan, swan, swan, I think.

In a drizzle, we walk up the street to hold onto china.

I made us miss the movie on purpose. I had intent. What was playing there was an inner city drama with subtitles. You'd watch it. What I wanted was to take you back to the bed, up the stairs behind my little wooden door. You must know. I can't say any more. How many times could one tell another he wanted to take him to bed? We were verging on the domestic drama, and we wouldn't want that ever, now would we.

What I settled for was let's go back and play a game, chess. We'd play by your rules. I allowed. You must know how much I ultimately had in this position. Here was my milky way. You were all dry pistons.

I offered you the towel, for your neck and head, because of the rain. It was that season.

Tricking every night was a sign of despair, you read to me from Anne Carson, and I as always paraphrased, just slightly, after I decked you out in jewels from the green box: a string necklace of cut glass, transparent pearls, a bracelet on a wire and an opal brooch.

Now look at yourself in the mirror.

It caught the overhead light in the room, making you glint all over with it, like seeds lit up.

I rearranged myself just for you, so you wouldn't see just how much I wanted you, would like to just insist on you.

Here, have a seat in all your finery on the old folded up futon we could easily collapse down into a bed. It's from a movie. Ready, and set.

I stand there trying to deny this one moment and another.

Forget, please, now, all that talk of the men who twined like you in the dark.

I'm trying to tell you I've sunk for you, would let you be the fairest one, the won one.

You're the engagement tonight, groomed with all that's left unspoken.

Outside this story you're reading, the cars are bleating plaintive horns. The drunks are driving by and shooting off mouths out the windows. Any minute now they'll start screaming louder and louder. I know.

I roll over here every night.

Up against your chest, I can hear your heart beat inside. We would be strong. We would still be just boys. You said you didn't want to see me any more. I didn't believe you. You no longer wanted to be sexual. I didn't believe you. It had never been that important to you. I didn't know how to answer.

You could care less what was in my pants.

I go looking, always, for someone to keep me from thinking about this frustrated exchange, noticing you aren't there any more, how quiet my bed has become. It will stay that way.

The bachelor, your dark twin, makes me stop and turn one night he looks so much like you. I am not expecting it. He comes back around the corner for me like you won't. He follows me into the fluorescence of the green grocery. We look at each other and drink together, his eyes almost hidden by the black hat he wears pulled so low. I close the door. This close, he doesn't look that much like you at all.

Outside, the men loom.

Up in my room, you are wearing a necklace of synapses.

You are going to make a cast of our bodies pressed together. In some lights, you still want me, but won't just let yourself have me. It has to mean something. It has to mean even more for you.

Inside, I am crashing against your chest. I have been trying to take away all those potentially garish layers, but then I know how I'd look, naked in the longing, left with little.

You're grey sweat trunks show how clearly you are excited. You're wearing nothing else to bed. We're going to sleep together.

Two boys like us are coming together. We are holding it in.

Outside the window, the limo has passed by to go pick up someone else, is circling all his bases.

I was scared off, too, my heart racing.

One night there was the man in the park near the bridge of the highway, after nobody should have been there. There were those couple of wet benches, the dark bulk of the planted trees. He was there another night on the end of that same bench. He told me to get lost, or he'd shoot me, if I got any closer, he was going to shoot me. He was not playing with me. Get lost.

I'm not messing with him.

He's not playing. Get lost.

He warned me again as he began to rise in the dark.

That night nine shots rang out, that night in my bed.

What I needed was this silence, before our next step is proceeding to touch.

He is turning off the lights, closing up the restaurant. I'd just wait. He might want. He's leaning behind the counter, and then we were both out there on the streets, turning the same corner. He was continuing to smoke, pacing, making small crunching circles on the side of the restaurant, perhaps wrestling with something.

You were out of town, still.

In the City of Brotherly Love, I imagined the men propositioning you. I thought of you getting even more lost with them, how they'd lead you on your way through wandering, your eyes so opened and curious, as you were looking for better prospects, affections, noise. I worried about you. You were gone for three days. I sat across the street on the steps of someone else's brownstone, while another bachelor continued around the corner with his cigarette, blowing his rings of smoke out. No words were exchanged. It was less like sizing each other up than general surrender to a situation with no standard.

We were unpractised and both partly to blame.

I usually sleep naked, but that would not be appropriate any longer, with you there. You were watching me turning off the lamp beside my bed. You could have seen me taking off jeans followed by a green football jersey so long worn the threads more and more disappear. I am undressing in the dark, though.

You can't see me pulling my legs into the boxers monkeys join hands across. You're going to stay here tonight. You're going to want me. In the light through the window, we're going to sink down together, come back together. I'm hushing up about outside now. That's not between us. What is here is our hands, twisted together, found again between our two bodies.

One of my legs rests between your legs in the way that keeps me up. You let me. You move your back, back yourself, your hips I take firmly in my hands, as you back up into me, keep me, hoping.

One of us might still roll over.

One of us might come up to on top of the other's body.

I won't be able to sleep. You neither.

You go for the jugular, my heart.

You keep this proposition close to sacred.

The bachelors fall short of our frustration, your resistance, and my hope.

Your mouth kisses open, slicking the two of our lips, as they become two of our matching parts met, our mouths almost the same.

With empty stomachs, we went to bed. Neither of us could eat much at the restaurant.

Suddenly taking you, in the middle of the night, in my bed, as you are sleeping in trust, would be like forcing you. I don't want to force.

In the morning, I settled for the kiss on your belly, around the button that closed your shirt. You hadn't dressed all the way to leave yet. The excitement was making your body hurt for it.

You were walking home the rest of the way, after our kiss on the corner. You got back a couple of days ago.

We'd go for a few more days. We'd go for a few more even.

We might do a little more the next time. You might let me nearer there where we twin.

Nothing could feel more consuming than this distance between us. I try to find the inevitable prolonging romantic. I try to find nothing more explicitly erotic. I try to believe you just might change your mind next time. I try to let nothing be more worth our time of night than to see if we'll come back together, if you'll return to the place I'm keeping for us, as I try not to demand any more from you than I expect from myself alone.

As you're leaving me, you don't see what I see. I'll tell you how I sit in the chair at a table near a window, looking for you in other boys, believing I might find you there. The walls in the new restaurant are being whitened. I'll tell you about an attempt to focus on making need not so desperate. I consider forgetting us being nothing or all. I'll try to find a place between.

Up the street, they are drinking already. The bars open early. You don't know what a boy like me is to do with himself.

Jane Rogers

Voyage

Stepping on to the ship, Anne feels a wave of relief. In fact she feels – imagines she feels – because how could it be true on a ship the size of a tower block, tethered in the flat oily filth of the harbour? – imagines she feels the iron deck rise a little, like a tiny indrawn breath, to meet her falling foot. Imagines she feels the movement of the sea, after the stillness of the land. Imagines, as she imagines the sea lifts her, that it will be all right.

Her cabin is above deck, as promised, but inside it's strangely dark – a reddish gloom, light through a closed eyelid. When the steward has put down her cases and unnecessarily pointed out the shower, Anne hands him the folded 1,000 Naira she's been clutching in her pocket and shuts the door after him. Why is the room so dark? The window seems to be blocked by something; she stares out and realizes it is the red side of a container, no more than twelve inches from her window. By craning her neck right back she can just glimpse a crack of sky above it. Perhaps they'll move it, maybe it's waiting to be stored below. There's an odd smell, cleaning fluid and disinfectant covering something else, something that sticks unpleasantly at the back of her throat. She runs her fingers around the window frame looking for a way to open it, but there's none.

Anne stows Father's case in the wardrobe and opens up her own. There are two plastic bags of dirty washing. She felt awkward about letting the houseboy do it, and couldn't do it herself because of the houseboy. But there must be a laundry room on board; or she could even use the tiny sink in the shower room.

Not yet. She locks the door then sits on the bed, empty hands on her knees. What now? Her instinct is to go straight out on deck, out of the artificially lit dimness of this cabin, but things are still being loaded, she can hear the shouts of men – the sailors, the dockers. She might be in the way on deck, they might stare at her. Better to wait here until they sail. Anne suddenly visualizes the crowded rails of a passenger ship, tiny figures leaning over to shout and wave goodbye, the answering calls and waves from the shore, the blue sea widening between them. There is no one here to wave her off.

She swivels round and swings her legs up on to the bed, leaning back against the wall. The stopping, being at the end of the list of things to do, is bewildering. Since she left home – since the morning of the Reverend Richard's phone call whenever it was, ten days ago – things that must be done have made stepping stones. She had to fly to Lagos, had to bury Father, had to clear his things; the past three days have been consumed entirely in begging and bribing her way on to this ship. To reach this empty space; to see if she actually feels anything.

The only time she's cried has been out of sheer weariness and frustration when the big uniformed man (Police? Army? She still doesn't even know who he was, or why he had the power.) told her the body must be sent home for burial, burial of an English tourist in Nigeria not being permitted. But he wasn't a tourist, she argued. And how can nationality be relevant to a corpse? Sweat glistened in the rolls of the official's neck above his khaki collar, and the little fan on his desk made slow eddies in the hot thick air. A part of her brain observed that its whirring motor was generating heat of its own which its spinning blades struggled to dispel; its functions cancelled one another out, leaving only the by-product noise. The fat man shook his head, the interview was over. When she got out of the room, hunching her shoulders and sliding her hands into her pockets, she touched the roll of notes Richard had made her count out – the bribe she should have offered. – and tears rose to her eyes.

Richard had sorted it out; requesting an interview the following morning, delicately placing the cash on the edge of the big man's desk as they sat down; nodding to Anne to hand over her father's passport when it was requested, although she wanted to keep it, although she knew there could be no official reason on earth why she must surrender Father's passport to this pig.

She can't sit in this strangely-smelling darkened room all day. It's hot everywhere of course but at least out there there may be a breath of wind, or a hint of coolness off the water. Once they are at sea she will leave the door open, let in some clean fresh air.

Taking her book and Father's hat, she braves the deck, turning left to head for the rail on the side away from the dock. She threads her way between containers, expecting any moment to be turned back or forbidden, but there's no one here. Between the last container and the rail, she finds a space a couple of yards wide, shaded by the container. The rumble of the crane and dockers' shouts and cries are all away behind her. She leans on the rail. The harbour is busy and filthy, every kind of rubbish floating on the oily water; she stands staring down at it blankly, nostrils wrinkling at the smell, both more disgusting and more reassuringly real than that inside her cabin. She is suspended until the ship moves; nothing can happen till then, it's no-time, like waiting in an airport.

Coming here hasn't helped anyone. Reverend Richard could have buried his visitor more efficiently without her, could have bundled up the books and papers and airfreighted the case back to England. A man's child should be at his funeral, she thinks. But he doesn't *know* she was there. It's a fictional transaction, she must derive satisfaction from knowing that if he had been able to know she was there then he would have been pleased, from knowing she has done the right thing although nobody is there to see it. 'God sees.' Oh yeah. She still feels that hot smarting adolescent resentment at what he has instilled in her, the nasty little judging eye. Well, are You satisfied? I came to Lagos and buried him. It has been horrible. Are You satisfied?

Once the ship begins to move it will be *her* life again.

'Hello.' A man has come round the container behind her; middle-aged, tall, a sheaf of papers in his hands, official. He extends a hand. 'Murbak. First mate.'

She can't place his accent. 'Hello. Anne Walker. I'm a passenger.'

'I know.'

Of course. There are only three passengers, the retired couple and her. Every member of the crew will know. Will she be the only young woman, and all these men? She can feel heat spreading across her face and neck, suddenly imagines the crew going about their business, glancing up surreptitiously at the passengers coming aboard, then meeting each others' eyes and winking. They might run a sweepstake on how many of them can make it with a likely female, they might joke about her in their quarters at night . . .

Why is she thinking this? For God's sake. The first mate stands still before her with a quizzical smile, she can feel him watching her traffic-light face. She turns quickly back to the rail, but he takes a step closer. There's an awful little silence, and she can't stop herself glancing round to see what he's doing behind her. Copying on to his papers a number stamped on the container. Why's it taking so long? She should ask if they are moving the red container. He's standing slightly too close. This is in her imagination.

'You know there's an area of the upper deck reserved for passengers and officers . . .'

So that's what it's about. 'I'm sorry, shouldn't I be—'

'No, you stay here if you like it, Miss Walker. You can go most places on the ship; I'll give you a tour once we're under way.'

'Thank you. Please call me Anne.'

'Anne.' He gives a quick nod, then goes.

The man was simply being polite. Probably passengers are his responsibility. She behaved like a fifteen-year-old. He'll think she is ridiculous. Why did she have to blush?

*

In the evening there's a meal where the captain welcomes them. They're still in dock, waiting, he says, for a tug to take them out. He's a small squat German with very precise English; he introduces four other officers, including the first mate she has met, and Mr and Mrs Malone, the other passengers. Conversation is strained, the Malones tell the table about other cruises they've taken, and why they always travel on cargo ships, while two of the officers sitting at the end conduct a subdued argument in

German. The first mate doesn't speak. Everyone at dinner is rather far away, just out of focus, it is all Anne can do to eat her food and drink her wine and haul herself to her cabin at the end of the meal. She's exhausted, but it's all right; there's nothing to do, she's not accountable to anyone here. Somewhere, appropriate emotions are stirring. There's an undertow, on which she's riding now, which is making her limbs weak and her eyes blurry, which is sucking her into oblivious sleep.

*

Anne wakes suddenly, to pitch darkness, head full of grinding noise. She thinks the cicadas have gone mad – turns to look for the window above Father's bed, where for the past nine nights she has lain watching stars and the moving lights of planes coming into Lagos – and realizes she is on the ship.

The noise must be engines. They are moving. She feels for the lamp switch and the room leaps into place. The clock says 01.58. She pulls on clothes and sandals and quietly lets herself out of the cabin, making her way between the dark hulks of the containers towards the ship's rail. She can feel the vibration of the engines through her feet, and has a flash again of that sudden excitement of stepping aboard. The ship is moving. And coming to the rail, suddenly the sea is open and silvered before her, covered in moonlight, with a cluster of yellow harbour lights on black falling away to the left. As her eyes adjust, the moonlight seems brighter and brighter, as bright as day, shining over a sea of mercury, filling the sky with pale light that almost obliterates the stars. The boat seems to move very fast, charging through the water, the shore lights dropping away even as she watches. Ahead is nothing but emptiness, a flat silvery plain.

The surface of the sea is metal, a fine foil; it undulates gently but never breaks, a lid hiding whatever is beneath. She imagines the things beneath: living things that eat each other, the seabed littered with bones of fish and empty shells and pearls, old oil cans and the glint of treasure and rusting metal of wrecks. A mirror image of the world above, she thinks, full of pursuit and capture, sex and death. They have put Father's coffin in a hole in the ground. Because they arrived two hours late at the graveyard, thanks to the roadblock and traffic jams, the gravedigger had gone, leaving a spade standing in the heap of earth to one side of the hole. And she and Richard took turns to shovel earth over the coffin. It was a relief to have a good reason for sweating.

She should have brought Father on the ship, to be buried at sea. Imagine sliding him from the deck, to crash through that molten surface and disappear into another element. Imagine slipping him into a world as wide and deep as the one he's lived in, imagine him floating and twirling down towards the depths, coming to rest at last among rocks and weeds and lurking sightless fish, imagine him rocking slightly, just a touch, with the deep swell of the sea. Instead of lying inert and weighted down by earth, to be baked by tomorrow's sun.

He's gone to his heaven, she reminds herself. It had better bloody well be true. Not in the earth, not in the sea, but in some mysterious golden space, some place of light and splendour. Irritation rises in Anne's throat. He's under that inadequate scraping of earth, why does he have to pretend otherwise? He is there like a pet hamster buried in the garden.

After a while the blank silveriness of the sea, the wrinkled mirror it presents to the pearly sky, seems almost offensive – like a person who blankly returns your look, refusing recognition. It is surprisingly cool; the first time in ten days she's felt cool. She turns and heads for her cabin, then detours to the lit doorway leading to the little passenger lounge and stairs down. (Companionways? Why? Do you go down them in search of companions?) She's wide awake now and reluctant to return to the confinement of her cabin; it's pitch black at night because of the container blocking her window. It defeats the point of the cabin being on deck. In the morning she should ask them to move it. Even a few inches would be better.

She heads down the narrow metal stairs, six steps and a turn, six more to the deck below, relishing the emptiness of the ship. There are little signs in the stairwells: DINING ROOM and LIBRARY, B deck; PURSER'S OFFICE, C deck. Like a doll's house. LAUNDRY is on D deck. At the bottom of the last flight of stairs she pushes through the heavy door into the corridor. It's painted grey; the metal floor rings under her feet. It feels as if she has strayed into an area where passengers are not allowed. But the whole ship is a working ship, and passengers are surely allowed to use the laundry. The doors on either side of the corridor are blank, not named or numbered, all painted the same dark green. It makes her think suddenly of a submarine, of hunched men in uniforms sitting watching each other, ears strained for the slightest sound . . . waiting. What's behind all these doors? Sailors' quarters? Suddenly, on her left, LAUNDRY. She pushes the door and is immediately in the warm familiar smell of soap powder and dryers. One dryer is on, the clothes inside flying round lethargically, flopping against the glass. Three old-fashioned top-loading washing machines stand with their lids up; against the wall opposite the door is a large sink with a bucket and clothes baskets piled beside it. The churning dryer suggests someone might return to fetch his clothes quite soon. Of course sailors work all night, they work shifts – watches. The idea of men crawling from their bunks and hurrying to engine room or bridge, peering into the darkness with a mug of tea cradled between their hands, glancing across lit panels of instruments and gauges, gives Anne a sudden warm feeling. They keep the ship humming on its way through the night. They make the night safe. Like parents used to.

She doesn't want to meet the man whose clothes are drying. She leaves the laundry and is puzzled for a moment over which way to turn. Left? Right? The corridor stretches away, exactly identical to either side. As she hesitates, there's a movement at the end of the corridor to her left. She doesn't want to meet anyone now. It's very late; they would think it strange, her wandering the ship in the middle of the night. She turns right and hurries along the corridor, looking for the heavy swing door. The person behind her is running. She can hear his bare feet slapping against the iron floor. He's running after her. She freezes, and glances back. The man immediately slows to a walk, his right hand is half raised as if to wave to her, or beckon. As he gets closer his walk becomes more and more hesitant. She makes herself turn fully to face him, waiting.

'Please . . .' The man stops. He gestures back in the direction he has come from. 'Please?' He's the first Nigerian crew member she has seen. He's panting and sweating from his run. 'Can you help?'

'I'm a passenger,' Anne says stupidly. She can't help, whatever it is, he should find another sailor. He's standing there staring and pointing, his breath coming harshly in the stillness of the corridor. The empty silence stretches away to either side of them. Through the corner of her eye Anne realizes the door to the stairs is just behind her, to her right.

'I'm sorry. I shouldn't be here, I'm just a passenger.' As she speaks she's turning, bolting, shoving her way through the door. She's running up the stairs as if he might chase after her. When she reaches the upper deck she stops and listens, holding her breath. Nothing. He hasn't come on to the stairs.

She pushes out to the cool of the deck. He should look for someone else who knows about whatever it is. She wouldn't have been any use anyway. She unlocks the door of her cabin. With the bedside lamp glowing and her books on the table it looks like a haven. She quickly locks herself in and gets back into bed. It's a while before she can stop shivering.

*

Anne wakes again at the same time the following night, 2 a.m., after two and a half hours' sleep. Why? She lies in the insistent blackness of her cabin, willing the outline of her window to appear; it must be a shade or two lighter than the walls, surely, even through the container is there? Her eyes can't distinguish any variation, though, and when she turns on the lamp she realizes she has not even been staring directly at the window, it's further along the wall than she remembered, she doesn't even have the shape of the room properly in her head.

The image of the Nigerian is haunting her. Surely it was a dream? He stands, hand half raised to catch her attention, to gesture backwards to whatever trouble it is he needs her help for. He needs her for something serious. How could she have run away like that? How come she hasn't thought of him all day? Why didn't she tell someone or ask someone or do something to make sure he was all right? He didn't want to harm her – look how hesitant he was – how dare she pretend to have been frightened by him?

She imagines Father's disappointment. He's looking at her with that very slightly puzzled look, almost kindly; he is mystified. 'But why didn't you ask him what was wrong? Surely you could have done that?' Always able to spot the right thing to do, as if it was obvious. It *is* obvious, she tells herself furiously. I must go now and see if the man's all right.

It is not a good decision, she knows that even as she dresses. Whatever was frightening last night will be equally so tonight. Why she has not dealt with it in daylight, with the humdrum running of the ship all around her, sailors coming and going, people to turn to, God only knows. In daylight it never even entered her head. Perhaps it really was a dream.

She lets herself out of her cabin, remembering fleetingly the relief with which she reopened the cabin door last night, the safe room and glowing lamp. If only tonight was over as well, and she was just going back to bed. But how ridiculous to make it alarming. She will go down to the third deck, walk to the laundry room – past it if necessary – check that all is quiet and well, and then return to bed. There's nothing else to do. Of course he won't be there again. The trouble, whatever it was, will have been resolved – even to go there like this is silly – she dodged it yesterday and now the time is gone. Isn't she only going back to salve her conscience?

She runs down the stairs quickly, nobody will see her, she'll be back in bed in no time. When it's done it can be forgotten, a small bad taste.

At the bottom of the third set of stairs she pushes through the heavy self-closing door and turns right along the corridor. This is where she stood as he spoke to her; this is where she turned to see him running after her; this is the laundry room doorway, where she first saw a movement off to her left. Everything is still and quiet. She will make herself go right to the end of the corridor. She passes green door after green door. How can there be so many rooms? Who are they all for? She has seen no more than half a dozen crew moving about the ship, and the other two passengers are in a cabin like hers, on deck. What's behind all these doors?

The corridor ends in stairs down. There are double doors, hooked open. She hesitates at the top, peering down, glances back over her shoulder at the silent empty corridor, then begins to descend, half crouching to see what is down there. The stairs let into a huge open area like a car deck on a ferry. The dim lighting reveals piles of sacks, and containers with black chasms of shadow between them. As she looks, the Nigerian suddenly emerges at the bottom of the stairs. She can't prevent a little gasp, an involuntary retreat back up one step. The voice of contempt in her head: Oh, how surprising. You came to look for this man and now you've found him. What a nasty shock. She forces herself to go down two steps. He's nodding at her.

'Thank you. This way.' It's as if no time has elapsed since last night.

Before she has responded he turns and heads towards the shadow between containers. There's nothing to do but follow him. No, you can't run away this time, this is allegedly what you came for. She forces herself down the steps and after the man's retreating back. As she moves into the darkness she thinks, but anything could happen. No one knows I'm here. Anything could happen. Why don't I go and tell an officer? But the man is moving on quickly in front of her, along the narrow gaps between containers. Already her view back to the stairs is blocked, it's too late to ask for help. She can't not follow; it's as if he is a magnet, she's dragged across the iron floor, unable to resist. The light gets dimmer, there are smells: sacking, dust, the bitter tang of cocoa. He must be some kind of watchman. That's it. He must be a watchman on the cargo deck, he probably has to sleep here to guard the cargo. Perhaps he's made a mistake and is afraid of getting into trouble. It will only take a moment to set him straight.

He stops and turns to her. 'Here,' he says softly, indicating the container behind him. 'In here.'

'What is it?' Anne can't imagine. Something leaking? Something spilt, maybe? Then she sees that the side of the container is missing. It has been taken off, like the back door of a lorry.

The inside is lit by a candle stub on the floor, which reveals looming dark shapes and shadows – a lair, a den. What's in there?

The man steps in and picks up the candle, raising it so that it sheds more light. The bulging shapes at the back are sacks, heaped up; the ruckle on the floor is cloth, blankets, rags. Suddenly Anne sees a face. A woman's face, on the floor among the rags. A black woman's face, eyes closed, the light gleams for a moment on the line of her cheekbone and jaw.

'What is it?' Anne whispers again, unable to make sense. Has the watchman found her? Found a woman here, hidden? Has he brought her here, and is she now dead? Something is wrong with her surely or she would move, she would look up.

'Please.' The man gives a slight nod towards the woman. He wants Anne to go to her. Why? Sweat suddenly breaks through Anne's skin, she opens her mouth to breathe but the air has become little tiny fluttering moths, just escaping her, just escaping, flittering away before she can get a lungful. Her eyes continue to search for detail; she can see the shape of the woman's bulk beneath the blankets. As she stands frozen, utterly unable to step into the box, she sees that the picture is Rembrandt's etching, *Nativity*; the man's and woman's faces illumined, the dark shapes around them an indecipherable clutter of shadows, and the heart of the image the tiny light of the hand-held lantern; thinks simultaneously, in this moment in which no time passes, that this is an image Father would have built a sermon on, the tiny Light of the World gleaming bravely amid so much engulfing darkness; thinks further, and still in less time than it takes to blink, of all the versions Rembrandt printed off, from the first where details are discernible, filling up with darkness all along the way, to the last where nothing but the flame and a glint of Mary's face are visible, blackness having swallowed the rest; considers (in no rush) the grimness of the artist's vision, the spreading swamping blackness, and counters calmly that it is a technicality, an etcher can only move to greater darkness, can only scratch away more of the increasingly black plate, it's the nature of the medium; and without breaking stride in the thought, without making a pause in the interaction between herself and the man, Anne steps into the box and crouches down beside the woman.

Who is clearly very ill. Her bones jut in the skin of her face, the sharpness exaggerated by the leaping candle flame. Her face is slick with sweat and her breaths are short and light, almost panting. Her body beneath the blankets seems swollen and mis-shapen; Anne realizes what a part of her brain at least has already registered. She turns to the man.

'Is her baby due?'

He shakes his head. 'Too soon.'

'But she's ill.'

'Yes. You can help her.'

'Me? I'm not a doctor.'

He watches her quietly. What can she say?

'We must get the ship's doctor, I'll run up and find—' She's rising, but his hand's on her arm, his fingers clench tightly around her wrist.

'No.'

'She needs medical help.'

'You tell no one.'

'But how can she be helped?'

'You tell no one.'

He is hurting her arm. 'OK. Is it . . . Doesn't anyone know you're here?'

He loosens his grip. 'If they catch us they send us back.' He sets the candle on the floor again. Anne slowly straightens up. The story begins to assemble in her head. No one knows. The woman is ill. They need help. They are stowaways.

Why me? Here in the middle of the sea in the middle of the night in the dark hold of a container ship, why me? They are expecting her to do . . . what? Something heroic. What can be done?

'Why have you asked me?' Anne cries in desperation.

'You are a woman.'

'But I don't know how to cure her.'

He shrugs.

'She could die.'

'If they send her back she will die.'

'But you must explain . . . tell them you're refugees.'

He shakes his head; turns abruptly and goes out of the box.

Anne is left staring at the sick woman. The sick pregnant woman. For God's sake, what can she do? She crouches again and touches the woman's forehead. Hot. Of course, she has a temperature.

Anne stumbles out of the box. The man is leaning against the side of the neighbouring container, face averted. 'Do you have water?'

He nods. Anne stands a moment, helpless, her thoughts flickering and stuttering like a video that needs tracking. She will go back up to her cabin and think what to do.

'I must go.'

He turns without speaking and leads the way back through the containers to the foot of the stairs. As she starts to climb he says softly, 'Thank you.'

Anne does not look back.

Alistair Elliot

The Chest of Drawers

The chest of drawers has legs.
It used to stand as square as Hamlet's friend,
as solid as a tower-block on its pegs,

a strongbox, where we store
your folded delicates and my ironed breastplates,
our armoury tactfully hidden in a drawer.

One day I was surprised to find
this chest, this quayside for the marriage-boat,
suddenly wobbly, as if undermined.

A floorboard's moved, I thought,
and touched one leg: it gave: it wasn't glued
or nailed in place, but screwed,

on wooden threads. All four were loose. This chest,
with its twelve lowered eyes
discreetly witnessing our hours of rest,

had secretly been dancing with itself:
years of soft shuffles, shudders of a drawer
being pulled, small earthquakes through the floor,

perhaps from traffic, tremors of the bed . . .
It has unwound the spirals of its wood:
and now it teetered, ready, unsteady,

to be off.

Jackie Kay

Not the Queen

Maggie Lockhart spent her life trying to work out what she'd done to deserve it. There are reasons for things. Things don't just happen, no they don't. Sometimes the reasons are a long time coming, but when they finally do, they are clearly printed like her pension slip. Most things Maggie worked out to her own satisfaction, though getting people to see the thinking behind the reasoning was hard because nobody took her seriously. Maggie didn't have the temperament for teasing; never had been good at being teased even as a child, before the nose and the mouth and the cheeks set, but even the most sweet-natured woman would have baulked at what Maggie had to put up with. No way in the creation of Christ was it easy going about the place as a kind of a live joke with The Face on it. Nobody could see her face without thinking of the other one's: not the man or the woman in the street, not the total stranger at the bus stop, not even her own family. And even she had the odd feeling when she glanced in the mirror that she wasn't seeing herself, but the bloody Queen. No, no seriously. All right, not dressed in those uptight suits with the buttons, in all sorts of colours from navy to pink to emerald green, with the scarves, and the bloody brooches and the silly hats, but the Queen just the same. Even with a fag dangling out her mouth and no make-up on, Maggie Lockhart had the bad luck of looking the exact spit of HM Queen Elizabeth II.

There had to be some reason she'd been given The Face. From her teens, Maggie had grown old with the Queen. The Queen was ages with Maggie; Maggie was ages with the Queen. Now they were both in their seventies and it still wasn't making any sense. Oh she had had her fill of it! Not a overly religious woman, Maggie had some vague notion of a grand plan. Life had to have some sort of purpose or what was the point of it all?

Twenty years ago, Maggie's car broke down on the M8 Glasgow to Edinburgh. When the AA man arrived, he gaped at her. 'Christ you gave me a fright there, Hen.' He lifted her bonnet and peered into her engine. 'Has anybody ever told you, you're the double of—' 'The Queen,' Maggie said, cutting him dead. 'Aye!' he said. 'I'm no kidding but it's a wee bit freaky so it is. Go and look away, will you, while I fix your motor cause you're putting me aff. Jesus whit a predicament fir ye. An A suppose this is jist gonna go oan and oan. Whit a burden fir ye, Hen.'

It seemed to Maggie that the AA man was the very first person to ever truly understand. She stood nodding on the hard shoulder, as the rain swept across the three lanes of the motorway, making the road glisten and sparkle like a ballroom floor. A wee tear came to her eye and rolled down her cheek. She wiped it away quickly. She dabbed the end of her round nose. In Maggie's head, her car had broken down for two reasons. The first was to stop her having a fatal accident. The second was to hear the AA man say, 'It must be a burden for you Hen.' Twenty years later, Maggie still hadn't got any further than that. A dour friend would say pragmatically, 'Well that was the face you were born wey,' which was all very well but she wasn't the one who had to go and get born wey the monarch's mug. Maggie couldn't joke about her face; it was no laughing matter. It had ruined her life. People thinking one thing about her and then the other. She suspected Some people chose her as their friend just because she looked like their stamps. Folk doing the big double take, folk on the make till they realized they'd got the wrong woman. Fancy your own face being a con; fancy feeling that you were going about the place trying to trip folk up. People following her around sniggering and whispering. There were even jokes about her. Some people would come and stand outside her small two-up two-down in Drumchapel. 'Have you heard about the Glasgow woman that's the spit of the Queen?'

Maggie was as bad as everybody else was. She looked at her own face and couldn't see the individual. Imagine that. The thoughts in her head didn't match her face; how many people had to go around thinking that their inside thoughts didn't tally with their face? Of course it was all right for Her Majesty. It was plain sailing for Elizabeth. She was the Queen. She could look in the mirror and believe it. Come to think of it, she looked like she did look in the mirror daily and say to herself, 'I am the Queen of England.' But what could Maggie say to herself when her reflection appeared before her? Not a lot. Ever since the AA man's pronouncement though, she did have something to say. She'd apply a bit of blusher, which made her look even more like *her*, and she'd say to herself, 'What a burden.' And on really rainy days she'd think, Why me? Are faces accidents? Do they mean anything?

It seemed to Maggie walking down Sauchiehall Street in town that her face weighed more than other people's faces, heavy on her shoulders. Going out shopping, people often just came right out with it, like the woman at the checkout in BHS who said, 'Oh my God! You're the spitting image. You gave me the fright of my life there!' Maggie was shy and didn't like talking to strangers particularly, never had not even as a child, but The Face made every stranger feel they could pass comment, just like that. She didn't need to have a dog or a baby for complete and total strangers to talk to her; she just needed to look like the notes in her purse. It was rude. Everybody was so rude, so out of order. Cheeky wee madam, Maggie thought to herself when a teenager insisted she was the Queen's twin hiding out in Glasgow. One of Maggie's small satisfactions was talking inside her head to herself throughout the length of a day. What a big stupid glaikit bugger, she'd think as some hefty big guy gave her the eye. Sometimes she wondered if the Queen ever did that, so similar were their faces. What did she really think about people when she was going about shaking hands and smiling and saying sugary yucky things?

She walked through the shop. Same as usual, several ignoramuses performed the open mouth. The Big Stare. She did her best to ignore them. Everybody knew the Queen. Everybody knew what the Queen looked like. Nobody would ever say to the Queen, 'You are the double of Maggie Lockhart,' though Maggie had a great dream the other night when exactly that happened. No, Maggie was the double of the Queen. It didn't work the other way round. The Queen was not the double of Maggie

Lockhart. Maybe that was what rattled her. How could you be nobody to yourself?

There are reasons for near enough everything. When the holiday to Tunisia fell through because the bucket shop went bust, Maggie knew that it was probably a good thing. Some terrible experience had waited for her there; she would have got mobbed, literally mobbed. One year as she'd stepped off the plane to Cyprus, a whole flock of people had gathered around her. Maggie had had to wave her hands, 'No, no, no, no! I'm not who you think I am,' until her Charlie made the crowd vanish. Oh, but Charlie loved it, the swine. The big limping swine loved to see her awkward and embarrassed and to take her arm and rush off as if the pair of them were famous. There was something about Charlie's attentiveness that drove her up the wall from time to time. She came close when he came back from London with a mug with the Queen's face on it. 'No many people can drink their tea and look at their wife,' Charlie had said, raising the mug. Maggie yanked it off him and put it in the box for the jumble.

On the other hand, there were times when it had its advantages. Charlie was always the one to look after her, particularly now they were getting on, the one who did the hoovering, the gardening in their small bit of back garden, changed the bed because he thought putting a duvet into a duvet cover was too much exertion for her. It was Charlie who always made the cups of tea, who'd bring a steaming mug to her in the living room. 'Yir tea, maam.' When they walked out, Charlie walked a couple of steps behind her, always on the lookout for any chancers. Once Charlie said to her, 'Dae ye no think we could dae wey a bodyguard fir you?' Charlie was always dreaming up schemes like this. Of course they never had the money, even supposing Maggie Lockhart wanted a bloody bodyguard.

It was a relief that she no longer worked as a wages clerk after all the comments she'd had to suffer year in year out. People saying, 'It's all right for some,' when she handed over the wages on a Friday. Wee Glasgow blokes all full of themselves as if they were the first ones on the planet to crack a joke. Yug. 'No wee smile? That's like her too. Have you noticed, she hardly ever smiles?' If Maggie had not felt so furious at The Face, by now she would have started feeling a strange sympathy for the Queen. 'Right soor puss. Doesnie even manage a real smile on Christmas Day, fir her own speech.' That was wee Edna. Wee Edna seemed to delight in discussing the Queen's personality with Maggie. 'Do you think she actually *feels* anything for her children?' wee Edna would say. Or, 'I think she's a bit obsessed with those corgis.' It didn't matter what Maggie said or what look she gave, wee Edna would read everything about the Queen and come into work announcing confidently, 'The Queen is blazing with Diana, absolutely blazing.' As if Maggie should care, as if any of it mattered to Maggie. 'It bores me to tears, Edna. I'm not the least bit interested.'

And, years before, it had seemed that no man would be brave enough to marry Maggie. Then Charlie did. And in bed that first night, to Maggie's absolute horror, he whispered, 'Who's my very own wee Queen then eh?' She leapt out of bed and made him swear never ever to say anything like that again or it would put her off. But it was clear to her looking into Charlie's small eyes that it was the very thing that turned him on. No many men got to see the Queen naked so they didn't no they didn't.

They were always the same age, Margaret Dorothy Lockhart and the Queen of England. There was never any chance of the Queen suddenly getting older and leaving Maggie to get younger or anything like that. So it was a lifelong thing, and after a while Maggie stared at photographs of the Queen in magazines and would make comparisons. She couldn't help herself, especially when they were both getting on. Not many people had a double to compare themselves to unless they were identical twins, and Maggie and the Queen looked the same, so much the same, that Charlie would say, 'I'm telling you! Put the pair of you side by side and pit her in your claes and you in hers and not a single bloody person in the whole of England wid be able to tell the difference!' Charlie could get quite het up, as if he was sitting on a goldmine and didn't know how to get at the gold. The Queen had bad posture; Maggie's was better. The Queen had good skin, better than Maggie's. (Mind you, think of all the expensive moisturisers.) If you could look into the Queen's eyes for a long time, you'd find that she was shy just like Maggie. The Queen's health was better than Maggie's was too. Maggie had bad asthma and would wheeze when agitated or nervous. Maggie also had irritable bowel syndrome and spent a good portion of her day these days on the toilet cursing and muttering to herself, which was her privilege. She allowed herself that, Jesus and fair enough too. When it came right down to it, Maggie didn't know much about the Queen. She knew her favourite dog and horse and castle because wee Edna was always reeling out the facts, but she didn't know anything personal. She didn't know if the Queen liked her nose, her eyes or her cheeks, if she thought she was attractive or handsome or plain. If she looked in the mirror and felt pleased enough or if she never troubled to think about it, if she just didn't have to think about how she looked at all because she was the Queen whereas Maggie had to think about it because she was not the Queen.

Maggie was shy and rather diffident, more like an Edinburgh woman, wee Edna was always saying. Never one to put herself first or forward, Maggie would have been perfectly happy going through life taking a back seat. But The Face made her take a front seat. There she was, stared at from the minute she got up to when she went to bed. When Maggie went to get her hair done, it was always the same. She came out with the bloody Queen's hair even if she'd asked for a frizzy perm. They even cut it when she said, 'I'm growing it.' Year in year out, hairdresser after hairdresser couldn't resist giving her that daft coiffeur, those silly smarmy marmy waves. She could have opened many a library or hospital or theatre, she could have cut many a ribbon. She could have gone about Scotland nodding seriously and saying a few judicious words before pushing people away with her strong handshake.

Once wee Edna and Maggie went to the bingo and Edna enjoyed all the people staring at Maggie as if Edna had taken part in creating her, as if she was a circus act or some bloody freak show. Edna didn't even concentrate on her numbers properly for looking at people looking at Maggie. When Maggie shouted, 'House!' somebody shouted, 'You're rich enough already,' and her row roared with laughter. Maggie couldn't be persuaded to go again. 'I'm just not putting myself through it,' she told Edna to Edna's great disappointment. Being out with Maggie caused quite a sensation, quite a commotion.

The day came for Maggie to do something. It finally dawned on her that there was no good reason for her having the Queen's face in the way that there were good reasons for other things in her life. She'd been patient for ages to wait and see what the purpose and the point of it all was. Always a bit philosophical was Maggie, always one to say reassuringly, if Charlie didn't get promotion, 'What's for you won't go by you.' Always one to believe that there must be some intention behind the smallest of things. No such thing for Maggie as coincidence or accident, things were meant to happen for some reason. So she'd put up with her face for years looking in the mirror and seeing herself and simultaneously the Queen. Well not for much longer. Maggie was no mug and it was time she asserted herself. She had been saving on the q.t. for some time and had a total of three and a half thousand pounds. It'd been a toss-up between really treating her and Charlie to a cruise or doing what she was going to do. But the cruise would have been nightmarish, port after port of people squealing. So that was that then – decided for her, in a way.

Maggie got up at seven. Her bag was already packed from the night before. As far as Charlie knew, she was going to stay with her sister for a couple of weeks. That would give her time to get over the bruises and let things settle. She was having the operation in London to be as far away as possible from home. On the train down, Scotland changed into England but she couldn't see the difference properly.

She'd already been down to London a few months before to see this particular man she was putting her faith in. She'd already told him what she wanted – a longer nose, higher cheeks, a different chin – and he'd told her that all that would involve an enormous amount of work and wouldn't be good for her face at her age. So they had settled on just changing the nose. The nose wouldn't cost too much and would change the look of the whole face.

Of course you get the wind up when you make a big decision

like that, and in the taxi up to the West End, Maggie was having second thoughts. Had she not just been a bit touchy all her life? Couldn't somebody who liked a good laugh have enjoyed herself with the Queen's face? Had Maggie used her face as a scapegoat to cover her own inadequacies? Would her life really have been different without the Queen's face? How? Because it was not as if she had the Queen's money or palaces or anything else, it was not as if she had benefited in any way. But then had she really suffered? Charlie loved her for being herself and looking like the Queen, but all husbands had funny ideas about their wives, didn't they? Some husbands liked to see their wives as wee whores as well as wives, so at least her Charlie wasn't that bad, and he'd never been violent and never ever aggressive and he'd treated her like his Queen. Christ, wouldn't most not well-off women give their eye teeth for her Charlie? What would Charlie say if she came back with a different nose? Charlie would be gobsmacked. He would hit the roof. He would say, 'In the name of Christ Maggie, could you no have consulted me? Whit were ye thinking of wuman?' And then he would probably cry. Oh God, yes. Charlie had only cried twice in his life – when his father died and when Scotland lost in '74 – and both times had filled Maggie with a mixture of pity and revulsion. Charlie hadn't just dabbed at his eyes, like she did, Charlie had gone for the whole waterworks, heaving and making a lot of noise and saying 'Oh Christ! Oh Christ' bawling his eyes out like a man who hadn't had a chance to cry since he was a boy. It was the thought of Charlie crying that changed her mind. To hell with it. Have the Queen's face and put up with it. Maggie looked out of the black cab window as it passed Piccadilly Circus only to see some people excitedly looking in. She gave them the smallest of waves.

Charles Fernyhough

Fado

> The description of the hippopotamus by Hero-
> dotus is far from correct.
>
> – George Rawlinson, translator's note,
> *Histories of Herodotus*, 1858

For his grief he had the *Histories*, all the calamities of antiquity
swept down on a tide of deaths, against which his own loss felt
like a solitary drop into a vast and vicious sea. The feeling of
having taken a wrong turning in life, which had dogged him from
the beginning of that dream-cluttered year, was made worse by the
fact that he could not, for the life of him, remember having taken
any turnings at all. There was not much he could do about his
shaking hands, the difficulty in hanging on to any thought for
more than a few seconds, except put it down to some nervous
reaction to his own jittery existence: an intolerance which, in his
walks along the disused railway line, had made him long for a
swift unscheduled train. Before he died, his father – that creature
of considered opinions – had told stories about a beach in India,
his winter home for nine years of frugal retirement and Stephen
had had these dreams too: of sunsets that dazzled the soul,
cancelled the creeping damp of an English winter, and might shed
some light on a deeper restlessness which sent his hand twitching
like a cardiograph over pages of blank paper and filled his
thoughts with glimpses of the sea.

In Goa his father had swum every day, listened to news of
wars and interest rates on his short-wave radio and set the world
to rights by candlelight during power cuts as tourists grumbled
in darkness at the big hotels. His letters, full of these minor
triumphs, were typed out in short misspelled sentences on flimsy

167

aerogrammes which ripped when Stephen tried to open them. A year on he was still sorting through them, laying them out in chronological order and laughing at their deadpan humour as he tried to piece together the story of his father's late-flowering happiness, as improbable and ordinary as the man had been.

He flew to Dabolim with the letters folded into a black note-book, a copy of Rawlinson's *Histories of Herodotus* that had turned up unexpectedly on one of their house-clearing trips, and a heavy leather rucksack, which he settled carefully in the overhead locker, glanced up at in moments of turbulence, and was still clutching tightly as he walked out of the airport building into the February heat.

*

Back in March Stephen had looked starry, touched by great-ness, his glassy skin and tragic thinness now apparently signs of strength and sinuosity, the marks of his survival. After the exhaus-ting roller coaster ride that had followed the first news of his father's illness – which struck him now as the sudden clouding over of a previously pristine sky – Stephen felt toughened and determined, and sometimes, if he admitted it to himself, halfway hopeful about the changes life after Dad would bring. Within three weeks of the funeral they had decided, almost without discussion, to give up their commitments in Oxford and move three hundred miles to a small clump of houses in the countryside north of Consett. Helen had accepted a post as a clinical psy-chologist in Newcastle, and Stephen was going with her. There was no job waiting for him. He needed, he decided, no one standing over him to make sure he used his time profitably. He had ideas that needed following through, fundamental ideas about how this stood in relation to that, and they were going to need stillness, northern silence, a view from a window, empty roads that he could fill with traffic of his own.

He explained some of this to Helen, who nodded profession-ally and gave out those efficient murmurings of assent that made him feel he was describing some new neurosis to her rather than his own plan for being cured. They had been together too long – seven years, four of them married – to question each other's right to feel happy. If, in those first few months, Helen had any doubts about the speed of her husband's recovery, she kept them to herself. He watched her in their new garden, wheeling a barrow of uprooted perennials, or caught sight of her down on the railway line, gathering blackberries in an old ice-cream carton. She had stuff of her own to come to terms with. Stephen would be around the house all day, the most qualified twenty-something for miles around, with nothing to occupy him except a bit of decorating and the sight of ten miles of countryside. Naturally Helen wanted to help, to support him in whatever it was he was wanting to do. And yet, as soon as he had finished his explanation and gone to sit down at his writing desk, she was worried. She had heard him out with sympathy, even shows of enthusiasm, but those months of doing nothing held possibilities that frightened her, made her retreat to places of relative safety where she knew the names of all the things that could harm her: monkshood, laburnum, the blood berries of cotoneaster, varieties of foxglove and creeping deadly nightshade, whose poison worked directly on the heart.

They had bought a small Victorian farmhouse in an acre of steeply sloping land nibbled at on all sides by ewes half-dead from lambing. Stephen had seen the view over the valley, the thread of the river curling through dark trees, and he had known that this was the place to begin his project, the germ of an idea which was slowly working itself up into an obsession. There were cracks in the walls you could stash treasure in, but the surveyor assured him that these were only surface problems, a characteristic of Victorian plasterwork and by no means indicative of any deeper realignment. The surveyor and the estate agent were closely related, and both were on brotherly terms with the builder who turned up one afternoon to offer his services. The price was out of their range, but his father's house had sold quickly on the back of the latest mini-boom to hit the south-east housing market, and years of renting a terrace in Oxford made them feel entitled to be skipping a few rungs on the property ladder. As for the plasterwork, Stephen could fill his days with a bit of DIY. The wisdom of buying into bricks and mortar had, after all, been one of his father's most unassailable certainties, and he was glad, even at this late stage, to be taking the man's advice.

They moved in at the beginning of August, at the end of a spell of rain which looked permanent but instead turned overnight into a heatwave. The last vanload of furniture from Dad's house in Kent vanished into the unfamiliar spaciousness of their new home. They left the tape on the packing cases and went outside into the garden, where his grandfather's antique wooden bench had already been set out for them by the removal men, and a huge sycamore was shaking its leaves in the breeze as though applauding their decision.

For two months the weather held. Helen met her colleagues at the hospital and made preliminary explorations of the obsessions, compulsions and hallucinations of her new patients. Stephen roamed the perimeter of their property, shirtless in the improbable heat, peering at cracks in the rendering and jotting down sentences on index cards. He lay naked on his grandfather's bench, reading of the insults done by Cambyses to the body of Amasis, king of Egypt, as butterflies scooted over the wall before him and the river sparkled half a mile below. At night they would lie together on a sunbed, the embers still chinking in the barbecue, warm and naked under a duvet of stars.

But with the first storms of autumn the doubts returned, and the months stretched ahead like fields to be crossed, an uphill struggle towards a horizon that, for all his searching, remained empty. The cancer that had killed his father seemed to have left some residue in Stephen, clogging his nerves and making his hands tremble with foreknowledge of disaster. The wind blew. Mornings he looked out and saw trees flattened in the valley, torn up by the force of the storm, and he sensed that something was trying to uproot him too, a nemesis that had been hunting him down for years but had only just found out where he was living. What had he done, or failed to do? What was he going to do now? He wrote in his books for hours, the house dark except for the moonlight cast across his desk and an orange glow from the stove. Upstairs, Helen would be waiting, ready to hear what he had to say, but death had closed him down like a lamp, tempted him with murky revelations when he wasn't supposed to be looking, and now he hid away like a clumsy adulterer, busy by night with secret writings, embarked on an affair that neither of them could understand.

A journey was planned. It had been decided early on, when he and his sisters were on their way back from the doctor's surgery with the death certificate, that they would lay Dad to rest a year on, off the beach where he had spent so much of his retirement. They would scatter his ashes in the bay and throw a party at Bosco's, and people would remember him over prawn papads and shots of *caju feni*. The anniversary would fall in February, a few days after Stephen's birthday. By then there would be no rain, the Christmas crowds would have dwindled, and the sun would not yet have reached the impossible ferocity of April and May when everyday life, already famously laid-back, slowed almost to a standstill. Stephen would stay for the month. He could decide his future in beach shacks, drinking lime soda sweetened with spoonfuls of sugar, and his project could take shape on warm evenings within earshot of the sea. The rest of the family – Helen, his stepmother and two sisters – would fly out later for the ceremony. Stephen would turn thirty in the bosom of his family, a few days before their trip out into the bay.

Lying awake, another day closer to their parting, Stephen stopped wondering where the wrong turn had been taken and considered instead whether he was about to take another – some correction, perhaps – the second wrong that might still make a right. He heard Helen's breathing in the twilight, a regular snag in her air passages that reached him like the ping of sonar, and he tried to imagine what depths she might be navigating, what miraculous underwater chasms her dreams left her free to explore. He longed to wake her, press for a glimpse of those shadowy places, but he was afraid that he was already missing from them, that she was getting used to his absence even before he set foot on the plane. Outside, the gale shuffled the roof slates and whistled through a gap in the front door, inflating the house like a huge leaky accordion sighing out a solitary winter blues.

On the morning of his flight they were up before dawn. In the car to the station he was caught out by tears, sobbing regrets for an action not yet taken whose outcome seemed to lurk in wait for him and would leave their love so cruelly exposed. The sun was rising over the cathedral, revealing the city through layers of pink and yellow mist. He promised to phone. He stood at the window and watched her small frame fade into a tightening angle of glass, her brown hair loose on her shoulders and her forehead high and unfurrowed, as the train hissed and slid away.

There was no god in the taxi. On the dashboard where the icon usually sat, garlanded with marigolds and flashing LEDs, there was only a rectangle of black vinyl relatively unbleached by sunlight – evidence perhaps of a hurried removal, a sudden apostasy on a mountain hairpin. No god suggested that the driver had no faith, and no faith meant no investment in the great cycle of being, every speeding Hindu's belief that at the moment of impact a better life was waiting to begin. Perhaps this meant that his driver, who had not so far spoken a word in any human language, was the kind of careful atheist who would avoid taking unnecessary risks with his passenger's life. The black Ambassador was scorching, the plastic seat almost liquid under his hands. Then again, Stephen thought, the absence of a god might simply prove that his driver did not value this life sufficiently to want to come back for another, and would try to kill them both on the first blind bend. Ever the professional, Stephen found himself checking the rear profile of the Indian for signs of suicidal depression. The fellow had grunted at his foreman with obvious irritation at being woken from his mid-morning snooze but now seemed cheerful, waving at thin men on scooters, their elegant wives with long skirts flapping out behind.

They drove along the coast road, against a sea stained red with iron, then inland across green paddy fields planted with giant hand-painted billboards. Last time – with Helen, four years ago – they had been advertising Thums Up and washing powder; now it was Pepsi, cut-price internet connections, mobile phones. Every patch of shade concealed signs of building: half-finished apartments in grey breeze block held together by messy white cement with the apparent consistency of toothpaste. The taxi was overtaking a rickshaw which was overtaking a Tata truck; a plaque on the truck's rear bumper requested, 'Horn OK Please!'

Stephen's man obliged cheerfully then pulled in sharply to avoid an oncoming bus, thus demolishing Stephen's theory that his driver was a cautious humanist for whom this life was the only one on offer. Suddenly the comforts of religious faith began to appeal as never before, and he hurried to summon up an image of Lord Ganesha: Ganesha, who looked after young Christian travellers in all their in-between days, who had kept him safe on that first night-time bus trip, eight years ago, when he was driven down from Bombay by three stoned teenagers who stopped to lay marigolds at a roadside shrine and then careered on down the mountainside with headlights switched off to preserve the bulbs, cheeky chubby Ganesha, whose kind elephant eyes had watched over him in auto-rickshaws and motorcycle taxis, who had righted the capsizing ferries and buoyed up the outrigged fishing boats, as they carried him, sinking only slightly less quickly than their engines propelled him forwards across the muddy waterways of his travelling years.

The bridge had still not been rebuilt after its last collapse, so they took a detour inland and crossed the river by the old ferry upstream. As they rejoined the new road the driver started singing, the light seemed cooler, and the colours of the earth brightened, red on green. Old women selling fish by the roadside looked up at them as they passed, as if they had word that something precious was returning and would at any moment pass by. No longer fearing for his life, Stephen took off his jacket, found his sunglasses in a pocket, and let the unfolding landscape draw him back through memory, like a convalescing patient on familiar streets, driven home after such a long time away. He felt across the hot upholstery and laid a hand on the leather bag on the seat beside him. In the pub at Gatwick he had found a chair for it across the table, as if saving a space for someone who would soon return and to which, in their absence, he would occasionally address a few words. All through the flight he had glanced up at the overhead locker, worried that heavy objects might be dislodged in transit and fall and injure other passengers. He had watched it pass through the scanner at Dabolim, his cargo appearing on the screen as an anonymous black rectangle, and had been ready to surrender the appropriate documentation, which would prove that he was not carrying proscribed drugs nor the instruments of terrorism, that he was a danger neither to the State of Goa nor to himself. But the scanner man was bored, or asleep, and wasn't even watching as Stephen swung the bag back on to his shoulder, caught out again by the weight of it. As he walked through the gate a sharp voice called him back, but the woman in the uniform only wanted the last stub of his immigration card, which Stephen handed over with a faint tilt of vertigo.

The car turned on to a raised road across bright green rice fields worked by women in red saris and plodding water buffalo, then dived into tree-shade past crumbling colonial houses where black-clad grandmothers sat on verandas, chatting in the old language. On one corner was a tiny whitewashed shrine housing the photographs of two young children, road-death icons draped with garlands of marigolds. Stephen recognized the church of Our Lady of the Candles, with its sky-blue plaster and bright golden bell, and as they drove past he heard music. People were carrying benches into the shaded courtyard and laying them out in rows, and Stephen wanted to announce that he too was bringing something to the feast, returning a displaced treasure to its rightful home. In the bag beside him was a plastic jar, the size and shape of a newsagent's sweet container; and in the jar was his father, fired to a temperature of nine hundred degrees, shaken down to a brown-and-grey powder, sifting in darkness on the heat-cracked road.

Tim Liardet

In Praise of the Tenor Sax

She made it to the festival and went off with the saxophonist.
Not for love, he was not the likeliest object;
not for looks, which in truth were rather ordinary.
It was not for his height or stature, which were about average,
or nothing her friends would choose to comment on;
not for the pencil-line moustache that hovered
on his lip like light, as if uncertain of its provenance.
It was not for his quietness or his sudden blushes
or the air he gave off, say, of a diffident clerk
or the middle way he kept between wallflower and roué
or the limited language he had with which to speak
but for the fact that once he got behind his horn
he blew out such a lifelike energy he turned into the fender
and funnel and valves of the 00:00 express
which laid down its own track in darkness and flashed
through station after station as if choosing to ignore
the signal cocked at danger and compulsion to ease off
the throttle at its limit, but which stopped for her.

Michel Faber

Beyond Pain

Morpheus, drummer of North Ayrshire's foremost death metal group Corpse Grinder, woke up on the eve of an Eastern European tour with a strange sensation in his head. He blinked and squinted in the surfeit of winter light beaming into the tiny flat through its uncurtained bay window. The cars parked on the street outside were white with a night's worth of snow, dazzlingly, belligerently white. Snowy cars had never worried Morpheus before, but they worried him now.

'I feel funny,' he said to his girlfriend Ildiko – in Hungarian. This in itself wasn't strange. The bed in which they lay together was in Budapest.

'Well, you're a funny guy,' said Ildiko, nuzzling her shaggy head against his shoulder. He stroked her under the sheets, mildly disoriented to find that she wasn't naked any more, but snugly wrapped in warm cotton. His palms, callused by years of drumming 240 beats per minute on such songs as 'Inferno Express' and 'Meet You In Gomorrah', lingered over the strange scab-like textures on her garment.

'What have you got on?' he said, and she sat up, displaying his own black Corpse Grinder T-shirt with its embossed silver letters on the back: European Tour 2002 – Budapest, Bratislava, Prague, Wrocław, Warsaw, and other places whose names had already been half-disintegrated by the washing machine. 'Hand-wash only,' the merchandise said, but let's face it, who hand-washes T-shirts?

'Looks good on you,' said Morpheus. It was a relief to be eyeballing something dark.

'I have a nice pink nightie you can wear, if you want.'

'Ha ha ha,' he groaned, wondering if the Hungarian for 'ha ha ha' was something subtly different.

Ildiko was the wittiest girlfriend he'd ever had. She wasn't a groupie; in fact she wasn't even particularly fond of Corpse Grinder. Her thing was ambient. But she liked him.

'I've got a strange feeling in my head,' he said.

'A pain?' she suggested, getting out of bed, her bottom amply covered by the hem of the XXL T-shirt. 'PREPARE YE!' said the slogan under the list of tour dates.

'Yeah, a pain,' he conceded, frowning.

'A . . . headache, then?' she said, pulling her toasty warm tights off the old cast-iron heating duct.

'I don't get headaches,' said Morpheus, wincing as she stepped in front of the window and blasted his eyes with a halo of fierce sunshine all around her silhouette.

'Well, you seem to have one now.'

'Maybe it's a . . . a . . .' He didn't know the Hungarian word for brain tumour. 'Maybe I'm going to die.'

She tossed his T-shirt back to him in order to put on a bra.

'Start with an aspirin,' she advised him.

'You know I don't believe in drugs,' he chided her, shielding his face with his massive sunlit hands.

*

It was true that Morpheus never got headaches. Even when he was a teenager in Maybole, just plain Andy Wilkie then, he'd never felt pain in any part of his body, except the blisters on his hands when he first joined The Unbelievably Uglies (later The U.U., then Judas Kiss, then finally Corpse Grinder). 'Pain is an illusion,' he used to say. 'Power of the mind, mate!'

It was true, too, that Morpheus didn't believe in drugs. Not many of their fans knew it but Corpse Grinder were an unusually straight bunch of guys, having long ago ejected and replaced members whose bad habits made them unable to rehearse the tricky time signatures of the band's music or endure the punishing pace of their concerts. When Corpse Grinder had still been based in Scotland, Neil the guitarist (Cerberus) used to get drunk occasionally, and Charlie the bass player (Janus) might drop an E on his nights off, but now that they were older and based in Budapest, they were as clean as Cliff Richard.

'Funny the way things have turned out,' Cerb would say. 'Ayrshire to Hungary. Back home, nobody wanted to know us; we'd still be playing in the local pub. Here, we're a stadium act.'

Morpheus would excuse himself when Cerb got started in this vein. At twenty-two, he was a bit young for dewy-eyed reminiscence. Besides, it wasn't quite true that Corpse Grinder were a stadium act; they only toured stadiums when they landed a support slot to a bigger group, like Pantera or Metallica. That's what this tour of Eastern Europe was all about. Despite the exclusive billing on the Corpse Grinder T-shirt, they were one of several warm-up acts for that hoary old heavy metal warhorse, Slayer. Thousands and thousands of Eastern European adolescents were primed to crawl out of the woodwork to see Slayer, and with any luck they would spare a cheer for Corpse Grinder too, and buy a CD or a T-shirt ('Hand-wash only').

*

'Maybe your neck is stiff, Morph,' suggested Ildiko. 'Maybe you slept in a bad position.'

'Yeah, next to *you*,' he grimaced, rubbing his temples experimentally.

'Stop grouching,' she said, fully dressed and efficient by now. 'I've brought you a coffee.'

'Not that Portuguese garbage in the blue and yellow packet?'

'No, it's Dutch. Top brand. Inferno Espresso.' She stared down at him poker-faced until he twigged she was joking.

'Ha ha ha,' he said.

A little while later, she convinced him to go for a walk in the fresh air. His 'bad head', as she diplomatically called it, might respond to oxygen and exercise. So the pair of them dressed up in their anoraks and gloves and fur-lined Polish boots, and took to the streets outside Ildiko's apartment. Morpheus wore dark sunglasses, a mainstream rock star affectation he usually avoided, but the sun on the snow was still fearsomely bright.

'Fantastic day, Ildiko!' called Hajnalka, the florist.

'Sure is!' she called back.

'That's all people talk about in Scotland, too,' muttered Morpheus, keeping his eyes on the footpath, where the footprints of pedestrians had scuffed the snow into a more digestible mud-grey. 'The weather.'

'Must be a human trait then, I reckon,' she said, leading him under the tarpaulin canopies of a street market.

The traders were out in force today. As well as the usual stalls of mobile phones, outmoded Italian leather jackets, counterfeit Gap and Adidas gear, bootleg Hollywood videos, blue-and-yellow packets of Portuguese coffee, Britney Spears calendars and discount confectionery, there were more traditional wares on offer: home-made strawberry jam, burnt-out light bulbs which people could buy for a few forints to 'swap' for functioning ones at work, reams of office paper, gigantic mouldy salamis.

'Would you like a Bounty bar?' said Ildiko, casting her eye over a trestle table loaded with chocolates from America via the Arab Emirates.

'I feel . . . There's a strange feeling in my stomach,' said Morpheus.

'You feel sick, in other words?' said Ildiko, buying a Mars for herself.

'I'm never sick,' insisted Morpeus, shoving his sunglasses up under his hood as he rummaged through some pirated CDs. There was a Slayer Greatest Hits, called *The Greatest Hist of Slayer*, as well as the most recent album by (of all people) Cradle of Filth. No Corpse Grinder, of course.

'You wouldn't want there to be, would you?' said Ildiko. 'You wouldn't get any money from illegal copies.'

'We've never seen any money from the official releases, either,' he grumbled. 'At least the pirates pay their own costs.'

Ildiko zipped her unopened chocolate bar into a jacket pocket. 'I want something nourishing first,' she said. 'Let's go to Café Kalvin and have a *Halaszle*.'

'I'm not hungry.'

'You'll need something inside you for tonight.'

It was the first time she'd alluded to the fact that tonight was showtime; the first gig of twenty-two, the firing-on-all-cylinders start to Corpse Grinder's highest-profile tour ever.

'Plenty of time,' said Morpheus, his eye caught by a glossy

magazine that looked as though it might be about thrash metal. It proved to be pornography for leather fetishists.

*

'Have some of my soup, Morph,' Ildiko urged him, stirring some cream into her *Halaszle*.

'It's too early in the day for anything fishy,' he said. The lights inside the Café Kalvin were nice and subdued, though the sight of the pale cream revolving in the dark soup around Ildiko's twirling spoon was making him slightly dizzy.

'It's one o'clock,' she reminded him. The gig at the castle was due to kick off at 7.30, with Corpse Grinder following Ferfiak (the home-grown pretenders) at 8.15. Morpheus, still helplessly staring at the swirling cream in the *Halaszle*, had a sudden vision of his band's ideal light show – flickering red strobes and sweeping white lariats of dervish luminescence.

'Gonna blow everyone away tonight,' he declared, picking up a fork and teaspoon, and drumming a high-speed fanfare on the edge of the table. Even through the tablecloth, his power and skill were unmistakable.

'Are you ready to order or what?' called the waitress.

*

Morph walked through the door under the sign that said GYOGYSZERTAR. It could have been the name of an Eastern European thrash metal or Goth group, but it meant 'pharmacy'.

'I have a headache,' he told the old uniformed lady behind the counter.

'Speak up,' she said, cupping one gnarled hand behind her ear.

'Headache,' he repeated, shamefaced.

'What have you tried?'

'Nothing. What have you got?'

She gestured behind her, at a wall of little cardboard boxes. Analgesia for every man, woman and child in Budapest, by the looks. Was there really enough pain inside a sufficient number of skulls to justify the existence of all these pills?

'I've heard aspirin's pretty good,' said Morpheus, wishing the old woman would take charge.

'In that case, you don't need to pay through the nose for a fancy brand name.' She seemed to be warming to him, showing a motherly side. 'We have mounds of no-name aspirin out the back. You can get a hundred of them for the same price as twenty Bayer.'

'I only need a couple,' pleaded Morph, wondering what he'd done to deserve a run-in with Hungary's only surviving pre-capitalist.

'I'll get you fifty.' She smiled, already moving towards the storeroom, as if he were a cheeky little boy at the baker's and she was about to sneak him a bag of yesterday's doughnuts.

A minute later she stood in front of him with a plastic bottle and a glass of water.

'What, here?' said Morpheus, alarmed.

'Certainly. No time like the present.'

He shook two pills out of the bottle and threw them into his mouth, quickly chasing them with a swallow of water.

'You've never done this before?' she said, as he half-choked and grimaced and drank more water.

'Arghhh,' he replied, shaking his head.

'Are you working in Budapest?' She could tell he was a foreigner, of course.

'I'm a musician.'

'Really? What's your name?'

'Uh . . . Andy.'

'English?'

'Scottish.'

'Beautiful place. What brings you to this den of thieves?'

Not enough demand for Corpse Grinder in Scotland, he thought. 'My girlfriend lives here.'

'That's nice,' she said, the corners of her eyes wrinkling benignly. 'That'll be a hundred forint.'

*

'How's the head?' said Ildiko as they walked back towards the flat. Drizzle was eating into the snow like a mist of acid. The parked cars were emerging from their white canopies like giant metal mushrooms.

'Worse,' said Morph. 'I shouldn't have taken those pills. Power of the mind, that's what's needed.'

Indoors once more, he allowed Ildiko to massage his neck and shoulders while he watched TV. With the remote control he turned the brightness down so far that the faces looked African.

'Maybe you should let the other guys know,' said Ildiko.

'Know what?'

'That you may not be well enough to play.'

'Of course I'll be well enough. Mind over matter.'

She kissed his head. Her fingers were tired from kneading his tense musculature.

'Hey, look!' he said. 'It's the lead singer of Ferfiak!' On the TV, a heavily tattooed young man was telling a journalist that his band was going to blow Slayer off the stage all the way across Europe. Then the bass player pushed forward, middle finger raised in defiance, and shouted in English 'We're gonna kick some asses!'

Morph and Ildiko cackled gleefully.

*

At six, Morpheus was on his way to the castle, to rendezvous with his fellow Corpse Grinders. It was a twenty-minute drive, with Ildiko at the wheel of her pirated Volvo. Morph was in the back, as the front passenger seat was taken up by a carefully balanced quivering transparent plastic bag filled with water and tropical fish. The exotic creatures swam backwards and forwards in their giant polythene placenta, the water vibrating to the thrum of the engine.

Morpheus was drumming against the back of the seat with real drumsticks, getting himself psyched up.

'Meetchooo in Gomorraaaahhhh!' he sang tunelessly, beating the hell out of the leather headrest.

'Maybe that's not so good for the fish,' called Ildiko over her shoulder. Her father had been waiting for these little beauties to arrive for months, and wouldn't be too happy if his decision to let his daughter pick them up for him from the city resulted in them being dead on arrival.

'Survi-i-ival of the fiiitte-e-e-est!' sang Morpheus, the title track of Corpse Grinder's first album. Nevertheless, he drummed less aggressively.

To be honest, he was feeling like hell, and even the exertion of hitting his drumsticks on the back of a car seat made the blood in his temples pound. He squeezed the sticks hard in his fists, breathed deep, pressed his knuckles into his leatherclad knees. The biker trousers, usually like a second skin to him, were cold and clammy. His bare arms were pale and goose-pimpled, but his anorak was on the front seat, a nest for the wobbling fish bubble, and the bother of extracting it seemed intolerably great. Always in the past he had driven to gigs wearing only his stage T-shirt; sheer adrenalin kept him warm, even if the car had no heating and the temperature outside was below freezing. Today he was shivering.

'Are you sure you're all right?' called Ildiko, when a sharp bend in the road provoked a heavy sigh from him.

'Aspirin poisoning,' he groaned. His stomach and intestines had turned to hard rubber inside his abdomen, a solid mass of anatomical sculpture with no fluid function. A dark mass of pain pulsed behind his left eye and brow; he pressed his forefingers against the bridge of his nose, harder and harder, until it seemed they were in danger of bursting through the bone of his skull (a very heavy metal album cover scenario, he had to admit).

'Stop the car.' His voice was alien to him, a weedy nasal sound, indistinct above the thrum of the engine and the rushing in his head.

'It's only another couple of minutes to my parents' place.' Ildiko checked the rear-view mirror, verified that there was a car jam-packed with post-adolescent Hungarians right behind them, a Peugeot crammed to the roof with excited young men ready to raaahk.

'I'm going to be—'

Morph lurched sideways, wound the window down at desperate speed, and heaved a hot gush of vomit into the air. It spurted out of his mouth and nose like beer from an agitated can and splattered the side of Ildiko's car, wind-blown, in a long yellow stream. Smoothly, Ildiko slowed down and pulled off the road, allowing the traffic behind to roar past.

Morpheus fumbled the door open and fell out on to his hands and knees in wet frosty grass. He vomited more: convulsive gouts that made his head hammer with agony. Ildiko's arm around his back triggered a fit of shivering.

'H-how are we doing for time?' he panted.

*

Morpheus woke up in a dark room surrounded by ceramic milk-maids and carved statuettes of reindeer. He was in bed – not Ildiko's aromatic little nest but a strange king-size rococo layer cake of quilts and embroidered coverlets and ironed cotton sheets and fur-lined pillows. He might have been an ancient warrior on a funeral bier, floating on to a dark lake just before being set on fire.

A crack in the bedroom door admitted a pale antique glow from the hallway. Ildiko's parents had always been wealthy, even before Hungary's threadbare Iron Curtain was impatiently swept aside. Their house was a Viennese-style monstrosity, a nineteenth century hunting lodge hidden inside a three-bedroom bungalow, a Black Forest gateau cunningly concealed in a Ryvita wrapper.

It was deathly quiet; usually when Morph visited, Pavarotti or Carreras was warbling from the superannuated sound system. He sat up in bed, finding himself dressed only in his T-shirt and underpants, light-headed and weak as a kitten.

'Ildiko!' he called softly.

She appeared in the doorway almost at once, holding a coffee mug shaped like a squirrel.

'A doctor came,' she explained. 'You've had a shot of pain-killer, and something for the vomiting. Migraine, he said.'

'The concert . . .'

'It's long over. Zoltan from Ferfiak filled in for you.'

'Zoltan? He belongs in a post office, stamping the Christ out of letters . . .'

'Maybe so. But he filled in for you. They're on their way to Bratislava now.'

'Bratislava? What?' He swung his legs out of the bed and tried to stand, but it felt as if two feet were insufficient for this.

'It's next day already,' Ildiko said, opening the bedroom curtains a bit. Undeniable daylight shone in. The dyed sheepskin rugs on the floor lit up caramel and gold. Morpheus noted that he could cope with these things now, that the sun was well within the range of his endurance. He was thirsty and a little peckish; his innards were empty as a bass drum.

'I've got to get to Bratislava,' he said. There was a crust of dried blood on his thigh where the needle had gone in. He didn't remember the doctor at all, though he vaguely recalled his own arrival at Ildiko's parents' place: the ecstatic barking of the dog, the embarrassment of being half-carried across the threshold, his limp arms slung round the shoulders of a midget middle-aged couple, the surreal passage past bookshelves crowded with Goethe and knick-knacks, stuffed antelope heads, crocheted farmyard scenes in teak frames, the door of the guest bedroom with the smiling graduation photo on it, the spare plastic goldfish bowl they'd given him to vomit in, the divine relief of being stationary and warm and in the dark.

'See if you can make it to the toilet first,' suggested Ildiko. Standing there cradling her squirrel mug, she looked calm and happy; she always enjoyed seeing her old room again, to remind herself why she now led a life of rumpled minimalism.

'I puked on your parents' hallway carpet,' said Morpheus, remembering suddenly.

'Don't worry, it fits right in,' said Ildiko. 'Besides, they're over the moon about their new cichlids.'

Morph pictured Mr and Mrs Fleps sitting in their front room, Pavarotti silenced, staring in trance-like devotion at their latest imported fish. He chortled and allowed himself to slump back on to the quilt.

'You look cute on this big bed,' said Ildiko, tugging the covers out from under him, tucking him back in.

'I feel like . . . like death warmed up,' he groaned, but this can't have been a Hungarian turn of phrase, because she replied, 'I don't think that's something my parents have in the house. How about a bowl of chicken soup?'

'Just . . . coffee, thanks.'

'How about a cup of tea, in a squirrel mug? Expensive English tea, bought by my daredevil dad on the black market in 1977. Maturing in the tin ever since, just waiting for you to come along.'

He closed his eyes wearily. 'My band has left me,' he said, in a voice from the Hadean depths.

*

By evening Morpheus was up and about, if a little shaky. In the same room with the benignly attentive Mr and Mrs Fleps, the over-friendly Alsatian and the successfully integrated tropical fish, he spoke on the telephone with Cerberus.

'Slayer have *had* it,' enthused Cerb in his strong Ayrshire accent. 'They're old men. We're gonna murder them all across Europe.'

'What about me?' said Morph.

'We'll save the death blow for you. Catch up with us when you can. Meet you in Gomorrah!' Cerb was raving, high on adrenalin. He was about to go onstage in Bratislava and sounded as though he was surfing a tidal wave of adulation, or had succumbed to a cocaine pusher.

'How are they coping?' asked Ildiko when he hung up.

'I don't know,' he said. 'OK, I think.'

Morph was hungry by now, but reluctant to endure a three-course meal under the watchful gaze of Ildiko's parents, the dog, two of El Greco's saints and the stuffed head of a fox.

'I'll take you out for a snack,' whispered Ildiko, assuring her parents that 'Andreas' needed some fresh air.

They left the house, blinded by the porch lights and stumbling hesitantly until they found their footing on the moonlit main street. Morph's legs functioned like newly purchased equipment, not yet broken in. He looked up at the sky, clearer here than in the city. The patterns of the stars were unrecognizable, nothing like the ones above his own parents' house in Ayrshire.

At the end of the street was a grocery shop, closed, and a tavern called the Blaha. They went in and seated themselves at a table, thereby doubling the number of serious diners though there were half a dozen folk drinking beer and wine. A trio of local musicians – guitar, accordion and drums – were playing restrained renditions of pop standards. Observing Morph and Ildiko's arrival, they judged that the demographics of the Taverna Blaha had changed sufficiently to justify a switch from Abba to U2. A cat-eyed girl Ildiko had gone to school with wandered over to take the order.

'*Somloi Galuska*,' said Ildiko, without looking at the menu.

'*Bacskai Rostelyos*,' said Morph, after some deliberation.

'Are you sure?' Ildiko whispered to him. 'So soon after chucking up?'

'Mind over matter,' he smirked.

The band played U2 until the food arrived, then slimmed down to a duo for 'Nothing Compares 2 U'. Morpheus watched Ildiko spoon her vanilla cream cake into her perfect mouth; Ildiko watched Morpheus devour his roast beef in tomato sauce.

'Does it bother your parents,' he said between mouthfuls, 'that we're not married?'

'Of course it bothers them, you idiot,' she said, and licked the icing sugar off her fingers with her long pink tongue.

'Then let's get married,' he said.

A cheer went up from the middle-aged folk at the bar. There was a scattering of applause. Morpheus assumed they were showing their appreciation for the musicians.

'Idiot, idiot, idiot,' sighed Ildiko, shaking her head. 'Come on, let's dance.' And she pulled him to his feet.

'I'm still woozy from the drugs,' he hissed in her ear as she pulled him close to her. The accordionist played a tremulous fanfare.

'I'll hold you up till the roast beef takes effect,' she whispered back.

The band, complemented to the full trio once more, launched into a slow waltz version of 'Loch Lomond'.

'I can't dance to this sort of thing,' Morph murmured anxiously into her hair.

'Just hold me tight,' she said, directly into the ear that was the less deafened of the two. 'Close your eyes, and pretend you're lying down by my side.'

Panos Karnezis

Deux Ex Machina

She came on the morning train, on Monday. She had been loaded on the cargo car together with a bale of hay and the bottom half of a scrapped boiler which had been hastily cut with an oxyacetylene torch to make a watering-trough. A king-size mattress was nailed on each of the wooden walls to protect her from the sharp bends of the track. She had a canvas bag roped to her croup between her legs to collect her dung, but by flipping her tail to swat the flies she had displaced it and it had served no purpose at all during the trip. The stationmaster became aware of the smell immediately he opened the door, even before his eyes had time to get used to the dark interior of the car. She came at 14.07 on the 11.03, and no one knew about her until then.

*

An hour earlier, the stationmaster finished reading yesterday's paper, cut it into square pieces several pages at a time, and walked to the small shack across the track. Pinching his nose he hung the pieces from a nail next to the toilet bowl and quickly got out again, closing the door behind him. Back on the platform, a young man in a suit sat on a bench and put his cardboard valise next to him.

'Are you sure I haven't missed the train?' he asked.

'Yes.'

The big clock above their heads showed 13.10.

'But it's over two hours late.'

'That clock is running fast.'

Pretending to check his watch, the stationmaster climbed the bench and turned the hands back three hours. There was a whistle in the distance and the young man stood, straightened his jacket and picked up his suitcase. A minute later a train passed through the station at full speed and threw him off balance. From the concrete floor he watched the open freight cars leaving the station in a cloud of air and gravel.

'It's iron ore,' the stationmaster explained. 'From the mines of the penitentiary.'

The stationmaster sat on the bench and took off his cap. He took a collapsed cigarette pack from under the lining and offered one to the other man.

'What do you sell?' he asked, after lighting their cigarettes.

'Encyclopaedias.'

'What sort?'

'Medical.'

The stationmaster shook his head.

'People don't get sick much around here. Maybe it's the fresh air. Or maybe because they die young, while they're still healthy.'

'Why do they die, if they're so healthy?'

The stationmaster took a draw from his cigarette and swallowed the smoke. 'I haven't thought about it before.'

They watched the train disappear over the horizon, bumping up and down on the uneven tracks, and there was silence again. A brief wind turned the blades of a water pump and brought over the smell of the shack from the other side of the track. The young man spat, disgusted.

'Virgin Mary. What's that smell?'

'Sanitary facilities.'

They carried on smoking.

'Our station is at the top of the Public Works list of repairs,' said the stationmaster after a while. The salesman did not reply. Above their heads, the carousels of gears ticked the minutes inside the old clock. The stationmaster listened to it with attention and pride; it never missed a minute. But the customer's always right, he thought, amused. A fresh cloud of smoke emerged from the hills and soon another train approached. This was a passenger train and was slowing down. The salesman combed his hair and picked up his valise, but put it down again when the train stopped at the water tower outside the station.

'This isn't your train either,' said the stationmaster, and stretched his legs. 'How much are the books?'

The salesman fell back on the bench.

'Much less than you'd expect. And you can have one volume free. Either the anatomy atlas or the digestive system.'

While the train was taking on water a woman climbed down and ran to the shack. But as soon as she opened the toilet door she closed it again. She covered her nose with her handkerchief and returned to the train. She wore a dress with stamped roses and a hat.

'How about the reproductive system?'

'That will cost you extra.'

*

They fetched the plank they had for unloading barrels but it was no good. When she put a hoof down, the wooden board arched and oscillated and made a hollow sound, and she backed into the car, neighing and refusing to walk down again. In the end, they took stones from the collapsed wall of the yard and built a solid ramp under the board, from car to platform – one to support an ox. But she did not trust them any more.

Passengers got off the train, made suggestions as to how to get the horse out of the car, and then started eating what remained of their provisions. They carried straw baskets, a pair of cackling hens hung upside down, a demijohn of wine, a braid of garlic. A man in a white hat and summer suit with a leather briefcase also climbed down from the train and wandered among the crowd. The stationmaster assumed he wanted to use the facilities.

'I'm afraid the toilet's broken, sir.'

'I don't understand.'

'Better wait until the next station, sir.'

When the horse neighed to greet him, the small circle of people stepped aside with respect, and he said that he was a solicitor from the capital on business.

He suggested feeding the horse sugar and they did. But only after she had eaten the whole stock of sugar cubes from the village grocer did she listen to their commands. Finally, when she stood on the platform, they were all so impressed they forgot that they had missed lunch, they could not smell her dung any more, and they ignored the fact that they would be drinking their coffee bitter for at least a week. For what they saw was a race-horse, an Arabian mare from Damascus which had won thirty-two races in her youth – although they did not know that then – and she still had a perfect set of teeth. She stood naked but for the halter and a rubber-stamped luggage tag tied around her neck with the name of the village on it, and her flanks were such a glorious sight that the men cheered, the women sighed, and the children wanted to touch. The encyclopaedia salesman compared her mane then to the tassels of the velvet curtain of the National Theatre, but no one acknowledged his simile because they had never been to the capital city.

'What's her name?' the stationmaster asked.

'History,' said the solicitor.

'Hell!' said a boy. 'They called her after a book!'

As if it were the beginning of a religious procession, the crowd started down the street with the mare in front. The solicitor was on one side holding her halter and on the other were the encyclopaedia salesman and the stationmaster, who had forgotten in the commotion to semaphore the train out of the station. The train driver was there behind him determined to see who the lucky owner of the mare was. Further back walked the train passengers, both those who were returning home and others whose destination was some other place along the line. The crowd took a short cut through the forest of listing crosses in the cemetery, turned left at the ramshackle telegraph office where the wasps had made their nests in the chinks in the plaster, and made a brief stop at the civil guard station with the withered flag. The corporal checked the papers of the solicitor and joined the procession.

When they arrived at the house, the solicitor knocked at the door. Silence. He knocked again. The door opened and a young woman with hands covered in dough squinted at the sunlight, and looked at the solicitor, annoyed. Then she looked at the horse, and last at the crowd.

'Where's your husband?' asked the stationmaster.

'He's not in. Some people work for a living.'

*

A boy found Isidoro in his plot and told him they were looking for him. The young man stopped working and leaned against his hoe. The words PROPERTY OF were painted on its handle, but the name had been ground away with emery paper. He had a brief look at his land. It was small and on such a steep slope that now he had worked the earth deep, the soil had rolled to the bottom of the hill and he would have to carry it back up bucket by bucket.

'Isn't that old Marko's hoe?' asked the boy.

'No, it isn't.'

'It must be. The blade's broken at the corner just like Marko's, and—'

Isidoro put his foot on the blade and pushed it into the earth.

'What's this about?' he asked.

'The horse.'

'What horse?'

'The horse that's so important it travels by train.'

*

Behind the bar of the coffee shop the landowner sat on a low stool. His eyes just emerged above the counter in front of him. He watched the door, every man that walked in, the traffic outside, and his eyes shone in the shadows like a swimming crocodile's. He wiped his forehead with his handkerchief and put his fingers deep into the brine of an open tin. When the waiter came he caught him eating the olives.

'Why don't you sit at a table like everybody else?'

The landowner wiped his fingers on his trousers.

'The doctor said I should stay out of the sun. And in any case, I've saved you a table.'

The waiter took the bucket and mop while the landowner searched the shelf for newspapers.

'Where's today's?'

'The train hasn't come yet.'

A customer walked in, leaving the door open. The wind from the direction of the station blew into the shop.

'Close that damn door,' shouted the landowner. 'My clothes will smell of shit.'

The customer obeyed silently.

'They should demolish that toilet at the station,' continued the landowner, addressing no one in particular. 'In fact, they should demolish the lot. It's a public danger.'

'It's required by law to have sanitary facilities in public places,' the customer offered.

'Why do I waste my life in this shit hole?'

'You're the richest man in miles.'

'What's the point when all I can smell is shit and I can't get my newspaper on time?'

He leaned against the wall and rested his legs on the gas cylinder of the stove. The waiter finished mopping and the sun on the wet floor made the round tables look like lilies in a pond. The landowner gazed beyond them to the square glow of a window where a cat licked its paw. Suddenly the cat jumped off and the face of a horse looked at him from the other side of the glass. Then a crowd of human faces covered the windows and it became dark inside the shop. A well-dressed man walked in. 'Send a boy to find him,' he said to the crowd who had stayed outside and watched quietly. 'I'll wait here.'

The landowner turned to the waiter.

'Who is he looking for?'

'The man you sold that useless patch of land to. Up in the hills.'

Later, when Isidoro came, the solicitor told the crowd about the mare. How she used to belong to an army general, a relative of Isidoro so distant he was not sure whether he was from his mother's side of the family or his father's, God rest their souls. In fact he was the cousin of Isidoro's wife's aunt, an eternal bachelor, a major in the war, a pagan repenter who had been told on his deathbed the pearly gates would remain shut like a constipated arse unless he demonstrated humility and the altruism of love. The major donated his fortune to the benevolent fund of his local parish, but it was not enough. He scratched his head.

Son of a bitch, he thought, those priests are worse than politicians.

Finally he remembered he once had had a family: a father, a mother who had a sister, yes, who had three children he used to play War of Independence with when he was a little boy until he had almost impaled one of his cousins in an attempt to re-enact one of the most moving pages in the history of the revolution. He called his solicitor then, and gave him orders to trace his closest relative.

'I have to put him in my will.'

'Which one, sir?'

'Any bastard you can find as long as he's a man, because only a man can care for my beloved History, the only female I loved in this life.'

He signed the inheritance papers, and two days later peacefully passed on.

'And now she's yours,' the solicitor said to Isidoro. He opened his briefcase and took out a typed page and a pen. 'Please sign here.'

'I know nothing about horses,' said Isidoro.

'You are twice lucky today,' the encyclopaedia salesman said. 'I have everything you need here.'

'You sell human anatomy books,' said the stationmaster.

'It's the same thing.'

*

The wasps appeared at sunrise, after the horse had spent a few days in the house. They found her from her smell, methodically searching for a crack in the shutters until their persistence had paid off. Then, encouraged by the warmth, they explored the rest of the house. It was a small rubble house with only two rooms, a bedroom and a kitchen, where they eventually made a banquet from the food shelves and the meat safe. The cobwebs on the lintel caught a dozen of them, but that was merely an inconvenience because of the strength of their numbers. Diamanda was aroused by the sound of their wings and, under the delusion of sleep, she believed it was the noise of a radio. But only for a moment, because soon she was awake enough to remember they could not possibly afford one.

She tiptoed to the kitchen door, opened it, and her eyes had only a few seconds to take it all in: there were wasps on the leg of lamb, on the bread, sucking the oil and bathing in the jar of molasses, licking the sugar and sipping the drops of lemonade on the table. Taken by surprise, the thick cloud of insects took flight and tried to escape not through the open window but through Isidoro's shaving mirror. Diamanda quickly closed the kitchen door and woke up her husband.

'What is it, woman?'

'I don't know why I ever agreed to marry you, but I know now why I should divorce you.'

It took Isidoro several hours to calm her down. Every time they heard steps or the hammering of donkey hoofs on the cobblestone path outside their house, they stopped until the sound had faded away, and then carried on arguing.

'Fine feathers make fine birds,' said Isidoro, and killed a wasp that had escaped through the kitchen window only to re-enter the house through the bedroom. 'People used to pity me for what that cheat the landowner did to us.'

'A plot on a slope we need ropes to get to!' exclaimed Diamanda.

'Anyway,' said Isidoro, regretting he had brought up that matter. 'Now, with the mare, I get free drinks and snacks, and people talk to me like old friends.'

'All they want to talk about is the horse.'

'It's talk isn't it?'

Diamanda closed the bedroom window. The wasps had managed to escape from the kitchen and were circling the house. In the garden the cat clawed the air.

'What are you going to do about the tools?' she asked.

'That horse was a God-sent gift. It will help us buy our own. Then I'll put them back in Marko's shed.'

'How's the horse going to help you do that?'

'I'm thinking of racing her.'

'You know nothing about horse racing!'

Before Isidoro could continue there was a knock on the door. It was the landowner. He walked in not waiting to be invited, shaking his handkerchief to get rid of the wasps.

'What do you want?' Diamanda asked.

'I have business to talk to your husband about.'

'The last time you talked business with my husband we almost ended up in the poorhouse.'

The landowner turned to Isidoro.

'I understand your uncle, son.'

'My uncle?'

'The major. I'm a widower. I can use some company, too.'

'You should remarry,' said Diamanda.

The landowner made an expression of displeasure.

'I want to buy the mare,' he continued. 'I will look after her well.'

Isidoro stood up. He was still in his woollen long johns and looked more stout than he really was. He felt as if a dream had come true. He felt lucky, like the time he had won his necktie in the church raffle, and proud.

'She's not for sale.'

The landowner looked at him for a moment. He then left without saying another word.

Diamanda sighed. 'We'll live to regret another of your decisions.' She opened the kitchen door a crack; at least the wasps had gone.

*

It was the same evening when the landowner sat with the priest in the coffee shop. They started by drinking coffee, then had a beer each, then the landowner suggested they had a couple of brandies.

'Why not?' said the priest.

'Will you be all right for matins, Father?'

'If you'd ever been to one you'd know it's only old women who come these days, and they're all deaf. I could recite the cup results and they wouldn't know the difference.'

They drank the brandy. A group of loud children were playing in the street. Then a woman came and sent them home, cursing and throwing stones at them as if they were stray dogs. After they were gone, the men in the coffee shop could hear the music on the radio, and the women sitting at the doorsteps could chat in peace.

'The man who couldn't afford a donkey now owns a race-horse,' said the landowner.

Father Yerasimo nodded in agreement. 'Who would believe it?'

'This country is on course for disaster, Father. The poor are too proud for their own good.'

The priest ordered another round of drinks.

'There's a lot to be said about the evils of pride.'

'By the way, Father, do you know about Marko's tools?'

*

For the rest of the week the wasps would come every day at dawn and circle the house for a way in, but they could not find one because Diamanda had put mosquito nets in the windows, Isidoro had blocked every crack in the walls with plaster, and the cooking fire was kept on day and night so that they could not get in through the chimney either.

On Sunday the rooster crowed earlier than usual. In bed Diamanda thought, This means a clear, sunny day. Just what the wasps love. It had rained the night before and soon the humidity added misery to the heat. Inside the house the smell of horse manure and urine from the cellar had taken over. Isidoro got dressed standing at the window, looking towards the hill where his plot was. Money was running out, spent on hay for the mare and the encyclopaedia payments. But he was not worried. He put on his only coat even though it was a warm day and did up all the buttons. He opened the door and jumped out. Before the wasps had time to attack him, he hid his head inside his coat. 'This is the siege of Constantinople!' he said and started walking fast, while the wasps fell on the coat like rain.

Half a mile down the road he took off the coat, hid it in the bushes while watching for neighbours, and in his short-sleeved shirt got back on the road and headed towards the square. There was plenty of time until the meeting. On a wall a lizard basked in the sun's rays and he clapped his hands to watch it run away. 'Fast, but not as fast as my horse, lizard,' he said. He looked up, and although he was far away, immediately recognized the priest from his black cassock. 'Damn,' he whispered and crossed himself. 'It's bad luck to see a priest early in the morning.'

'I didn't see you today at church, Isidoro.'

Isidoro kicked a stone.

'Well, I'm busy these days, Father.'

'Lay not up for yourselves treasures upon earth, where moth and rust doth corrupt, and where thieves break through and steal.'

Isidoro shrugged his shoulders.

'I'm poorer now than I ever was, Father.'

Father Yerasimo stroked his beard.

'You know, old Marko's lost his set of tools.'

Isidoro avoided the priest's eyes.

'I know nothing about that, Father.'

'But if you ever do, you'll make sure Marko gets back his hoes.'

'Why is Marko bothered? He's old. He doesn't work the fields any more.'

'A sin's a sin, son.'

'Yes, Father.'

'You used to be a good Christian, son.'

'I am, Father.'

'I'll investigate that.'

After the priest had gone, Isidore spat on the ground. 'Priests aren't happy unless they see you in a pine box,' he told himself. 'I'm not a thief. All I need is one race, one win, and I'll buy Marko and everyone else ten hoes each.'

In the coffee shop he greeted the other customers and took a seat to wait. It was 10.30 and the 07.35 was due at any time. He ordered coffee and then decided to buy everyone else a drink with the last of his savings. When he turned to give his order, he saw the landowner's eyes fixed on him from behind the counter. That bastard crocodile is everywhere, Isidoro thought calmly. But today's my day.

The other men asked him questions about the horse, and he answered all until the train whistle interrupted them. A few minutes later the first passengers crossed the square. Isidoro watched impatiently, trying to determine who was his man. Soon the square was empty again but for a boy playing with the stray dogs. Isidoro grew impatient. He won't come, he thought. What a jinx, that priest.

The boy was the first to see the little figure walking from the road that led to the station. He was dressed in dark clothes, patent leather boots, and a hat. Isidoro walked out to meet the stranger and led him to the coffee shop. When the visitor entered, everybody stood as if he were a guest of honour.

'Thank you for coming,' Isidore told him.

'I'm afraid I don't have much time. The train's leaving soon.'

'As I said in the telegram,' started Isidoro, 'I have a horse. A racehorse. I would like to get into partnership with someone who knows about racing.'

'I was surprised to hear that someone owned a racehorse in this—'

But he did not finish his sentence.

'Yes, History is a great horse.'

'Did you say History?'

'Maybe you've heard about her. She's a champion.'

'Everyone in the business knows about History. She was a champion indeed. A very rare mare.'

'Well, I own her now. Inheritance, I won't bore you with the details. I'm thinking of racing her.'

'Racing her?'

'Racing her, yes.'

The man had some brandy and smiled. 'The fact is,' he said, 'that horse has no racetrack value any more. She's too old.'

Isidoro and everyone in the coffee shop went silent.

'And she's not a workhorse, either,' the man added. He stood and checked his watch. 'I guess she's only good for walks now. I hope you'll enjoy riding her.'

Suddenly, a laugh began from behind the counter like the cackle of a hen. It was the landowner, sitting on his low stool and holding the folds of his belly like an accordion, spitting olive stones with every breath. Everybody else was silent. The waiter collected the empties and returned to the kitchen to wash them in the sink. He turned on the tap all the way in order for the running water to cover the laugh, but it was quite unstoppable now, louder that the wind in Isidoro's land where only rock grew, or the drone of the wasp cloud and the sound of Diamanda's insecticide bomb. It was worse than the smell from the station every time it blew towards the village, and worse than the pestilent air inside Isidoro's house.

The moment Isidoro picked up the knife from the table, the laughter became the sound of dynamite in his ears, and he could already see himself in the iron mines of the penitentiary, shovel in hand and a civil guard behind his back with a rifle, lazily smoking and keeping an eye on him. But the image did not discourage him, and he slowly walked towards the man behind the counter. The landowner fell off his stool as he tried to back off. He had nowhere to hide. The only way out was past the young man who shuffled his feet, still coming.

He would have killed him then if it were not for Diamanda, who walked into the coffee shop that very moment and, seeing what was happening, stood between them.

'Isidoro,' she said. 'You are about to sign another contract without having read the small print first.'

Isidoro stopped. His face was blushed. He looked at his wife and finally dropped the knife, ashamed.

*

Father Yerasimo sat at his desk with a cup of coffee, a plate of meat, and the oil lamp next to his notebook. He did not have much to do for the next day: a one-page sermon, a few lines for a lamentation, and a letter to the bishop in the district capital. It had been a strange few days. But now old Marko's tools had been returned and he had given Isidoro absolution and a promise not to notify the civil guard – but only after the foolish young man had agreed to the donation. As far as Father Yerasimo was concerned it was a fair punishment.

He started the sermon. Writing about the rich, the poor and those in between, he became so absorbed that at some point he imagined he was Archangel Michael and his pen was his mighty sword. He had to stop then, because he realized he was committing the deadly sin of pride. To get his mind off it, he picked a slice of the cured meat he had kept for himself before sending the rest to the poorhouse. He tasted it. 'Sweet!' he exclaimed. 'A God-sent gift. That horse saved Isidoro's soul and will feed the poor, too.' And he proceeded to eat everything on his plate, stuffing his mouth as if he had not had anything for days.

Gloria Evans Davies

Schoolboys

Schoolboys uproariously
enacting a scene from Hamlet
with a sheep's skull
as they plagued a grave-digger
in Dyffryn Road cemetery.

Brythyn

Brythyn
drunk on his way home
sings to Ebrilla
the cow
an arm around her neck,
                        drunk too
staggering and mooing
in the field of the cider apples.

Georgina Hammick

Green Man Running

BEFORE

There were three gates to the Top Pasture. Two of these gave on to adjoining grazing; the third, which opened on to a narrow, high-hedged lane, was only ever used when there were sheep on the grass. When cattle were on it the lane gate was kept shut and secured to the gatepost by a chain. This was because although the lane was the shortest, by far, route to his farmyard, bad experience had taught Michael Bucknell that to attempt to drive cumbersome animals, not fitted with brakes or gears or super-grip tyres and weighing half a ton apiece, down Breakneck Hump, was a mistake. In any case, to reach the farmyard, it was not just a matter of driving the stock downhill. At the bottom of Breakneck the lane veered sharply right and at once began an almost equally steep climb up a hill named Gray's Rise, a climb that cows and heifers and steers were unwilling to make. The road route from the Top Pasture to Bucknell's cattle sheds was acknowledged to be a roller-coaster ride, the people who appreciated it best being teenage boy bikers, madcap motorcyclists and, in hard winters with the lane closed by snow, tobogganists.

When, one sunny October afternoon, someone unhooked the chain on the lane gate, managed to kick the gate open a few feet but then, on account of the claggy turf and dung and thistles surrounding the gate, failed to shut it properly afterwards, it did not take long for a curious bullock to notice and to barge a way through to freedom. The rest of the herd followed.

Out in the lane, the cattle turned left. The angle of the gate dictated their course, though in all likelihood, since left equalled downhill, they would have turned left anyway. The leaders at once mounted the verge and began to graze or to relieve themselves, but were kept on the move by the bump and bore antics of the curly-headed, leaky-nosed, mud-caked bully boys in the rear.

Twenty yards further on the lane's leisurely descent ended in a bend, and the precipitous incline of Breakneck began. The unwary bullocks, moving together as one, plunged over the crest like a waterfall. Pell-mell. Helter-skelter. Faster and faster. Faster.

*

A mile away, approaching Gray's Rise from the opposite direction, behind him the distant mass of Brown Clee Hill, on his left and closer the quarried jags of Titterstone Clee, was Billy Martin in his Ford pickup. The pickup, last of a series of beaten up vans and pickups and jalopies Billy had snatched from the breakers and scrounged replacement parts for, and – once he'd got the camshafts, or big ends, or gearboxes into more or less working order – drove through the lanes like Jehu, had a load of logs on board. The load consisted of oak, apple, ash, and some make-weight birch that invariably found its way into the loads and that certain customers complained about. It burned like matchsticks, they argued; it sputtered and spat great sparks that could leap a fireguard and set the house on fire.

It seemed to Billy as he rattled westwards that the whole world was on fire that afternoon. For one thing there was this all-over hot and excited feeling he had that made the palms of his hands so slippery he was finding it hard to keep a grip on the steering wheel. For another, the sun was dropping by the minute and everything its rays touched on – corrugated barn roofs, brilliant verge grass (so bright and fresh and green after recent rain you could almost believe it was spring coming), hedgerow oaks, hawthorn leaves and berries, tags of hay and straw in the hedge that the bale trucks had left behind – was red-gold and aflame.

*

Billy was the second youngest of five brothers, the sons of Jack Martin, farm labourer, and his wife Linda, whose maiden name had been Carter. Jack and Linda had known each other since junior school and they got married in 1948, when he was eighteen and she sixteen. It was quite usual in those days for young people to marry in their teens; at least half the couples Jack and Linda knew tied the knot before they were twenty. They did this even when there was no baby on the way and no real reason to.

Before Linda nabbed him there had been girls galore after Jack. He was considered a catch, not because he had brilliant brains or ambitions – he had neither – but because he was tall and darkly sexy and according to some looked a lot like Gary Cooper. He had a dry wit too, and the deadpan, cynical-seeming remarks he came out with, which disconcerted those who didn't know him well, made Linda fall about laughing.

Linda wasn't a looker in the head-turning way Jack was. She was only five feet tall and her head seemed a shade too big, her face a shade too broad, for her diminutive hands and feet. But she was slim in those days, and vivacious and warm-hearted, and her large blue eyes were unusually sparkly. By nature an easy-going person, she took life as it came, which was just as well as how it came was hard and sometimes cruel. For example, her firstborn, a girl, had a heart defect and lived only two days. Then the second child, Malcolm, was partially deaf and developed epilepsy when he was three. And it must have been around this time that Jack tripped while felling an ash with a chainsaw. The saw all but removed his arm and the healing of it – though the pain never left him – kept him off work and wages for the best part of a year.

Money was tight enough anyway in the Martin household and it got tighter as more babies came along. Linda was not a moaner. She didn't complain about Jack's forty-Woodbines-a-day smoking habit and the chunk it took out of the housekeeping. Nor about the tied cottage they shared with successive dogs and cats. This was the middle strip of a red-brick Victorian terrace of three two-bedroomed cottages, bang on the road but not on the bus route, two miles from a shop, six miles from the town. The only form of heating the cottage had was a chokey coal fire in the front room and an unreliable coke stove in the kitchen, and the slates that blew off the uninsulated roof stayed where they fell. There were no plumbed-in baths in the terrace, and no inside toilets either. Not, that is, until 1968, when Jack's employer and landlord, possibly under pressure from the council, had the roof felted and three lean-to bathrooms built on at the back. But he forgot to instruct the builders to put in a damp course, and so before long a green, black-spotted mould decorated the bathroom walls.

Life was better in summer. The children could be turned out into the vegetable patch, and on sunny days Linda sat on the step and rocked the pram and watched the older boys fighting and the nappies blowing, and the clouds flying and Jack's brown hens nodding their way through the cabbage stalks. As a child she had been walked by her mother to the fields at haymaking and harvest times and spent whole days there. The days of farmworker family picnics were long gone by then, but when Jack was cutting grass for hay or silage she and her little ones would park themselves under a hedge and turn their heads to follow one man and his machine, and the tall grass falling over itself in their wake.

*

It was 1970 now, and all but one of the Martin boys were grown men. The three eldest had left home. Malcom and Kirk were married. Malcolm, who still suffered regular but unpredictable fits, was temporarily out of work. Kirk, a meat packer in his wife's home town four counties away, had three kids of his own. Unmarried Lionel, Linda's favourite, worked as a shepherd on a big estate near Leominster and had a centrally-heated bungalow all to himself. The only two left to keep her and Jack company in the evenings and to share the back bedroom were twelve-year-old John, a gentle, pink-cheeked cherub of a boy, and Billy.

Billy was known to his log customers as the Wood Boy, even though chopping and splitting and delivering logs for J & M Forestry was mainly an autumn and winter job and only one of several things he did. He was a general farmhand who liked variety and hired himself out on a casual basis to whoever needed and paid him most. Tractor driving, muck spreading, fruit and grain and potato harvesting, coppicing, sheep dipping, lambing, calving, bale stacking, hedge laying, ditching, grave digging – these were all tasks Billy could turn his hand to and, more crucially, stick at till the job was done. A tearaway in his boyhood, useless in class (though Miss Spindle, who taught the juniors, would never hear a word against him then or afterwards), he had had to work doubly hard to earn his present reputation as a reliable if short-term grafter, especially since, in his early teens, he'd been up before the magistrates in Mill Street more than once for joyriding.

Billy was twenty now and hadn't been in trouble for three years at least, if his appearance suggested otherwise. He was the tallest in his family, six foot three, raw-boned and cavernous, and the clothes he habitually wore – a dirt- and grease-stiffened jacket that had once been Sunday best for his father, a sweat-dark T-shirt (in winter a rough-rib polo neck), a pair of diesel-stained jeans that had originally been a stonewashed blue – hung off his back or flapped unprepossessingly against his legs. The rancid smell these garments gave off was unignorable indoors. Anyone standing at the regulars' bar in the Crown or in the cigarette queue in the shop had no need to turn his head to know that it was Billy Martin who had just blown in.

Then there was Billy's pallor that no amount of sun and wind managed to whip into the ruddy, pre-leather tan his brothers had, and his haphazard gait, and his stoop, and the diagonally chipped front tooth he broke tobogganing down the Double Dingle on Whitcliffe Common that showed up unmissably when he smiled and which gave him a gipsyish, if not actually criminal, air.

Billy was not unpopular, however. The three old men, all in their eighties, who passed their days on a bench outside the Crown liked Billy because he always found the time to stop and say, How ya doin then? and to wait for an answer, which not many youngsters could be bothered to do. Desmond Bucknell, ten-year-old son of farmer Michael Bucknell, liked Billy because whenever Billy was doing a job for his dad he'd allow Desmond to work alongside, talking to him as though they were mates and the same age. The majority of Billy's peers, the boys he'd bunked off school with, and fished with, and gone night-poaching with, had left to seek their fortunes in Bridgnorth or Worcester or as far afield as Birmingham; nevertheless the few who remained got on all right with him. Also, and surprisingly – for he fitted nobody's idea of a ladies' man – girls seemed to have a soft spot for Billy. His crinkly mane, parted in the middle Jesus-style, was in fashion that year, which might have had something to do with it. Or perhaps the attraction was not so much Billy as his lurcher dog, Yellow, a familiar sight in the back of the pickup where he acted as quivering lookout atop the log pile. Whatever the reason, when Billy played pool on Saturday nights there was very often a shy or sly sixteen-year-old hanging around the pool table, or making up to Yellow in a corner.

Today, instead of his usual outfit, Billy had on a clean white T-shirt with cap sleeves, a worn but clean pair of denim flares held up by a leather belt, and a tan suede jacket with a V of cowboy-style fringing across the chest and back. The clothes – jeans noticeably short in the leg – belonged to Billy's brother Lionel, and the reason Billy had borrowed them was a girl he'd recently met at a youth club social in the town. The girl, Marianne (he did not ask her other name), told him she was certain to be elected Rose Queen next year – Just you wait and see. She said she worked in the shoe shop in Broad Street but was going to pack it in soon because she was sick of the sight of feet. This remark, or maybe it was the way she said it, made Billy hoot.

Marianne had wide green eyes and straight blonde hair that tipped up, and bounced, on her shoulders. She had a naughty look and laugh, and Billy was smitten, the first time such a thing had happened to him. At the end of the evening he asked her out for a drink, or for a Sunday stroll along the Bread Walk, if she'd prefer a bit of air, but she said she wouldn't go out with him unless he had a wash and smartened himself up.

To his astonishment, Billy heard himself tell Marianne he'd do that. He heard himself say he'd meet her at the Buttercross after work Friday. They'd go for a drink at the Globe, and he'd be so damn smart and clean she wouldn't recognize him.

Marianne rolled her eyes when Billy had finished. She said, The Globe? You're expecting *me* to go to the *Globe*? It's the Feathers I'm used to. It's cocktails in the Feathers or nothing, *if* you don't mind.

Billy wasn't offended at all. He could tell Marianne was having him on about the Feathers. He knew she'd never set foot in the place, no more than he had.

*

Billy had two other jobs to do before he could get himself to the Buttercross. After he'd delivered his wood load – to a middle-aged couple called Tilson, newcomers to the area who'd recently moved into the Red Cottage, Bitterley – and stacked the logs (if the Tilsons wanted them stacked and were prepared to pay), he had to take a Land Rover wheel, belonging to Mr Johns, one of the bosses at J & M Forestry, into the garage for repair. Mr Johns said that if it turned out the damage could be fixed then and there Billy must wait and bring the wheel back with him.

Normally Billy wouldn't have minded hanging around for as long as it took, or longer, because the forecourt attendant was a mate of his; but he didn't want to be late for Marianne. Time was tight enough anyway: as well as the logs and the wheel he had to do some grocery shopping for his mother. As soon as he'd mentioned he was going into town she'd found a pencil stub and written him a list.

It was hot in the cab and Billy had the windows down to allow the through-draught to cool his face and neck. The pickup had no sun visor and the angry red ball was slap in front of the windscreen now; except when a hedgerow oak or a barn fleetingly eclipsed it, the dazzle was blinding. He kept scraping the hedge. He kept having to stamp on the brake and stick his head out of the window to check there wasn't a truck or a tree heading straight for him. At the same time he had the radio on and was singing along to Mungo Jerry and 'In the Summertime'. The song had reached number one in June and stayed there. Even now that summer was over it was still high in the charts and Billy was sick to death of it. A week ago he would have switched off or fiddled around with the radio, but today was different, the song itself different. Today the words might have been written for him. The weather was fine and he had women, or rather a woman, on his mind.

Sing along with us, dee dee dee dee *dee* . . .

He was singing along with them – thumping the steering wheel to the rhythm, sticking his head out of the window, thinking about Marianne, thinking about her hair, trying to picture her mouth, imagining how she would look (and how he would feel) when he first caught sight of her at the Buttercross – as he passed the red sandstone wall at the entrance to Bucknells Farm and rattled along the ridge leading to Gray's.

At the start of the drop he put his boot on the brake but did not change gear. In his book it was chicken to change down for hills. He only ever changed down if he could see something bigger than him coming up.

*

Carnage was the word the headline writer on the *Advertiser* chose to describe what happened when pickup and bullocks collided in the little well at the bottom of Breakneck and Gray's. Seven prize-winning steers killed outright. Eight more so badly injured – some by flying logs – they had to be destroyed when the vet got there. A pet dog, belonging to driver of the vehicle Mr Billy Martin and thrown clear in the impact, struck and killed on the verge by a Land Rover wheel.

Astonishingly, Billy was not killed, although the head and chest and spinal injuries he received provoked the general whisper that it might have been better if he had. Better for Billy and better for his mother, who was going to have to look after him.

The report of the tragedy took up most of the front page and spilled over on to page 3. On page 2, along with a picture of the wrecked pickup, were articles dealing with issues arising from the accident. One, headed 'Pickup Had Bald Tyres', listed all the defects the unlicensed uninsured pickup had and called for tighter MOT controls and more frequent police spot checks. The logs in this case were green, it was pointed out, which meant they were particularly heavy and injurious; wasn't it high time all wood loads were tarpaulined and roped by law? Another item, 'Ramblers Blamed for Open Gates', centred on the danger posed to cattle and livestock by urban visitors who either did not know or refused to observe the countryside code.

A third feature, in heavier type than the rest which gave it a funeral look, was a verbal portrait of Billy pieced together with the help of people who'd known him all his life. The heading – NO ANGEL, BUT HIS HEART IS IN THE RIGHT PLACE – came from a telephone interview with Billy's one-time teacher Miss Spindle, retired now, who said that Billy was one of the few of her pupils who could be relied on to keep in touch: He'd always drop in for a cup of tea if he was passing. She was disappointed and surprised, she said, that Billy's vehicle had not been taxed or insured, but put it down to forgetfulness: I'm sure he meant to do it. He was a reformed character in most ways. Billy's parents and brothers refused to be interviewed (Billy was in intensive care and they had been warned he might not survive) but Linda's cousin Ted Carter, a poultry farmer over Market Drayton way who didn't keep up with that side of the family, spoke, he said, for all of them: It's a tragic waste. The lad was just beginning to make something of his life. We're just hoping he can come through this. We'll give him all the help we can. He's got everything to live for.

*

No, said Desmond. No, I didn't. I never leave gates open. You know I don't.

I won't be angry with you, his father said. Not if you tell me now.

Well I didn't. It wasn't me, repeated Desmond.

His father was rolling a pencil around on his desk. He called it a desk, though what it was was an oblong of laminated chipboard supported either end by a metal filing cabinet. He left the pencil alone and began shuffling a stack of papers. He stood them upright, sorted them the way he wanted them, laid them down flat, squared them up. Then he picked up the pencil and began chewing the end of it.

I hope you're quite sure about this, he said, taking the pencil out of his mouth and examining the bite marks he had made. If you're not sure, if you're not absolutely certain about it, now is the time to tell me. We all make mistakes, lad, he added after a pause. I do. We all do.

They were in the farm office, a cell-like room with metal windows set too near the ceiling to see out of or to clean, which led off the boot room (which led off the scullery, which led off the kitchen). The office smelled strongly of old tin ashtray, and also of rubber boots and oilskins. Behind Desmond's father, on the cream-gloss brick wall, were framed photographs, ages old some of them, of prize-winning cattle and sheep and pigs. The men, in overalls or long aprons, who stood beside these animals, keeping a firm hand on the head-collar rope, were Desmond's father, or else his grandfather, or else his great-grandfather. Above them, a foot or so off-centre of the wall, was a large electric clock. As Desmond looked at the clock, mentally shunting it to the left as he always did, the big hand, seemingly stopped, jumped five minutes all at one go. *Clunk.*

I didn't do it, Dad, really, Desmond said.

You see, it's important to have trust, for people to be able to trust each other, his father said, looking up abruptly, straight at Desmond. I need to trust you, you need to trust me. Otherwise—

I know that, Desmond said. But I didn't leave the gate open. I can promise you that.

His father put the pencil down and began rolling it again. I know you were in the Top Pasture on Friday afternoon, he said slowly, because Don saw you on the hazel track when he was checking the troughs. The pump's playing up, but I daresay you know about that. You were nutting when he saw you, Don said. You had a stick and you were bashing the hazels to get the cobs down.

Well it was half-term, Desmond said, so— He stopped. I didn't do any damage to the bushes. I don't think I did. No, I'm sure I didn't.

I know it was half-term. I know that *now*. But I forgot it when the police came round. I had to tell them where everyone was and what they were doing Friday afternoon. I told them you weren't anywhere near the Top Pasture because I knew, I thought I knew, you were at school. Or on the bus coming home from school. No one can be certain, of course, exactly what time the lane gate was left open.

But I helped you with the milking, remember? Desmond said. I don't do that on school mornings.

As I say, I forgot about half-term, his father said. That's really what I'm trying to say to you, that we can all forget things. We can forget to shut a gate, and afterwards we can forget, we may be able to forget, that we forgot to shut it. Sometimes it takes something or someone else, to jog our memory. Don't you find that?

Clunk. The minute hand on the clock jumped another five minutes. I climb gates, you know, Desmond said. I hardly ever go through them. It's easier to climb over them. Saves a lot of time.

Don said you had a bucket with you to put the cobs in – a black plastic feed bucket – is that right?

Yes.

Don't you want to sit down? his father said. There's a chair right beside you. Oh, all right then. Desmond sat down.

His father pulled a packet of Embassys from his jacket pocket and after it a box of matches. He shook out a cigarette, put it in his mouth and struck a match. The match went out; he struck another. He began smoking the cigarette slowly, taking long, slow, noisy inhalations of breath. How did you get to the Top Pasture, by the way? he asked eventually, directing a volley of smoke at the ceiling. Did you go via the Six Acre or did you go by road?

I went by road; I biked there. I biked to the bottom of Gray's, and I left my bike in the hedge, and then I walked up Breakneck. And then I climbed the gate.

See anyone? In the lane or anywhere?

No, said Desmond, after a pause.

I imagine you threw the bucket over before you climbed the gate? his father said. That would be the easiest thing to do. Chuck the bucket into the field first, and then climb over. Is that what you did?

Yes. I think so.

But coming back? his father said, stubbing out his cigarette in the tobacco tin lid he kept on his desk and used for an ashtray.

The lid was emptied from time to time but never washed, so that a silt of hardened and sour-smelling black ash covered its surface. But coming back? he repeated. That wouldn't have been so easy, would it? I mean to say, the bucket was full then so you couldn't chuck it over else you'd have lost all the cobs you'd collected. It's not that easy climbing a gate – an old, mossy, slippery gate – carrying a bucket, is it? And those feed buckets are cumbersome enough when empty. I've been trying to put myself in your shoes, and I think I'd probably have decided it would be simpler to—

I managed it though, Desmond said. It can be done. I managed it all right.

Clunk.

You're shivering, lad, his father said. I don't think you've got enough clothes on. It is a bit fresh in here, mind. Switch on the fire if you want it.

I'm not cold, Desmond said. There were huge shaggy cobwebs in the windows and on the ceiling, and he took a good look at them. There were spiders in those webs, very likely.

Well, we can't sit here all day, his father said. I've got work to do and I expect you have. He sat back and locked his hands behind his head. He addressed his next remark to the ceiling: You like Billy Martin, don't you, D? You've always got on well with him?

Desmond noded

Billy's going to be in a wheelchair for the rest of his life, did you know that? If he survives he'll be in a wheelchair.

Oh. Desmond said it so quietly it sounded more like a breath or a sigh.

He's almost certainly got brain damage. They don't seem to know the extent of it yet or what it'll mean. It may mean . . . He tailed off. Well, off you go then, D. His father got to his feet.

When Desmond was at the door his father said, The insurance assessors are coming this afternoon. There was a fair bit of money tied up in those steers, as you can imagine.

*

It was perhaps six months after this interview that Desmond changed his name. The name he chose was Dexter, after the

Sussex and England batsman and test match captain, E. R. Dexter (Cricketer of the Year, 1961). Desmond had never watched Ted Dexter play; he was too young. But he had seen him in some old test footage they'd shown on television. And there were photographs of Dexter – about to take delivery at the crease, hitting out, running – in a cricket annual he had. He liked the look of Ted Dexter, and the style of him. He liked his name.

Well, that's a pity I must say, Desmond's mother said when Desmond announced his decision and asked his parents to call him Dexter from now on. Desmond was my father's name, we named you after him. I know you never knew your grandfather Newell, he can't mean much to you, but I do think it's a pity. I don't like the name Dexter very much, do you, Michael? Not as a Christian name. It sounds American.

Oh, let the lad do what he wants, Michael Bucknell said, helping himself to potatoes. I was never that keen on Desmond myself. It wasn't my choice. Anyway, it won't make much difference because we hardly ever call him Desmond, do we? We call him D.

They were at the big kitchen table, eating supper, just the three of them because the girls were out. Elizabeth, aged eighteen, had gone to the cinema with her boyfriend. Anna, thirteen, was having her weekly piano lesson in the town.

If I was going to call myself after a cricketer, after a batsman, it wouldn't be Ted Dexter I'd pick, Michael Bucknell said. No, I'd go for the best. I'd go for Donald Bradman. Bradman Bucknell – now that sounds impressive. I quite like the sound of that. He took a piece of gristle out of his mouth and put it on the edge of his plate. On the other hand, I quite like the idea of a farmer's son choosing to call himself after a breed of cattle. We kept a small dexter herd here at one time, did you know that, D? Tough little fellows but not a patch on our Herefords. Pass the mustard, would you lad?

I don't know what his teachers are going to say, Margaret Bucknell said. Desmond Bucknell's the name on all his school books. I think he'll find he has to be Desmond at school.

Desmond Hogan

Winter Swimmers

Winter swimmers, you brave the cold, you know you've got to go on, you make a statement. A tinker's batty horse, brown and white, neighs in startlement at the winter swim. A man rides a horse on Gort Hill, disappearing on to the highway. Tinkers' limbs, limbs that have to know the cold to be cleansed.

'The tinkers fight with one another and kill one another. If someone does something wrong they beat the tar out of them. But they don't fight with anyone else. You never see a tinker letting his trousers down,' a woman whispered in Connemara, sitting on a wicker pheasant chair. The flowering currant was in blossom outside the window.

A traveller boy in a combat jacket with lead-coloured leaves on it stood outside his Roma Special, among washing machines, wire, pots, kettles, cassettes, tin buckets.

In early summer the bog cotton blew like patriarchs' beards, above a hide, the stems slanted, and distantly there were scattered beds of bog cotton on the varyingly floored landscape under the apparition-blue of the mountains.

I was skipping on Clifden Head when a little boy came along. The thrift was in the rocks. 'Nice and fit.' He wanted to go swimming. But he had no trunks. 'Go in the nude,' I said. 'Ah, skinny-dipping. Are you going again?' I was drying. 'No, I'll go elsewhere and paddle.'

'I used to pass him in the rain outside his caravan,' the woman in Connemara told a story before she went to mass, about a tinker man who died young, standing in an accordion-pleated skirt, 'sitting by a fire against a wall. "Why don't you go inside?" I'd ask him. "Sure I have two jackets," he'd say. "I have another one inside. I can put on that one if this one gets wet."'

'Are you a buffer or a traveller?' a tinker boy asked me. On their journey there are five-minute prayers at a place where you were born, where your grandmother died.

There was a traveller's discarded jersey in a bush. Buffer – settled – travellers stood in front of a cottage with the strawberry tree – the white bellflower – outside.

A traveller in a suit of mosque blue came to the door one day to try to buy unwanted furniture, carpets. 'He had a suit blue as the tablecloth,' went the story after him. Part of his face was reflected in the mirror. It was as if a face was being put together, bit by bit.

A traveller youth in a cap and slip-on boots which had a triangle of slatted elastic material held his bicycle in a rubbish dump against a rainbow. The poppy colours of the montbretia spread through the countryside in the hot summer. There were sea mallows between the roads and the sands. You felt you were nuzzling for recovery against landscape.

The sides of the sea road towards fall were thronged with hemp agrimony. The seaweed was bursting, a rich harvest full of iodine. As I was leaving Galway the last fuchsia flowers were like red bows on twigs the way yellow ribbons were sometimes tied around trees in the Southern States.

'Now therefore, I pray thee, take heed to thyself until the morning, and abide in a secret place, and hide thyself.' You felt like a broken city, the one sung about in a song played on jukeboxes throughout Ireland. 'What's lost is lost and gone for ever.' In May 1972 you heard a lone British soldier on duty sing 'Scarlet Ribbons' on a deserted sun-drenched street in that city.

Old man's beard grew among the winter blackthorns in West Limerick. Tall rushes with feathery tops lined the road to Limerick. Traveller women used to fashion flowers from these rush tops.

The bracket fungus in the woods behind my flat was gathered on logs like coins on a crown, stories.

On the street of this town the Teddy boy's face came back, brigand's moustache, funnel sidelocks, carmine shirts, the spit an emblem on the pavement. He had briar rose-white skin. 'They's come in September and stay until confirmation time,' a woman in a magenta blouse with puff sleeves whispered about the travelling people. When I was a boy travellers would draw in for winter around our town.

A pool was created in the river behind the house in which I was staying and I swam there each morning, the river, just after a rocky waterfall, halted by a cement barrier. On this side of the town bridge the river is fresh water. On the other it is tidal. Swans often sat on the cement barrier when only a meagre current went over it.

On this side it is a spate river, and the current, always strong at the side, after rain, is powerful. I did not gauge its power and one morning I was swept away by it, over the barrier, as if by a human force. I had no control. There was no use fighting. I was carried down the waterfall on the other side of the barrier to another tier of the river, drawn in a torrent. I saw a pegwood in red berry on the bank. I got to the side, crawled out. In ancient Ireland they used to eat bowls of rowan berries in the autumn.

One morning I tried the tidal part of the river at the pier called Gort. In Irish, *gort* means field, field of corn. It is very close to the word for hunger or famine, *gorta*. The flour ships from Newcastle and Liverpool used to come here. People would carry hay, seaweed to the pier. A slate-blue warehouse shelters you from view.

When I was a boy they used to hold a rope across the river at the Red Bridge, someone on either side, swimmers clutching it, and then the swimmers would be pulled up and down. I remembered a man drying the hair of a boy in the fall of 1967.

I had a friend who used to swim naked when he found he had a place to himself. One day someone hid his clothes in the bushes and a group of girls came along. He hid behind a bush until they went.

He was writing what he called a pornographic novel for a while. As we passed some travellers' caravans one autumn day he told me a story. A boy, a relation, a soldier in Germany, came from England, slept in the bed with him. At night they'd make love. The evenings during his visit were demure. They'd have cocoa as if nothing had happened. My friend had a modestly winged Beatle cut, wore vaguely American plum or aubergine shirts with stripes of indigo blue or purple-blue.

A traveller in a stovepipe hat called to the door one afternoon and offered five pounds for a copper tank that was lying behind the house, his hand ritualistically outstretched, the fiver in it. I couldn't give it to him. It was my landlady's. The copper tank disappeared in the middle of the night.

An English gypsy boy with hair in smithereens on his face, his cheeks the sunset peach of a carousel horse's cheeks, in a frizbee, carnelian hearing aid in his left ear, on a bicycle, stopped me one day when I was cycling and asked me the way to Rathkeale. I was going there myself and pointed him on. In Rathkeale rich travellers have built an enclave of pueblo-type and hacienda-type houses. They were mostly shut up, the doors and the windows grilled, the inhabitants in Germany, the men tarmacadaming roads. A boy with a long scarf in the lemon-yellow of the Vatican passed those houses on a piebald horse.

I moved down the river to swim in the mornings, nearer the house where I lived, and swam among the bushes, putting stones on the ground where there was broken glass. There'd been a factory opposite the pool.

When I was a boy it was an attitude, swim in rain, ice, snow, brave these things, topaz in the auburn hair of a boy swimmer.

A group of young people used to swim through the winter. Even when the grass was covered with frost and the blades capped with pomegranate or topaz gold. They'd pose for photographs in hail or snow. I was not among them but later I had no problems swimming in winter, in suddenly after some months of not swimming, of taking off a Napoleon coat in winter and swimming in winter in the Forty Foot in Dublin or on a beach in Donegal. There was something benign about these young people. Mostly boys. But sometimes a few girls.

One day in Dublin I met one of the boys just after his mother died. It was winter. We didn't say much. But we got on the 8 bus to the Forty Foot and had a swim together. He went to the United States shortly after that.

Some English gypsies were camped outside town and one day a boy on a Shetland pony, with copper crenellated mid-sixties hair and ocean-ultramarine irises, asked me, 'Did you ever ride a muir?'

'Look at that horse's gou,' he said referring to a second Shetland pony a boy with skirmished hair was holding, 'Would you like to feak her?'

It's like a bandage being removed I thought, plaster taken off, layer and layer, from a terrible wound – a war wound.

Christmas 1974, just before going back to Ireland from London, I slept in a bed with an English boy under a bedspread with diamond patterns, some of them nasturtium-coloured. He had liquid ebony hair, a fringe beard. He wore a bewhiskered Afghan coat, spears of hair out of it. In his bed his body was lily-pale – he had cherry-coloured nipples. On our farewell he gave me a book and I put the Irish Christmas stamp with a Madonna and Child against a mackerel-blue sky in it.

All the journeys, hitch-hiking, train journeys, overlap I thought, they are still going on, they are still intricating, a journey somewhere. It's a face you once saw and it brushes past the mikado orange of southern Switzerland in autumn, a face on a station platform. It is the face of a naked boy in an Edwardian mirror in a squat in London with reflections of mustard-coloured trees from the street.

When I returned to England in the autumn of 1977 I went on a day trip to Oxford shortly before Christmas with some friends and we listened to a miserere in a church and afterwards sat behind a snob-screen in a pub where tomtits were back-painted on a mirror. A boy in a sailor jersey was reflected in the mirror. It was another England. I was sexually haunted. By a girl I'd loved and who'd left me. By a boy I'd just slept with.

In Slussen in central Stockholm I once met a boy with long blond centre-parted hair, in a blue denim suit, and he told me about the tree in central Stockholm they were going to cut down and which they didn't, people protesting under it. I bought strawberries with him and he brought me in a slow, glamorous train to his home on the Archipelago, a Second Empire-type home. There were Carl Larsson pictures on the wall. It was my first acquaintance with that artist. He sent me two Carl Larsson images later. Images of happiness.

Years later I met that boy in London. He was working in the Swedish army and leading soldiers on winter swims or winter dips.

At the Teddy boy's funeral there were little boys in almost identical white shirts and black cigarette trousers, like a uniform, girls with bouffant hairdos, shingles at ears, in near party dresses, in A-line dresses, in platform shoes, in low high heels with T-straps, with double T-straps, carrying bunches of red carnations, carrying tulips. In ancient Rome, after a victory, coming into Rome, the army would knock part of the city. At the Teddy boy's funeral it was as if people were going to knock part of the town.

The Teddy boy wore a peach jacket in the weeks before he was drowned. He was laid out in a brown habit. My mother said it was that sight which made her forbid me swim at the Red Bridge with the other young people of town. In the summer when I was sixteen I tried to commit suicide by taking an overdose of sleeping pills at dawn one morning. I just slept on the kitchen floor for a while. At the end of the summer a guard drew up on the street opposite our house in a Volkswagen, the solemn orange of *Time* magazine on the front of the car. He'd come to bring me to swim at Red Bridge. Years later, retired, he swam in the Atlantic of Portugal in the winter.

At the end of summer of 1967, when I was sixteen, I started swimming on my own volition.

In early February the wild celery and the hemlock and the hart's tongue fern and the lords and ladies fern and the buttercup leaves and the celandine leaves and the alexanders and the eye-bright and fool's watercress came to the river bank or the river. There was the amber of a robin among the bushes who watched me almost each morning.

Here you are surrounded by the smells of your childhood I thought, cow dung, country evening air, the smell the grass gives off with the first inkling of spring, cottages with covert smells – the musk of solitary highly articulate objects – and a mandatory photograph on the piano. My grandmother lived in a house like the one I lived in now. She had a long honed face, cheekbones more bridges, large eyes, Roman nose. She was a tall woman and spoke with the mottled flatness of the Midlands.

Here's to the story tellers. They made some sense from these lonely and driven lives of ours.

When I was a child in hospital with jaundice there'd been a traditional musician who'd been in a car accident in the bed beside me. There were cavalcades of farts, an overwhelming odour as he painfully tried to excrete into a bedpan behind the curtains, but the insistent impression was, in spite of the pain, of the music in his voice, in his many courtesies.

You heard the curlew again. 'The cuckoo brings a hard week,' they said in Connemara. One year was grafted on to another. 'March borrows three days from April to skin an old cow,' they'd said a month earlier, meaning that the old cow thinks he's escaped come April. Two swans flew over the Deel and the woods through which golden frogs made pilgrimages among the confectioner's white of the ramson – wild garlic – flower, soldering stories. On a roadside in County Sligo once I sat and had soup from a pot with legs on it with a traveller couple. Now I knew what the ingredients were – nettles, dandelion leaves.

With May sunshine I started to go to Gort to swim each day. Traveller youths swam their horses in the spring tide, up and down with ropes, urging them on with long pliable horse goads with plastic gallon drums on the end. One of the traveller youths had primrose-flecked hair. Another a floss of butter-chestnut hair. Another, hair in cavalier style. 'You've a decent old tube,' said the boy with the primrose-flecked hair.

During the day I noticed his hair had copper in it. One evening during spring tide I saw him stand in a rose-coloured shirt, not far from cottages, the river where it was bordered by yellow rocket, holding a baby and watching great masses of yellow rocket float down.

The first poppy was a bandanna against the denim of the bogs of West Limerick.

In the evenings of spring tide when the travellers came along and swam their horses I was reminded of Saintes-Maries, which I'd visited twenty years before, when the gypsies would come and lead their horses to the water on the edge of the Mediterranean. To Saintes-Maries had come Mary, mother of James the Less, Mary Salome, mother of James and John, and Sarah, the gypsies' servant, all on a sculling boat. There were bumpers by the sea and in little dark kiosks jukeboxes with effects on them like costume jewellery. Lone young gypsy men wandered on the beach, great dunes on the land side of the beach. A little inland, horsemen with bandannas around their noses rode horses through the Carmargue. Back briefly in the river pool one evening I found the traveller youth with the cavalier hair shampooing himself after a swim. His underpants were sailor-blue and white.

Later that week when I came to Gort the boy with the primrose-flecked hair was there alone with his horse, a Clydesdale, ruffs at his feet. A few days' growth on his face, he was naked waist up. There was an imprint outline of the tank top – the evidence of hot days, his nipples not pink, hazel – a quagmire of hair under his arms, freckles berried around his body. His body smelt of stout like the bodies of young men who gathered in my aunt's pub in a village in the Midlands when I was a child. A rallying, a summoning in the body to dignity.

I am in the West of Ireland I thought. Illness prevents me from seeing, from looking. Like a soot on the mind. Sometimes I raise my head. Like Lazarus recover life especially vision.

One Friday evening as I cycled home from Gort the youth with the primrose-flecked hair was sitting on the town bridge with two of the varying set of youths who swam horses with him. His lips were more autobiographical in the near darkness. Friday evening was ammoniacal evening. He wore a Western shirt with parabola-shaped flaps with crystal buttons, buckled shoes, his hair brilliantined. Another youth had pomaded hair like a bunch of black grapes, wore incised boots. The other had a Tony Curtis quiff and a duck's arse. He had shoes of such bright and unusual sand colour that they would seem prohibited everywhere else.

The youth with the primrose-flecked hair introduced himself. 'Cummian.' And he introduced the other two youths. 'Gawalan. Colín.'

'You need a relationship,' he said.

When the tide came in in the evening again and his horse had a wounded leg and he tied it to the ships' rung on the pier and it would stand in the water for hours. Cummian stayed with it and he'd watch me swim and between swims he'd tell stories.

'There was a man, a homosexual, who worked in the factory. Some of the boys liked it and went with him.

'There was a man who fucked his mares. He tied them to trees.

'Someone sold a horse to a man who lived on Cavon Island off Clare and the horse swam back across the Shannon estuary to West Limerick.'

Two traveller brothers troubled over a horse at Gort, their voices becoming muffled. They seemed to wager the tide. The river had a mirror-like quality after rain. Late one evening Cummian was sitting in the bushes to one side with some men, one of whom was holding a skinned rabbit. Boys would often fish on the pier with the triple hook – the strokeall – for mullet. On the far side young men would hunt for rabbits with young greyhounds. On summer nights travellers would draw up on the pier in old cars – Ford Populars, Sunbeams. In Scots Gaelic there's a word, *duthus* – commonage. That's what Gort was, people coming, using the place in common. The winter, the dark days were a quarter I thought, now I have to face people, I have to communicate. There was often a bed of crabs on the river edge as I walked in.

'If I wasn't married I'd get lonely,' said Cummian one evening.

Water rats swam through the water with evening quiet, paddling with their forepaws. The tracks of the water rat made a V-shape. Sometimes in the early evening there'd be a harem of traveller boys on the pier in the maple red of Liverpool or the grey of Arsenal or the red white of Charlton FC or the grey white of Millwall FC.

'Where are you from?' asked a boy in a T-shirt with Goofy playing basketball on it.

'You don't speak like a Galway man but you've got the teeth.'

Cummian would tell stories of his forebears, the travelling people, beet picking in Scotland, hop picking in England. 'We eat bread with green mould here.' Wrote an ancestor of sojourning in Scotland, 'We lie down with manikins.' That ancestor used to write poems and publish them in *Old Moore's Almanac* for half a crown. Sometimes he got four and six pence. 'Some of them were a mile long,' said Cummian.

'They used to stuff saucepans with holes with the skins of old potatoes and they'd be clogged. They used milk cans especially. Take the bottoms out of milk cans. Put in new ones.'

With his talk of mending I thought, recovery is like a billycan in the hand, the frail, fragilely adjoined handle.

In the champagne spring tide of late July Cummian rode the horse in bathing togs as it swam in the middle of the river. One afternoon there was a group of small boys on the pier fishing. One had a Madonna-blue thread around his neck, his top naked, his hair the black stamens of poppies.

'I'll swim with you,' he said, 'if you go naked.' I took off my togs. They had a good look and then they fled, one of them on a bicycle, in a formation like a runaway camel.

Sometimes, though rarely, traveller girls would come with the boys to the pier, with apricot hair and strawberry lips, in sleeveless, picot edge white blouses, in jeans, in dresses the white of white tulips. Cummian's wife came to the pier one evening in a white dress with the green leaves of the lily on it, carrying their child.

Cummian was a buffer, a settled traveller, and lived in one of the cottages near the river, incendiary houses – cherry-, poppy- or rosette-coloured – with maple trees now like burning bushes outside them. Guinea fowl ran outside one of them.

Sometimes in the darkening evenings there'd be fires by the lane above the road alongside the river. Children gathered around them. There'd be horses outside the travellers' cottages, a jeremiad for the days of travelling.

One night travellers were having a row on the green by the river. There was a moment like the retreat of Napoleon from Moscow, hordes milling across the green. Cummian, holding his child, looked on pacifically. 'You're done,' someone shouted in the throng.

There was a rich crop of red hawthorn berries among the seaweed in early fall, at high tide gold leaves on the river edge. Reeds, borne by the cork in them, created a demi-pontoon effect.

A woman in piped white shoes with block high heels came around the corner one day as I stood in my bathing togs. 'This

place used by black swimmers during high tide. Children used
swim on the slope.'

A swan and five cygnets pecked at the bladderwort by the
side of the pier and the cob came flying low up the river, back
from a journey.

In berry, the pegwood, the berberis, the rowan tree were fairy
lights in the landscape. The pegwood threw a burgundy shadow
on to the water. With flood the reflection was the cinnabar red
of a Russian icon.

One day in early November Cummian was on the pier with
his horse alongside a man with a horse who had a sedate car and
horse trailer. The grass was a troubled winter green. The other
man, apart from Cummian, was the last to swim his horse.

'He likes winter swimming,' Cummian said of his. 'Like you.
He'd stay there for an hour. And he's only a year.'

With the tides coming in and going out there was a metallurgy
in the landscape, with the tidal rivers a metallurgical feel, something extracted, called forth. A sadness was extracted from the
landscape, a feeling that must have been like Culloden after battle.
On Culloden Moor the Redcoats with tricornes had confronted
the Highlanders.

'Why do you swim in winter?' asked Gawalan who was with
Cummian one evening.

'It's a tradition,' I said. 'I used to do it when I was a boy.'
Which was not true. Other people did it. I did it later, on and off
in Dublin.

Jacob Böhme said the tree was the origin of language. The
winter swim sustains language I thought, because it is connected
with something in your adolescence, the hyacinthine winter sunlight through the trees on the other side of the river. It is connected
with a tradition of your country, odd people – apart from the sea
swimmers – here and there all over Ireland who'd bathe in winter
in rivers and streams.

A rowing boat went down the river one afternoon in late
November, a lamp in front of it, reflection of lamp in the water.

Gawalan and Colín went to England. They'd go to see female
stripteasers first in the city and then male stripteasers.

With November floods there were often piles of rubbish left

on the river bank. A man in a trench coat, with rimless-looking spectacles, cycled up to the pier one evening. 'I hear them dumping it from the bridge at midnight. It kills the dolphins, the whales, the turtles. You see all kinds of things washed in further down, pallets, dressers.' He pointed. 'There used to be a lane going down there for miles and people would play accordions on summer evenings. A boxer used to swim here with wings on his feet. There was a butcher, Killgalon, who swam in winter before you. He swam every day up to his late eighties.'

The river's been persecuted, vandalized I thought, but continues in dignity.

Early December the horse swam in the middle of the river, up and down, and I swam across it. The water rubbed a pink into the horse.

Hounds, at practice, having appeared among the bladderwort on the other side, crossed the river, in mass, urged on by hunting horns.

A tallow boy's underpants was left on the pier. Maybe someone else went for a winter swim. Maybe someone made love here and forgot his underpants. Maybe it was left the way the travellers leave a rag, an old cardigan in a place where they've camped – a sign to show other travellers they've been there – spoor they call it.

Towards Christmas I met Cummian near his cottage and he invited me in. 'Will you buy some holly?' a traveller boy asked me as I approached it. Cummian's eyes were sapphirene breaks above a Western shirt, his hair centre-parted, a cowlick on either side.

There was a white ironwork hallstand, an overall effect from the hall and the parlour carpets and wallpaper and from the parlour draperies of fuchsian colours and colours of whipped autumn leaves. He sat under a photograph of a boxer with gleaming black hair, in cherry satin-looking shorts, white and blue striped socks. On a small round table was a statue of Our Lady of Fatima with gold leaves on her white gown, two rosaries hanging from her wrist, one white, one strawberry; on the wall near it a wedding photograph of Cummian with what seemed to be a pearl pin in his tie; a photograph of a man with a smock of hair, sideburns, John Bosco face, holding a baby with a patina of hair beside a young woman in an ankle-length plaid skirt outside a tent.

We had tea and slices of lemon gateau.

Christmas Eve at the river a moon rose sheer over the trees like a medallion.

Christmas Day frost suddenly came, the slope to the water half covered in ice. In the afternoon sunshine the ice by the water was gold- and flamingo-coloured.

Sometimes on days of Christmas the winter sun seemed to have taken something from the breast, the emblem of a robin.

Cummian did not come those days with his Clydesdale. I was the only swimmer.

I was going to California after Christmas. I thought of Cummian's face and how it reminded me of that of a boy I knew at National School, with kindled saffron hair which travelled down, smote part of his neck, who wore tallow corded jackets. His hand used to reach to touch me sometimes. At Shallowhorsemen's once I saw his poignant nudity, his back turned towards me. He went to England.

It also reminded me of a boy I knew later who smelled like a Roman urinal but whereas the smell of a Roman urinal would have been tinged with olive oil his was with acne ointment. One day after school I went with him to his little attic room and he sat without his shirt, his chest cupped. There was a sketch on the wall by a woman artist who'd died young. He used often to walk with his sister who wore a white dress with a shirred front and a gala ribbon to an aboriginal Gothic cottage in the woods.

He went to England in mid adolescence.

He was in the FCA and would sit in the olive-green uniform of the Irish army, his chest already manly, framed, beside a bed of peach crocuses on the slope outside the army barracks which used to be a railway hotel, a Gothic building of red and white brick, script on top, hieroglyphics, the emblems of birds.

It snowed after Christmas. The trees around the river were ashen with their weight of snow. There were platters of ice on the water.

As I cycled back from swimming, Cummian was standing

with two traveller youths in the snow. There was a druidic ebony greyhound in historic stance beside them. Their faces looked moonstone pale. I knew immediately I'd said something wrong on my visit to Cummian's house. It didn't matter what I'd said, it was often that way in Ireland, having been away, feeling damaged, things often came out the way they weren't meant. Hands in the pockets of a monkey jacket, hurt, Cummian's eyes were the blue that squared school exercise books were when I was a child.

There was a Canadian redwing in the woods behind my flat who'd come because of the cold weather in North America. Never again I thought as I was driven to Shannon, the attic room of beech or walnut, a boy half naked, military smell – musk – off him, a montage on the wall. Choose your decade and change the postcards. Somebody or something dug into one here.

I have put bodies together again here I thought, put the blood or strawberry terracotta bricks together.

In San Diego next day I boarded a scarlet train and a few days later I'd found a beach, the ice plant falling by the side, plovers flying over, where I swam and watched the Pacific go from gentian to aquamarine to lapis lazuli until one day, when the Santa Annas were blowing, a young man and a young woman came and swam naked way out on the combers, then came in, dried and went away.

*

The Red Bridge, a railway bridge, always porous, became lethally porous, uncrossable by foot. Cut off was an epoch, gatherings for swims.

People would trek over clattery boards who knew it was safe because so many people went there.

In the fall of 1967 trains would go over in the evening aureoles of light, against an Indian-red sun. You'd hear the corncrake.

A little man who worked in the railway would stand in the sorrel and watch the boys undress.

Shortly before he died of cancer he approached me, in a gaberdine coat, when I was sitting in the hotel, back on a visit. He spoke in little stories. Of Doctor Aveline who wore pinstriped suits, a handkerchief of French flag-red in his breast pocket, and always seemed tipsy, wobbling a little.

Of Carmelcita Aspell whose hair went white in her twenties, who wore tangerine lipstick and would stand in pub porches, waiting to be picked up by young men.

Of Miss Husaline, a Protestant lady who went out with my father once, who didn't drink but loved chocolate liqueur sweets.

Of the bag of marzipan sweets my father always carried and scrummaged by the rugby pitch; squares of lime with lurid pink lines; yellow balls brushed with pink, dusted with sugar, with pink hearts; orbs of cocktail colours; sweets just flamingo.

And he spoke of the winter swim. 'It was an article of faith,' he said.

Tiffany Atkinson

Tea

You made me tea
while I shook the rain from my jacket.
You stooped to fit into the kitchen,
but handled the cups as if they'd been
the fontanelles of two young sons
whose picture sits in the hip of your 501s.
We spoke of – what? Not much.
You weren't to know how your touch
with the teaspoon stirred me,
how the tendons of your wide, divining hands
put me in mind of flight.

You wouldn't have known
when you bent to tend a plant
that your shirt fell open a smile's breadth.
You parted the leaves and plucked
a tiny green bud. Best to do that
with the early ones, you said.
I thought of the salt in the crook
of your arm where a fine vein kicks.
Of what it might be like to know
the knot and grain and beat of you;
the squeak of your heart's pips.

Mark Illis

There's a Hole in Everything

Had to learn one of Hamlet's I'm-so-depressed speeches last night. 'Oh that this too, too solid flesh would melt.' You do just want to slap him sometimes. In class today, remembering it and writing it down, I'm watching people's eyes glaze and their lips move as they pull words out of their brains. I wouldn't mind if my flesh melted, ran down my body in a thick lava flow so I was sitting in a puddle of myself. What would Mr Jeffers say? He'd say, 'Rosa, go and see the nurse.' I'd have to scoop my melted flesh into a plastic bag and take it with me.

I actually love the quiet bits of lessons when everyone's working and all you can hear is the sound of pens on paper. The air seems to get thicker with the strain of people thinking, so if you put your hand up it would move more slowly. I lose three marks, all for punctuation which I don't think is fair, but I still come top.

'Hey, Rosa.' Natalie James bends to have a word on her way out, smiling like we're best mates. 'Your fan club meets this lunch time.' I look back at her, meeting her eyes, but I know my cheeks are red and I can't think of a word to say. She just winks at me and walks away. I sit still and let everyone go, everyone moving past me and round me like I'm a blockage in a drain.

So me and Shelley bunk off. Shelley's my best mate, and she's up for it, no hesitation. We stroll out of the gate then run down the road, sprint, my bag's thumping my hip, my shirt's tight round my shoulders, some old lady's staring at me as I run by her, but I don't care. When I leave that school I feel like a weight is being lifted off me.

Me and Shelley talk like American airheads.

'So you'd say what? About Mick? You'd say he was hot?'

Shelley grins. 'Hot, sure.'

'But really?'

'Yeah, really. I think about him when he's not there, and everything.'

'At night you think about him?'

'Stop it. Yes.'

I laugh, and so does Shelley, long, shivery giggles. 'At night you think about him?' I say it again and we laugh again, at my syntax as much as anything. Shelley doesn't mind me using words like syntax, she likes that I'm clever.

We find another tester to squirt on our already smelly wrists and throats. Shelley sniffs, serious and wrinkling, like a connoisseur.

'Hmm,' she hums. 'Sea air, petrol notes and a hint of banisters.'

'Polished?'

'Polished.'

Shelly chugs cider from her Coke can. I pick up a lipstick, Damson Blush, glossy, waterproof, twelve-hour life, and drop it into my pocket.

'And a hint of chandeliers,' I say, but we're both laughed out, so we head for the exit.

*

Dad gives me his dad-smile as we're eating. His skin's getting saggy and his lips are always dry, but I like his hair, thick and short and greyish-black like an old soldier.

'What did you do today?'

Bunked off, drank two cans of cider, nicked a lipstick and a CD, got thrown out of three shops, and tormented Shelley's younger sister, I don't say. I don't even say who I've been with, because ever since that thing about the dress with the sequins my parents think Shelley is a bad influence. I say, 'Mooched around some shops, went back to someone's.'

'Buy anything?'

'A CD, a lipstick, a sandwich.'

'What more could anyone want?'

He says things like that. Thinks he's funny.

Mum looks at me, maybe a bit too casual. 'Everything OK?'

I shake my head. 'Fine.' I can suddenly sense one of those situations coming up, where I get talked at in an understanding way. *You're not a kid, but you're not an adult either.* 'Homework,' I say, getting up.

Dad likes to have the last word. 'And by the way, you stink.'

I give him my look, mouth twisted like Granddad after his stroke, and leave him and Mum to whatever they do with themselves.

*

Finish my homework with the music up loud in my headphones. It's about Hamlet and Ophelia. She beseeches him to listen to her, but he's too bothered about his own problems. That makes him a jerk, in my opinion. She doesn't say beseech but I use it in my essay because it's currently my favourite word. When someone beseeches you, you have to notice, because it means they're really giving it everything. Whatever it is they want must matter more than anything else.

When my homework's done I lie on my bed with a book, not reading it, just staring at it. Then I put it down and stare out of the window at the sky. Uncle Frank used to lie on the grass with me in the park. We'd lie on our backs and watch the clouds moving and bumping into each other. I'd say, 'That one looks like a fat man swimming,' and he'd say, 'That one looks like a piano that's fallen into a tree.' He didn't try to be funny like Dad, he just was funny. I thought so, anyway. He told me he'd once found an ear in the grass, a real human ear, and it was only much later I realized he'd got that from some film he'd seen. For a long time I looked for ears like other people look for four-leaf clovers. He died, which made my mum cry for a week. I thought for a long time they might have made a mistake, that they buried someone else and he'd just turn up one day. I didn't think it exactly, but I hoped it. When I remember him, I usually think of lying on the grass beside him. He said you could feel the curve of the world beneath you, and he said if you looked at the sky long enough you felt like you could almost see the stars, even though the sun was shining. He was right about both those things.

My older brother's never home, mostly, and evenings are

boring. I write my diary and then listen at my door and tiptoe out on to the landing. Voices downstairs. They've turned off the TV and for once they're talking to each other. I sit at the top of the stairs where I'm just out of sight and eavesdrop. I think I'd make an excellent spy.

Dad: 'I dreamt she was falling over. She was at the top of the stairs and she was about to fall down them and I couldn't catch her.'

Mum: 'Dreams. Dreams are overrated.'

Dad: 'But you know what I mean.'

Mum: 'The question is what to do about it.'

Dad: 'When I was fourteen I was the same. In a few years this'll probably be just a blip.'

What to do about what? Me and Shelley talk about this whole exchange on the phone. How parents think they know you, but they don't. How after the talk about periods you get all the lectures – cigarettes, alcohol, drugs, sex – and after that you're pretty much on your own.

Shelley goes, 'They mean well,' and I'm like, 'Duh. So what? They don't even know what's happening in my life.' Mum used to be a physio before she started training in counselling. I think she should have stuck with pulled muscles.

Shelley goes, 'Have you tried telling them?'

She means about Natalie James and the fan club and everything. How they hate me because I'm clever, or else because they just like having someone to hate. Of course I haven't tried. It would be too embarrassing, and if I did and they went to school to complain I think I would actually physically die of embarrassment. There'd be an autopsy, George Clooney out of *ER* would cut me open and look at my heart and push his finger around in my guts and he'd take off his mask and point those big brown eyes at Mum and Dad, all sad and softly spoken but accusing. 'You should never have put her through it,' he'd say. 'This girl died for nothing.' Or, no, 'This beautiful girl died for nothing.' My mum would be crying, Dad would be looking at his shoes, and George Clooney would be literally holding my heart in his hands.

'You thought you knew her,' George would say, 'but you didn't.'

Me and Shelley can talk about stuff like that. She doesn't think it's weird that my George Clooney fantasy has him doing an autopsy on me.

*

Natalie sits on her desk staring at me. History is always worst, because Miss Hinde is always late. There could be ten minutes of this.

'So Rosa, how's things?'

Gravity is on Natalie's side, people are drawn to her, their heads all turn towards her. Even mine does. Me and Shelley read *Company* in a shop and it said visualize your personality. I picture Natalie's as a great big wave that grabs other people and sucks them in and pulls them along in her direction. You almost can't blame her for enjoying the power she has. I think she knows it might not last and she's making the most of it. It's just some lucky mix of people, circumstances and her nasty streak all combining to make her the one everyone looks to. She came up with the WE LOVE ROSA badges, and began the campaign about my so-called body odour. Stealing my things – a hairslide, a biro – that was Natalie's idea too.

'Who's Shelley?'

I keep ignoring her, but I start to bite the inside of my mouth. She picks up a book and shows it to me. It's my diary. She flicks through it.

'Me and Shelley, me and Shelley, me and Shelley.'

This is very bad.

'Who'd be sad and stupid enough to be your friend?'

Please God, let Miss Hinde come in now.

'Know what I think?'

Yes, I do know, but I don't want to hear it.

'I think Shelley's your imaginary friend. It says she lives on Bywell Street, and Suzie lives there and she doesn't know a Shelley. Is that true Rosa?' She sounds almost caring. 'Is she your made-up friend?'

I get up, slow and controlled, put my history books in my

bag and take my diary from her. She doesn't stop me. Then I walk out of the class. Natalie says goodbye. No one's laughing. It feels like it's gone beyond laughing.

No one tries to stop me as I walk down the corridors and out of the door. I've noticed that; if you look like you know where you're going and what you're doing, people tend not to question you.

Uncle Frank got depressed before he died. One of the things he said was, 'Afternoons are hideous, Rosa, hideous. You've lost your energy from the morning, and you haven't got your evening vibe going.' That's what he said. I never really get an evening vibe going, but as I walk out of school I know what he meant about afternoons.

The time is what he called the drifting middle of the day. The road's empty but I can hear the thrum of traffic, the whine of brakes like whale song, the wheezing of exhausts. I keep walking, slow and calm, listening to the air move in the trees. A TV is flickering behind a window. Uncle Frank said if you were quiet enough yourself you could hear everything. I hear a baby crying, and a dog barking and scrabbling at a door. The sun, behind a cloud but near to the edge of it, makes the light dramatic, makes me feel like I'm in a film. I get that sometimes, the feeling I'm up above my left shoulder, looking at me. Sometimes everyone else is looking at me at the same time and I'm like them. I'm thinking, *What's wrong with her? She's pathetic, why doesn't she fight back or something?* Other times it's like now, I'm alone and I see this girl just walking down the road and I feel a bit sorry for her. I wish things could go better for her. I don't know if it happens to everyone or if it means I'm going mad.

Things I want.

One: I want Natalie James to die or have a disfiguring accident or have to move to Iran because of her dad's work and wear an all-over veil.

Two: I want someone to use the word *beseech*. And it wouldn't sound stupid, it would be exactly the right word. It would be best if it was a boy using it, talking to me, but even if it wasn't I'd like to hear it; I'd like people to speak like that and mean it.

Three: I want nothing else bad to happen.

I'm on my back in the grass. As far as I can see the whole park is empty, everyone is somewhere else. Uncle Frank said if someone on another planet was looking at our planet, we wouldn't be lying under the sky, we'd be part of the sky. I like that. Part of someone else's sky. I pull up a blade of grass with my fingers, scrunch it up and smell it. I'm trying to feel the curve of the whole world under my back but I can't, it's just the park. School's a mile in one direction, home's a mile in the other, and I'm stuck between the two. And of the two people I care most about, Frank's dead and Shelley's gone missing.

I turn my head and there she is.

'Kill Natalie,' she says. 'Just kill her. Kill her. Seriously.'

Me and Shelley met at primary school. We promised to be best friends for ever. Pinpricks in palms, hands squashed together to mix our blood. Hamlet was wrong, you think you're solid but actually you're not. Look closely enough, look at the back of your hand, smooth and creamy as custard, you'll see you're full of holes. I like that, because it means I might still have a little bit of Shelley in my veins and she might, wherever she is, have a bit of Rosa pumping round her body. That's the way it is with real friends, you're part of each other. She moved away with her family after she'd been there for a term and a half. We managed a couple of letters, that was all. I've never seen her again. She's not an imaginary friend though, she's a might-have-been friend, a should-have-been friend.

'Follow her into the toilets. Your mum's letter opener in the throat, from behind. Wash your hands and walk away. Kill the bitch.'

*

My duvet smells biscuity, my *Hamlet* smells of clean pages, I've got sensuous essential oils burning. All this should be calming and restful. 'Oh that this too, too solid flesh would melt.' I should be feeling OK now.

There's a knock. 'Can I come in, Rosa?'

Mum's got her hand in her hair. It's curly and dark same as mine, only longer. Her nose is bigger than mine and she's got a whole flock of crows' feet. I know she's upset about something because she's used my name, because of the hand in the hair and because her eyes have gone small. She sits on my orange beanbag with the big brown flowers on it, her knees higher than her shoulders. It's from the seventies and I refuse to throw it away. She shifts beans with her bum till she's comfortable.

'So.' Her eyes move over my school shirt on the floor, the sticky plate on the desk, my tipped-over bag, my *Buffy the Vampire Slayer* poster. 'Heard you disappeared in the middle of school today?'

I shrug, tell her it's my period.

'Miss Hinde says it's happened before, and lately she says you've seemed quiet. Preoccupied?'

Uncle Frank once said that the first big surprise about your parents is that they don't know everything, and the second big surprise is they're not as stupid as you think. He was definitely my favourite relative, but he would go on a bit sometimes even before he got depressed, and you'd get the feeling he really liked listening to himself. On the day that he took the pills he rang up my mum and wanted to talk to her. She was busy so he asked her to put him on to me. She looked at me, I remember, eyebrows raised, and I nodded and took the phone. He seemed just the same as he'd been recently, going on, listening to himself, not completely making sense. Eventually we said bye and apparently he did it not much later.

Mum stayed in bed for a week, but we had a long chat, her in the bed, me sitting on it. She told me, with her eyes all baggy and red, that neither of us could have made any difference, that Uncle Frank had made a decision, a selfish one and a wrong one and a sad one, and we shouldn't feel guilty about it. I think she's right. What he didn't do was beseech me or her to listen to him. He was more Hamlet than Ophelia, all shouty and intense and actually a bit scary.

Mum's doing her quiet thing, waiting for me to say something.

'Ever wanted to kill anyone?'

This makes her go all thoughtful, like she's remembering something. I don't want reminiscences, so I start again.

'What would you do if I murdered someone?'

'I think I'd still love you. You planning to?'

'Not sure,' I say.

For some reason this reassures her. She sinks lower in the beanbag. She looks really uncomfortable.

'If I wanted to change schools, could I?'

'Maybe. You going to tell me what's up?'

I've been reading Sylvia Plath and Virginia Woolf, leaving them lying around sort of as a hint. *Hello? I'm not very happy.* Mum doesn't like hints, she likes things out in the open. That's her counselling.

'Say you beseech me.'

'What?'

'Seriously. Without being sarcastic or anything. Please?'

She's sitting there staring at me with her knees near her ears, probably wondering what drugs I'm on.

'Rosa, I beseech you to tell me what's wrong.'

So I do.

Christina Koning

Just Like a Young Girl Should

When Kitty was seventeen she knew all about love. That day in assembly when Jennifer Moynihan did the solo in front of the whole school, she knew things were never going to be the same again.

> Jesu, lover of my soul,
> Let me to Thy bosom fly . . .

The sun coming in through the windows of the hall in a haze of dust motes to strike Jennifer Moynihan's pure profile; the wiry springs of her red hair haloing her face; the way her imperfect soprano cracked on the penultimate line: all these filled Kitty with delicious confusion. *Lover of my soul.*

As time went by, she got to know about different kinds of love. She lived in a small town; there was not too much to do on a Saturday night. Every week, the local art college put on dances, though. At one of these, she met Alain. A-l-a-i-n, not A-l-a-n, he was quick to inform her. The redundant 'i' was critical. It was something he never let you forget, the thing that gave him *cachet*: his foreignness.

Alain was thin, with narrow bony hips she could hook her thumbs into and a talent for French kissing. Kissing was a serious business in those days. You had to get it right. On Saturday nights in the sweaty smoky dance hall with the music so loud you couldn't hear yourself speak and the strobe lights flashing like the onset of a migraine, she practised kissing with Alain. One night, as they sat together in Alain's father's car, Alain got her to unzip his trousers and take out his warm and surprisingly agile cock. When you took it in your mouth there was a salty stuff, viscous as school semolina.

'What do I do now?'

'Swallow it, silly.'

Kitty did as she was told, pleased to have passed this first test without a hitch.

Alain was beautiful, Kitty decided. His eyes (which were closed just at present) were the colour of black tea. His eyebrows ran in a single line across the bridge of his nose. Best of all was his hair, which was straight and black, and fell to his shoulders. Wisps of his hair got in Kitty's mouth when they kissed, until Alain flicked it away. It was a habitual gesture: kiss; flick; kiss.

'Next Sunday,' Alain said with his eyes still closed.

'Next Sunday?'

Kitty felt she was being stupid. Alain had that effect on her. It was because he was older, of course. Nineteen. When he and his friends from the art college were together, she hardly dared to open her mouth, for fear of saying something naive. Somehow, she always managed to say it anyway.

Alain sighed deeply and opened his eyes. 'Next Sunday my dad'll be away,' he said.

Kitty nodded, afraid of saying something that would betray her incomprehension. It was the first time Alain had mentioned either of his parents to her. His mother, she knew, was dead. She had learned this, and other essential facts about Alain, from his friend Phil.

Phil was the only one of Alain's friends with whom Kitty felt at ease. With that red hair and snub nose, and eyes so deep-set they disappeared when he smiled, he wasn't what you'd call good-looking; but that, at least, made it easier to talk to him. You could talk to Phil about anything. After a while, she even got to like his face.

Phil had a way of collapsing with laughter at something Kitty had said (usually something not intended to be funny), which was flattering if a bit unnerving. Standing in line at the college bar, she would say something and Phil would pretend to fall over with amusement. Sometimes they'd be laughing so hard they'd end up clutching each other, breathless and spluttering, while Alain looked on with a quizzical smile.

It was Phil who told her about Alain's mother and about Alain's problems with his father – a stern and difficult character,

Phil said, with inflexible views on certain subjects, Alain's friends in particular. Phil, it emerged, was banned from the house, for what especial misdemeanour he refused to say.

'He says I'm a bad influence,' Phil murmured, his eyes winking with amusement in their fleshy pouches. Kitty laughed, of course, when he said that, and Phil laughed too, and they were both shaking with laughter when Alain returned from the bar with plastic glasses of foamy lager for him and Phil, and a sweet cider for her.

*

'Next Sunday, then.' Alain kissed her on the cheek by way of dismissal, leaning across to open the passenger door. She got out, still faintly mystified.

'See you.'

But Alain did not reply, intent on tuning the car radio to his preferred station. *Radio Caroline seven days a week* ... Then he flipped his long hair back and drove away without a backward glance.

It was her friends who put the whole thing into perspective.

'You'll be alone with him, won't you?'

'Alone in the house . . .'

'Alone in his room . . .'

'You'll have to take *precautions*.'

By the time Sunday came she had worked herself into a pleasurable state of anticipation.

It took her a while to decide what to wear. There was her new blue dress, which Alain hadn't yet seen. She tried it on. The reflection in the bedroom mirror was disappointingly wholesome. Sweet. Not at all the effect she'd wanted to achieve. She settled, in the end, for what she hoped was casual sophistication. Velvet flares and a skinny sweater which clung to her insignificant bosom with pleasing emphasis.

She wished there was more she could do about her face. Her cheeks were the worst thing: a healthy unfortunate pink instead of the pallor to which she aspired. She did the best she could with plenty of white powder, and outlined her eyes and lips in Purple Haze.

Sitting next to a glass mosaic pillar in Di Marco's Ice Cream Parlour, Kitty found herself regretting the lack of social poise which had made her suggest this as a meeting place. But it was the only place she knew and a convenient distance from the bus stop. It was here she and her friends met after school, to discuss boys, swap cigarettes and compare homework. On weekdays, it seemed a cheerful enough spot, its mirrored walls resounding with the loud chatter of girls in navy uniforms, its atmosphere a heady mixture of frying food, illicit cigarette smoke and steam from the espresso machine. Now it seemed sad; deserted.

At a table across the aisle from hers, the only other customer, an old woman so bent she hardly reached the table, scraped the last spoonful of ice cream from a metal dish. The melancholy waitress, whose sombre beauty reminded Kitty of the Andrea del Sarto *Madonna* on the art room wall at school, wiped the sweating table tops with a slimy cloth and sighed, glancing from time to time at the clock.

She had given up hope of seeing him when Alain turned up. Looking up miserably from *Good Morning, Midnight*, it took her a moment to realize who it was, so casually poised in the doorway. Alain's narrow velvet jacket and bell-bottom jeans gave him an elongated silhouette which struck her as unimprovable. Suddenly breathless, she watched him cross the grimy mosaic floor, which sparkled like diamonds in the late afternoon sun.

'What a fuckin' awful dump,' he remarked, glancing around at the place, with its chipped glass pillars and fly-specked mirrors, its plaster display models of tutti-fruttis, banana splits and knickerbocker glories grown dusty in their glass and chrome mausoleum.

He accepted a cigarette from the stolen pack in her bag. 'Let's split,' he said.

In the car he seemed distant, preoccupied. For a panicky moment or two Kitty wondered if he'd changed his mind about wanting to see her. Maybe something had come up. Things often did, in Alain's mysterious social arrangements. But if he was having second thoughts, he did not admit it. When they got to his house he made her wait in the car while he checked that they had the place to themselves. Only when he was certain of this did he signal that she should follow him inside.

The house, it seemed to her on a first impression, was very much a man's house. Functional. Even a bit drab. Everything was brown or shades of brown, Kitty noticed, nervously scanning the room. Brown curtains. Brown cushions. Brown chairs. There were few ornaments. Men don't like ornaments, she had once heard someone say. Here was proof. On the otherwise bare teak mantelpiece was a photograph in a silver frame. A pretty dark woman in a boxy, out of date suit. Kitty felt she should say something.

'Is that your mother?'

'Uh-huh.'

Alain was digging around in the Swedish-style sideboard for glasses and a bottle of Bacardi. They drank the first glass sitting side by side on the settee, which was upholstered in a brown tweedy fabric that made Kitty think of one of her father's old jackets. She sipped her Bacardi cautiously, trying not to think about her parents. She'd told her mother she'd be at Claire's all evening, revising.

After a minute or two, Alain slid his hand under Kitty's jumper so that it was resting on her bare stomach. She closed her eyes for a second, letting her head fall against his shoulder. This must be what it felt like, she thought. Being in love.

'Come on.'

Feeling a bit queasy and light-headed from the drink, Kitty followed Alain upstairs. On one wall of his room, Jimi Hendrix stared moodily out from under the brim of a black felt hat. Arranged on the chest of drawers beneath the poster were candles, a small brass holder for joss sticks, and an orange paper flower. A shrine, of sorts. Opposite this, Kitty couldn't help noticing, hung a large Airfix model of a Lancaster bomber.

Alain drew the curtains, although it was still daylight, and lit the candles. He selected an LP and put it on the turntable. Then he sat down beside her on the bed and – suddenly playful – blew in her ear.

'Hey, baby,' he said.

This was his name for her. Baby. On the whole, she rather liked it; although there were times when she wondered if he was trying to tell her something. 'You're such a *baby*, Baby,' he'd say, after some further demonstration of hopeless naivety on her part: a failure to recognize the latest single by the latest band, or an inability to comprehend basic terminology – getting stoned, getting laid, getting blown.

In the beginning, he'd seemed to find her ignorance rather charming. Just lately, she'd detected a note of exasperation creeping in. 'I don't *believe* you,' he'd say, shaking his head. 'You're something else, you know?' As if she were doing it on purpose. But he was being nice enough to her now, singing along to the record – something about not being a schoolboy and knowing what he liked – while he fumbled with the hooks of her bra.

Kitty's skin, which had been on fire, now started to feel like ice. When she was naked, he removed his own clothes. In the flickering half-light, he was even more beautiful than she had imagined: slender, white, his dark hair falling across his face as he leaned to embrace her. His tongue felt slippery as a fish in her mouth; his cock hard and rubbery at the same time.

'It's all right,' he whispered fiercely. 'I won't get you pregnant.'

It took him a while to get it in.

'Does it hurt?'

'A bit.'

He stopped and lay still for a minute, breathing hard. She could feel his heart beating against his ribs.

'Want me to stop?'

'No.'

He thrust again and this time, astonishingly, she felt herself open to him. This is it, she thought with a wild joy, this is what it's like.

But just as she was starting to get the hang of things, it was all over. She heard Alain mutter something about needing to be careful; then he pulled out, only just in time. Stuff spurted out all over Kitty's stomach. For a little while they lay without moving while the air chilled around them. The last track came to an end, but the record went on going round and round, scratchily, in the silence.

Alain rolled off her, and went to fetch some Kleenex.

As Kitty was getting dressed she noticed she had started to bleed. Alain said nothing, but gave her a handkerchief which she folded into a pad. Months later, she found it hidden among her things, its triangular bloodstain faded to a brownish-yellow.

*

At school the next day, the encounter, a little disappointing in reality, acquired significance. Claire burst into tears when she heard Kitty had gone 'all the way'. Even girls who ordinarily ignored her betrayed an interest. She found she had joined a select group of initiates.

When Alain had not phoned after three days Kitty set aside her misgivings and decided to phone herself. She planned what she was going to say, and how she was going to say it. Insouciance was the key. He mustn't think she had been in any way put out by his neglect.

She was disconcerted when a strange man answered the phone, Alain's father, apparently. Remembering what Phil had said, she did her best not to antagonize him, although in fact he was much kinder than she had been led to expect. But she couldn't help feeling he was being evasive.

'Alain's not here, I'm afraid. Yes, I'm sure he'll ring you as soon as he gets back. No, I'm afraid I can't say when that will be . . .'

It was the same each time she called. Clearly, her messages weren't being passed on.

Kitty tried a different approach. Surely Alain's father, however much he disapproved of Alain's friends, wouldn't stoop to intercepting his letters?

Dear Alain, Hope things are OK with you. I rang you last week, but you weren't in (obviously!) so maybe you could call me, if you're not too busy . . .

Mysteriously, there was no reply to her first letter; nor to the second or third. Perhaps he was away, she thought, or doing exams, or ill (she made herself quite miserable over this last possibility). Surely, after all they'd been to one another, he wouldn't just drop her, would he? There had to be a reason.

But it wasn't in fact until some time later that she saw Alain again. It was at the end-of-term dance at the art college. The place they'd first met.

She was with her friends; he was with his. Everything was just as it had been, except that they were no longer together.

It was strange and not very pleasant, thought Kitty, seeing someone you'd once been so intimate with pretending not to see you. At first she wasn't sure if he had seen her.

But then he turned to say something to his companion – it was Phil, she saw – and both glanced in her direction.

Over the course of the next couple of hours, Kitty got drunk on warm sweet cider and danced with anyone who would have her. They were playing that song again, the one he'd played her that night in his room when it had seemed like the beginning instead of the end of everything.

It was a song that, adding insult to injury, she was to hear a lot that summer. One of those songs which take you back to the time you first heard it, and which, for years afterwards, can conjure up that particular moment, that mood, that person. But she didn't know that then. All she cared about was showing Alain what a good time she was having without him.

Her head aching from the noise and the drink, she took refuge in the ladies' room. Here, girls made faces at themselves in the glaring mirror, rounding their eyes in comic surprise as they wielded mascara wands, stretching their lips wide as they put on fresh lipstick. It was peaceful sitting there on the cold tiled floor, listening to the conversations over the sinks and to the gentle hissing of piss against porcelain, but after a while Kitty thought she had better move.

As she came out, the first person she saw was Phil, falling down the stairs which led to the floor above where the dancing was. He picked himself up, laughing, and lurched towards the plate glass doors which led outside. It took her a second or two to realize that the boy he was with was Alain.

Kitty didn't think he had seen her. She made a move towards where he and his friend were standing, holding on to each other for support. Phil seemed the drunker of the two, kept from falling only by the surrounding press of bodies. She began to push her way through the crowd of people around the exit, some trying to get in, others as determinedly trying to get out.

All she wanted to do was see him, she told herself. If she could only speak to him, it would all be all right. Phil would back her up, she felt sure. Everything would be explained.

By the time she reached the doors, there was no sign of Alain or Phil. They must already have gone outside. As she went to follow, her path was blocked by a bouncer in a shiny tuxedo.

'Where do you think *you're* going?'

Scowling, he stamped her hand with purple ink.

Groups of people were standing around outside, smoking and talking. Some had started to walk towards the gates, in search of taxis, although the dance was not yet over. After the heat and noise, the silence seemed immense. The air smelled fresh and cold. A light sprinkling of frost covered everything. As she stepped on to the lawn, she felt it crackle like glass beneath her feet.

The contrast between the heat she had just left and the cold outside had a sobering effect. The warm mood of hilarity which had cocooned her all evening had gone, leaving a bleaker consciousness of things. It was freezing, she realized. And what she was doing out here, wandering around distractedly in her soaked shoes? Her friends would be wondering where she'd got to.

But as she was turning back she heard a soft noise, like laughter.

At the side of the building was a small area planted with shrubs and young trees. Raw brick had been disguised with densely growing thorny plants, which formed a kind of screen behind which it was possible to stand, at least partially concealed. She had stood here once with Alain.

She peered into the darkness.

As her eyes adjusted, she could see two figures standing against the wall, half-screened by the bushes, kissing mouth to mouth. The headlights of a passing car picked out Phil's red hair and the white, upturned face of his friend, her one-time lover.

As she watched, the red-haired figure sank to his knees. Long white fingers twisted themselves in his hair as he went about his work. The dark face of the standing figure was in shadow, but she knew that the eyes would be closed, in perfect surrender.

Taking care to make no noise, she took a step backwards, then another. When she had satisfied herself that she had not been seen, she turned and walked quickly back towards the lights.

Ruth Padel

Black Coral

I was never your devoted lover. It was gossip,
    That. All wrong. I am the Amur Leopard no
        One knows about, the thirty-fifth, each eye
An emerald. I'm passing by Quo Vadis,
    St Anne's Court and Sunset Strip

On a summer evening trembling – water-muscle
    Breaking on the knife-
        Edge of a dam – with promises of headlong
Encounters that might change
    A life. I never ended everything between us so

You wouldn't lose your house and kids,
    Endanger school fees and the tax rebate,
        Your salary, your mother's Irish bonds.
That wasn't me. It was a question of identity,
    Mistaken. Poachers will get me anyway by and by.

So the mafia can re-package me
    As *os pantherii*, yellow pills in ivory hexagons
        Brush-painted with the Cinnamon Tree
Hieroglyph, the remedy
    For impotence in Hong Kong.

But I'm still leopard now, frostfur, quicksilver, planting pug-
    Marks all the way down Dean Street, past Café Lazeez,
        Trying not to hear through the open door
Of the Crown and Two Chairmen pub
    That ballad you used to sing. 'You Needed Me'.

I'm watching saffron awnings spill white zeds of light
On Il Siciliano's pavement tablecloth.
But catching my own reflection, rippling over
A Choi Sun figurine, the god of wealth (riding
A tiger, holding a block of gold) in the window of

The Wen Tai Sun News Agency, gives me –
Or let's take this out of self and call my leopard 'her' –
A shock. She pauses on the dimpled granite kerb
Of Chapone Place. She's all herself, and free,
But this whole territory's patrolled

By her lost mate. She's wearing her endangered heart
On every nerve-end just in case
His silvery silhouette and head-on-one-side smile
Pad up at the Webshack Internet Café.
Dean Street? This is Dream Street. There is nothing here,

No one to marvel at the sole
Nivalis in the wild zoologists still
Haven't counted. She'd send statistics reeling if they spied
Her rosette jigsaw of
Black coral, broken daffodil.

*

She's considering gateways to another world.
Stars of Orion's Belt, the Inca site
Of ultimate creation,
Obsidian mines at Tuetihuacan,
Haunted by the gentle kinkajou,

The Pyramid of the Sun she climbed
In the Avenue of the Dead,
Bristling with the Storm God's hooky heads
And water-lilies streaming from his mouth,
Or the cloisters at Quetzalpapalotl,

Palace-of-the-Quelza-Bird-and-Butterfly,
  Guarded by parrot-gods with mica flames for eyes.
    She's got to send her leopard mind
Elsewhere. She really, *really* doesn't want to face
  What she's learning now about that mate of hers,

The centre of her jungle for five years. She's mourning
  His integrity. In a minute she'll have to stop
    Believing he was good. Let her concentrate, instead,
On theatre lighting. Stage directions, say,
  For *Beauty and the Beast*.

                  *

The palace is a star in the wrinkled forest
  And Beauty has to go there of her own free will.
    Though she's afraid (she'd be mad not
To be), she tells her dad, 'You mustn't doubt the Beast.'
  When she steps into Beast's kingdom, avenues

Of paper pear-trees blossom, and the audience
  Hear tambourines. For this castle is the world
    Of melody. Every action in it, every thought,
Has its music counterpart. The clockwork servants
  Brushing Beauty's hair are shimmery chromatic scales

On pipes and mandolin. Beauty warms her hands
  On the coal-scuttle's mystic grin
    And we suddenly get guitars. Everything
Is moonsilk, lemonpale; invisibly policed.
  The carpet blushes peach for her delight.

Glass cases, caught in tinsel flakes of light from candelabra,
  Glitter with cup-hilt rapiers, schiavonas – blades
    Inlaid with jade and mother-of-pearl
And a white-enamelled, silver-chased estoo.
  Beauty come to rest on a golden swing

That represents her heart. She's utterly at sea about who
    She's supposed to be or what she's in for, but she has ghost-
        faith
        In a Beast she's never seen. She can even hear him breathe.
'I'm aware you'll eat me Beast,' she says into the wings.
    Judging by the noise, Beast must be ravenous:

His breathing is miked and amplified, the rasp
    Of Lord Darth Vadar in *Star Wars*. When Beast appears
        On stilts, a towering hedgehog-stork
In oriole feathers, whiskery chestnut fur, he has the face
    Of a rubicund wart-hog

But you see the actor's mouth behind the mask
    And living, vulnerable eyes – a sheepdog
        Listening for thunder – under diamond paste
Tears. When he smooths his fur-wrist ruffles (Beast
    Is fond of money and its fabrics) we can hear

Tchaikovsky strings in dominant sevenths. Sonic fire-
    Works – Roman candles, ripping to explosion
        In crashing north-east wind.
'All my rooms,' he says, 'are made
    To please you. All I want to do is give you joy.'

He may even think he means it. But, no getting away
    From it, she's a prisoner
        In his gold-plate masquerade
His Salon of Small Clowns in *millefiore* pink,
    His Hall of Singing Triangles and Mirrors.

                    *

That night she dreams she's dancing with a prince
    In snowy *crêpe de chine* and crimson
        Turban, sash and scimitar, purple sash. Next day
She finds a locket on the floor
    In the Chamber of Longed-For Harmonies.

A clash of cymbals as the audience glimpse
    The face within. That prince again, the one
        Poor Beast is desperate to become.
Corridors echo with his whisper, 'Set me free.'
    The prisoner, you see, is Beast – in the pelf and whirl

Of his own image, an the enchanted-palace way
    He looks at things. But rescuing him will be a daunting task.
        What'll it take from *you*, girl? How if you give up your
           life
To save him from himself? What's real in him? Suppose
    He can only operate behind a mask

Or in a dream? Even princes are fiction,
    Mostly. What's the betting there's a man in there
        You'd turn out not to like? Too bad. Beauty has no
           option –
That's the deal. Only someone who can treasure Beast,
    Trust him for what he is, can set him free.

      *

Beauty, the Stage Directions have decided,
    Must be generous and strong. Believe in him, devote
        Herself to his angry need, and long
For that wire breath on her throat at night. She's got to say
    With ninety-nine-carat genuine delight,

'My beloved is asleep all round me. This
    Is who I am. I'm his.' She must feel welded to him,
        Welcome him in every orifice.
Any chamber he can find in her shall be his earth.
    She will protect him from

That sense he labours under that he's got a skin
    Too few (instead of many).
        She must adore his Sinbad tongue
Dancing sambas over hers, become
    A passionate, prime-time fan of the prince within –

Beast Beautiful, Beast Hero, Beast of the Golden Sword –
    Whilst loving, open-eyed, what he is now.
        She's got to calm his *Kidnapped* panic at
A giantess in the sky, the mother-witch
    Who turned him into Beast. Beauty's got to cherish

(And keep mum about it) Beast-as-he-doesn't-wish-
    To-see-himself; as terrified. She knows
        The prince inside him won't survive
Without her. She goes on, however raw things get . . .
    What happened? There was rescue, yes,

But it didn't take. Maybe the witch-spell was too strong.
    Beauty escaped. She did it for his sake
        (He was torn in two, and holding him
Was trying to lullaby an earthquake),
    But also, if she's honest, for herself.

This is the Amur Leopard on the hotline to your heart, calling
    From the Soho Theatre bar. The nearly-to-last
        Snow Leopard, hoping to help you feel
More easy with what's happened. You were my care.
    I must have been your lover, after all.

But the man you were with me
    Was an endangered species, and has left the world.
        Beauty slinks back, to find her sweetheart sinking to the
           ground
In the Walk of Withered Roses: treacherous, and blank
    About it. No more songs. And no other way to tell

This story, play this scene, apparently; though I,
    In every alias I can think of, hanker after one that's kinder
        To them both. The Beast (or prince, whatever) falling
Back in her arms that always, always, wished him well, to –
    What did you expect? To die.

Claire Keegan

Salt

I married Billy Fennell in a cold lambing season. Before I reached the chapel snow was falling and while we stood at the altar, taking our vows, I knew the snow would last. Billy was wearing a navy-blue suit that was far too small for him. If I'd known he was going to wear navy, I'd have worn green. In any case, there we were, wearing the same colour. Behind Billy's back the Station depicted Jesus falling for the second time. Jesus was down on his hands and knees. A soldier was standing over him with a whip. During the sermon the priest belched and talked about love and respect and the serious nature of the commitment we were about to undertake. I wondered how you'd spell commitment and then he started the consecration. The serving boy was nervous about ringing the bell at the wrong time and my heart went out to him but the priest gave him the nod. Finally, he blessed us and made us sign our names. Out in the graveyard cherry blossom mixed with the falling snow on a lather of wind and when we ran down to the photographer's office the sign said it was closed. I was glad to be married and did not mind about the weather. We walked across the Slaney Bridge to the hotel and ate roast beef and cabbage and watched the birds panicking on the lawn.

Nobody came to our wedding. Our marriage was witnessed by a cousin of Billy's who owned the sweet shop next to the chapel gates and a layman from the boarding school who read the lesson. My father did not approve of me marrying Billy – he would not say why – and my mother was dead. She did away with herself when I was a small child and I can't remember much about her except that she forbade me to eat the berries off the yew and made me drink goat's milk when I was sick. Even to this day, I can't abide the taste of milk. Billy's father was in bed with pleurisy the day we married and his mother was in the nursing home in Baltinglass. He had no siblings and I had only the one brother who went off to England shortly after my mother's funeral and I hadn't seen him since. I came from people who were distant but Billy wasn't like that; I knew that if I died Billy Fennell would eat me sooner than bury me.

When I first saw Billy I was leading my father's brood mare around the ring at the Tinahely Show. She was a red chestnut who stood 16.2 and always won first prize. Some said we should stop entering her but my father paid no heed. Billy stood outside the ring and stared at me. He wasn't afraid to stare. After I got the ribbon my father took the reins and somebody from the *Farmer's Journal* came and took his photograph. Billy came over and asked me about her pedigree, who she was by and out of, and took me to the tent for sandwiches. I ate five ham sandwiches with mustard and then he bought me a big geranium at the ICA stand and we went to look at the poultry. I was thinking about rearing turkeys and selling them at Christmas to make a few bob but then I saw my father. He turned pale when he saw me with Billy and bade me load up the mare and come home.

'Don't you know we're late for the milking as it is?' he said when he got me in the car, but it wasn't true. When we got back to the yard the cows hadn't even come down as far as the Pond Field gate.

Billy wrote shortly after asking to see me. I made the mistake of showing his letter to my father.

'You're going nowhere with any man till you've come of age,' he said. 'You may write and say so.'

Billy wrote back and said he'd wait. When two years passed, I met him every Friday at the end of the avenue. He was unlike any man I'd ever met. He never tried to take advantage of me. My father wouldn't let him set foot on the land but I didn't care. Rain or thunder, I walked to the road of a Friday and, rain or thunder, Billy's car was parked on the road. In fact I preferred rain and thunder, those nights when we would drive out to the cliffs to watch the sea going mad and talk about the past until it grew dark.

Billy was a big man with long arms and his voice was the sound of hill water running over stones. Sometimes, when we were courting, I closed my eyes and imagined him asking me if I had shut the hen-house door or if there was a clean shirt in the house. His eyes were a dark creosote brown, the same as mine. I was, in truth, afraid of him even though he was never but tender towards me. I often wondered what he saw in me, for I took after my mother's people; I had nothing only a small build and a fine imagination. After two years of courtship that began and ended at the end of my father's avenue, I married this plain-spoken man and went to live with him on the back of Mount Leinster. My name was Rose Tyrell before I married. I was twenty-three years old and Billy was past thirty. I'd never asked his age. Neither one of us believed in God. We believed in land and trees. We believed in ghosts and the things that can't be named and neither one of us took the sun's rising or rainfall for granted.

*

We were hungry on our wedding day. Billy asked for more spuds and gravy and got the girl to bring hot apple tart and custard. I've no time for apples. It was apples all year round in my house: apple tarts and pies and jellies and jams and sauce. People were always coming up to the orchard after a storm with basins, saying 'Ya don't mind us taking the windfalls?' without waiting for an answer. After a few years we got wise and bought sows who shook the apples out of the trees and fattened. I wanted something bitter in my married life. I wanted sloes. I wanted salt. I had a taste for salt which never went away even when the desire for bitterness did, but I ate the custard and Billy gave me the skin off his.

Across the room a middle-aged woman sat staring at me. Even at a distance I could see that her powder was far too pale for her complexion, same as she'd dipped her face into a bag of plain flour. She watched me for a long time before she came over.

'Well, Billy, aren't you the sly one? I'm after hearing the news above in the sweet shop,' she said. 'Half a Bunclody will be bawling tonight.'

'Rose, this is Mrs Byrne.' He stood up and looked down on her. It wasn't the first time I'd seen him scare people away with his size.

'Ah now! None of this missus carry-on. Call me Nan.'

'Nan's our neighbour, Rose.'

Her eyes were taking root in my hair, crawling down through my navy-blue suit to the patent leather of my wedding shoes. 'Make sure and call in some evening when you're settled, Rose.'

'I will of course,' I said.

She looked up at Billy. 'Well, I won't keep yez. Lovebirds.' Her teeth were false. 'Good luck now! Ye will need luck same as the rest of us.'

She laughed a terrible laugh and went away and Billy looked at me. It was the first time we had looked at each other properly since we'd married. I knew he was glad to have me as his own and not to have to drive thirty miles to speak to me. Now that we had crossed the starting line I was impatient to get on with it, to get out of my good clothes, and begin. My clothes were a nuisance; the elastic in my knickers was tight and my wool blouse made me want to claw my skin till it bled. I used to do that when I was a child, scratch a hive until it bled, prefer the sting of a wasp to falling into nettles. I'm a woman of extremes. I'd rather be hurt than annoyed. That afternoon, I wanted to lie down naked, outside, and let him see me naked. I wanted him to show me the harm he could do me without doing me harm. I wanted the trees to get out of our way and the river to freeze. I wanted five seasons and the heavens were far too low on that, my wedding day.

'You'll have a drink, Rose.'

I shook my head.

'Come on, so.'

When we went up the street the car wouldn't start but the butcher boy gave us a push and we started on the run and turned back in the direction of Mount Leinster. A veil of snow covered Bunclody that Tuesday afternoon. Rooks were repairing nests in the sycamores above the stream and the crows looked savage balanced on the electric wires. When the shop lights went out I thought the power was gone but then we met a hearse on the Co-op road and I knew it was only a funeral.

I was his wife now. Christ, to be his wife, it felt so strange. I had lost my name, my father's name, and exchanged it for another.

I resented this, felt bitter that I could have no name of my own. And then I remembered that time he went off to Leitrim and was gone for a whole fortnight and wrote how he'd missed me on the Friday night, how he'd gone away from all the men in the field admiring the Suffolks and clenched a thistle so he'd have a good reason to feel pain. When the men stared, he didn't care. All he could think about was me stepping over the threshold of my father's land, to him. He said the day would come, and now the day had come. I felt hot. I am hot-blooded and seldom feel the cold. I've gone swimming in October. Billy grabbed my knee in a donkey bite so hard it pained me. When I flinched he laughed and I was afraid of him again.

He kept on driving, past farmhouses that reminded me of December months on calendars. The steep mountain road got steeper until the dwelling houses disappeared and the land turned stony. Mount Leinster's mast shone red and then I saw a shelter bed and a slate roof. The car lurched as we passed over the roots of a tree. Billy's house was covered in ivy. A rusty combine stood outside the front door but Billy drove round the back and stopped in the yard. There were fertilizer bags and dunghills high after the winter months but the diesel tank looked pretty in the snow and his sheds were granite. When I stepped out the wind made the heaving conifers moan and somewhere a wood pigeon called out, who are you? who are you? who? who? and two black dogs flew around the side of the house and stopped dead and bared their teeth until Billy told them to lie down.

The kitchen smelled of glue and mutton grease. No light was burning and the fire was out but when my eyes adjusted to the darkness I saw an old man, perhaps the oldest-looking man I've ever seen, leaning over an upside-down bicycle mending a puncture.

'What are you doing up?' Billy said.

'Ah, I was fed up.'

'Aye. A fine day for mending bicycles it is, and you would pleurisy. It's in your bed you should be.'

'Bed! I've spent half me life in bed. I'll die in that bed before long.'

'Rose, this is me father,' he said. 'Da, this is Rose. We're after getting married.'

'Married?' He stopped and straightened himself. He wasn't tall. 'Well, now, I thought you might be going to a wedding would the suit but I'd no notion it'd be your own.' He held out his hand to me. 'It's dirty but it's decent,' he said. 'I go be the name of Martin.'

His palm was cold and slippery like a bar of used soap.

'Would you like tay? Put the kettle on the gas there Billy and give the woman something.'

'We had a feed down the town.'

'Sure we'll have a drop so. It's not every day we've a wedding in the house.'

He went to the dresser. It was a big dresser with odd plates leaning against each other and a marmalade cat sleeping on the top shelf behind a jar of weedkiller. She stretched herself when Martin got the bottle but she didn't wake. Then a creature ran out of the dark and gave a great bleat and nuzzled Billy's leg.

'Don't feed her,' Martin said. 'She's had one. She'll get a pot belly and die if ya keep feeding her.'

When Billy lit the gas fire I saw woodworm in the ceiling boards and lamb droppings on the floor, and on the mantel two china dogs whose ears were gone sat staring off as if they could see the future. We drank whiskey out of dusty tumblers. I had never drunk in the afternoon. Martin looked like he was perishing with the cold but I knew by him that he was thinking hard, putting things together in his mind like a man trying to solve a piece of long division, but he kept on sanding the tyre and stuck a patch over the hole.

'There now,' he said. 'That much is done. Good health!' He looked into my eyes and raised his glass. He'd no trouble facing me and he had the bluest eyes I had ever seen. I wondered what age he was. I wondered Billy hadn't told him about us but then all Billy said was that he had the pleurisy. I drank the whiskey and didn't care. It was my wedding day. I was out of my father's house and had entered another where people did not mind about small things like shite or weddings or snow. We drank and said little for a long time. There was no clock ticking on their wall. I wondered if they cared about time.

'I have to strip!' I said.

The men laughed.

'Good girl!' said Martin.

'Go up to the room there,' said Billy.

I didn't know where the room was but I found it. He'd brought my things up from home the last time he'd called. It was the first time he'd set foot on my floor but my father said nothing that day. He sat outside with the black knife, cutting seed potatoes. I used to like that job when I was a child. He had taught me to find the eyes and to cut between them so they would sprout when they were in the clay. That day he just looked at us, finding the eyes, and now I wondered if I would ever see him again.

The room must have been Billy's mother's room. I saw a cat on the window sill, a beautiful dark brown cat curled up breathing faintly, but when I touched her I realized it was only an old fur cap. I knew by the way my things were that Billy hadn't touched them. I was glad of that for no reason except that I believed the man I had married was not eager to know anything he should not know about me. Billy always said that people find out things soon enough and the less said the better. He said he'd courted other women, women who went through him like he was nothing, only a chest of drawers. He said I wasn't like that. I was like the salt wind that cuts the trees down to size. We would last, he said, because of that. We would last.

The relief of taking off my wedding clothes was without comparison. I felt free again although, now that I think about it, freedom was a thing I wasn't used to so it might have been something I felt for the first time. I took off every stitch and pulled on a dress and jumper and work socks and when I went back down the men were drinking at the gas fire and it struck me that Billy and his father got along better than any relatives I had ever known.

'I'm an old man now,' Martin said. 'The longer you live, the less you know, but I've a feeling ye two will get along.'

'It'll soon be dark,' Billy said. 'I better go up the fields.'

'Ah, the fields!' said Martin. 'Do you know anything about the treachery and seduction of land, Rose?'

'I was hoping I'd left all that behind me.'

'Behind you?' he said. 'Nobody laves a thing behind them, girl, especially them that tries.'

'And you? Did you lave nothing behind?'

'I did me best. That's why I'm still walking around, the tormented man I am, girl.' He laughed until I thought he was going to cry.

Billy stripped to his vest and pulled a pair of trousers from a rope over the hearth. I had never seen his legs. They were the whitest, hairiest legs and he was unashamed, as well he might be. There were patches on his shins where the wellingtons had rubbed them bare. Then he pulled on a jumper I hadn't seen in ages.

'Well, Billy, there's nothing I know about you at all and now I'm thinking that maybe there's nothing I don't know just the same,' said Martin.

I wanted to sit on Billy's lap. He was such a big man I thought he could protect me from the world but in truth he made me feel afraid. I need to feel afraid. Happiness makes me uneasy. I am one of those women who expects the worst. I court the worst. Pain is to be expected. Happiness is altogether another thing. When happiness comes it's sudden but I'm never ready and then it passes.

'Ye are cut from the same cloth, yez are. I know!' Martin shouted. 'Rose! This house hasn't seen a woman since Ruby left for Baltinglass. Well, I'm off to the graveyard.' He got up and went to the font beside the back door and blessed himself and shook holy water on us the way my father used to sprinkle it over new calves.

'The graveyard!' he shouted, and stumbled to bed.

I liked him, this man who blessed us and knew nothing of our marriage. I did not care that my husband married me unknown to his father or that my father wouldn't come to the chapel or that my mother was dead or that I had not seen or heard from my brother in years. I didn't care about anything except that I was on Mount Leinster, married to Billy Fennell.

When Billy opened the door the snow was more than a foot over the ground.

'Lord Christ almighty!' he said. 'The ewes! We may fetch them in. Will ya come Rose?'

Billy whistled the dogs and they appeared like two willing shadows out of nowhere and we climbed his fields whose ditches ran behind the yard and made a boundary with the wood. His flock was speckled-faced, the black Suffolk crossed with the stubborn Border Leicester. The dogs responded to Billy whistling, going left and right and crouching when he bade them. The ewes wanted to go with the snow, not against it, and I knew they'd smother in the drifts if we left them out. We brought the flock home to the yard and divided them into sheds and sorted out which lambs belonged to which ewes. It wasn't easy. There was awful confusion with the ewes roaring and the lambs bleating and us, with the dogs snapping, trying to get them paired off into all the sheds. The ewes were demented, sniffing under lambs' tails and plucking them away to save their own milk for their own but finally we sorted out who was whose. Billy brought bags of nuts down from the loft on his back and I filled barrels with water from the pump but Billy refused to let me carry anything. The ewes were thirsty and it took over an hour before they quietened. One ewe was down. Billy felt her tits and looked under her tail and got a bowl of hot water and washing-up liquid from the house.

'You're in the deep end now. Your hand is smaller nor mine, Rosie. Lather it well.'

I did. I pushed my soapy hand into the ewe. She was lying there straining with her eyes bulging out of her head. I felt so sorry for her, I would have done anything.

'Can you feel the feet?'

'I think so.'

'Do you think there's one or two in her? How many legs?'

'I can't feel but the one, Bill.'

'Aye. There's the trouble. One leg is turned. Now, you've to pull the other foot round, the feet should be together otherwise the shoulder'll get stuck. Now wait, wait till she's ready. When she stops pushing, you push the lamb back into her and bring the foot round. It'll be no bother to you. Be aisy.'

Billy talked to the ewe calling her 'Magsy, Magsy, poor Magsy' and I found the other foot and pulled and soon a speckled face slithered out, a wet ewe lamb. Billy cleared the mucus off its nose and blew into its mouth but it didn't move. Dead weight is a thing I recognize.

'We're too late,' I said.

He took the lamb by the front feet and plunged it in the water bucket and threw it on the straw. We waited and nothing happened. An eternity passed and I saw my mother hanging from a length of clothes line and then the dead lamb shook her head and splattered us.

'Thank God!' I said.

Billy laughed. 'Doesn't matter how long you farm,' he said. 'You always get a kick out of that.'

The ewe came over and licked her lamb and when she got up she stumbled and went, blindly, to suck. The ewe stood, hating us, and let her milk down.

'Aye, she's only the one in her, same as me own mother,' he said. 'Go on now, good girl, and get the beestings.'

The lamb sucked and its tail turned into a crazed thing. It made me think of the stubborn beech leaf autumn cannot blow away. I've always thought it must be lovely to have a tail, and wondered what it is that humans have now that the tail is gone. I have never minded facing anybody but when people look at me from behind it makes me uneasy, as though I'm deformed because I've no tail. It's not something I can explain. I suppose everybody has a physical shortcoming that makes them uneasy and that is mine. Billy brought down a fresh bale of straw and shook it out over the floor and we washed our hands in the basin of dirty water.

'You did well,' Billy said. 'You have the touch. I didn't like to say an'thing but that was close. And you know that's the worst of farming: the losses. People say you expect the losses but in truth you never do and when they come they're fresh, and worse than the one before.'

I was sweating. Billy was watching me.

'Come here to me,' he said.

He held me for a long time. His arms tightened round me and I felt caught in the jaws of a trap.

'You're mine now,' he said. 'There's no going back, do you hear me, Rose?'

'I'll never go back.'

We stood there for a good while, facing each other.

'You're thinking.'

'I'm thinking it'd be lovely to have a tail.'

'You have a tail,' he said. 'Come here, I'll show you.'

He stripped me and I was afraid of him again, afraid his savage might would rise up and hurt me or, worse still, that nothing like that would happen, but it was slow and strange and painful and in the end, easy. It was easy as ripping a seam. I conceived a child that night. I knew this the way, without reason, I feel dread under happy circumstances and it comes to pass.

I got up. I walked to the shed door. Outside, the snow was still falling. I imagined it was falling nowhere else in the world but there, on Mount Leinster, for us. My wedding gift was snow. Wind made the clouds race, made savage attempts to lift the corrugated iron off the rafters. In a gust I heard cones falling off the larches. I thought of the seeds scattering, falling on infertile ground, and the waste of that. When I turned, Billy was dressed, and the lamb looked older.

'What did the landlords leave us, Bill?'

'Trees,' he said.

'Aye.'

'You'll catch your end, Rose.'

He dressed me. He wiped blood off my thighs with his sleeve and sat me on his knee and pulled my socks up over my bare feet and turned my dress right side out and buttoned my coat and took the afterbirth out on a shovel and threw it to the dogs.

'Jaysus, Rosie.'

That was all he said, and I said nothing.

'I love the way you say nothing,' he said.

The wind blew all that night. It swept the snow into the corners of the yard. It filled the dip tub and did its best to tear the ivy off the walls. Billy slept in his jumper and snored. At some point I woke and heard a door bang shut or perhaps I dreamt it. I remembered Billy grasping the thistle, me taking the thorns, the proof of his love, out of his hand with a shirt pin when he came home. Memory is strange, almost as strange as time. That night, lying there in the shelter of my husband's body, listening to the wind, I believed no harm would come to us. I believed that nature would have the grace to withhold her claws and keep us from all the betrayals every mortal who walks the earth endures.

Biographical Notes

Tiffany Atkinson was born in 1972 in Berlin. She teaches English and writing at the University of Wales, Aberystwyth. She has twice received first prize in the BBC Radio Young Poet of the Year competition, and more recently won the Ottakar's and Faber annual poetry competition. She is currently completing a book on critical theory and working on her first poetry collection.

Patrick Clinton was born in Belfast in 1951. He grew up in Melbourne, Australia, and trained as a commercial photographer in Sydney. Patrick has had various occupations and has lived between Ireland and Australia for the past twenty-five years. He now lives in Co. Wexford, Ireland. His previous publication, *Late Harvest*, was published by Roundstone Press.

Jenny Diski has written eight novels, a collection of short stories, a volume of essays, and a travel memoir. Her new travel book, *Stranger on a Train*, from which this extract is taken, will be published by Virago in the autumn of 2002. She was born in London in 1947 and now lives in Cambridge.

Isobel Dixon was born and educated in South Africa, and subsequently lived in Edinburgh. She now works in London as a literary agent. Her first collection *Weather Eye* was published by Carapace Books (South Africa) in 2001.

Bill Duncan has had poetry, fiction and non-fiction published widely, with work broadcast on BBC Radio 3. His first collection of short fiction, *The Smiling School for Calvinists*, was published by Bloomsbury in May 2001. He lives in Dundee and teaches at a secondary school.

Alistair Elliot was born in Liverpool in 1932 but after years in the United States, Scotland and Iran, has spent most of his life in Newcastle. Since taking early retirement from librarianship he has published his collected poems (*My Country*, 1989) and several other books with Carcanet Press and Bloodaxe. Diana Rigg took his version of Euripides' *Medea* (produced by Jonathan Kent) to Broadway in 1994. His last book was a parallel-text version of Valéry's *La Jeune Parque*.

Anne Enright lives in Dublin. Recent stories were published in *The New Yorker, Granta* and the *Paris Review*. Her last book *What Are You Like?* (Vintage) received the Encore award and was shortlisted for the Whitbread prize.

Gloria Evans Davies was born in Maesteg, South Wales. She has written two books of poetry published by Chatto and Windus, *Words For Blodwen* and *Her Name Like the Hours*. She has contributed to various publications such as *The Oxford Book of Welsh Verse In English*, the *New York Times*, and the *Times Literary Supplement*.

Michel Faber was born in Holland in 1960. He lived in Australia from 1967 to 1993 and then moved to Scotland. His short story collection *Some Rain Must Fall* won several awards and his novel *Under the Skin* was shortlisted for the Whitbread and sold to fourteen countries. Other books have included *The Hundred and Ninety-Nine Steps* and *The Courage Consort*. He is working on a giant Victorian novel and more short stories.

Gerard Fanning lives in Dublin. He has published two collections of poetry with Dedalus Press. *Easter Snow* (1992) and *Working for the Government* (1999). He was awarded the Rooney prize in 1993.

Charles Fernyhough was born in Essex in 1968. His first novel, *The Auctioneer*, was published in 1999, and has recently been translated into German. He has written extensively on the Russian psychologist Vygotsky, and is now a lecturer in psychology at the University of Durham.

Maggie Graham was born in Ayrshire, Scotland, and educated at Glasgow University. She was the winner of the Robert Louis

Stevenson 2000 prize, and her first novel *Sitting Among the Eskimos* was shortlisted for the Saltire first book award. Her second novel *Precious Little* will be published by Review in July 2002.

Lavinia Greenlaw has published two books of poems, *Night Photograph* (1993) and *A World Where News Travelled Slowly* (1997). Her novel, *Mary George of Allnorthover*, appeared in 2001. She lives in London and works as a freelance writer, reviewer and broadcaster. This is her first short story.

Georgina Hammick is the author of two collections of short stories, *People for Lunch* and *Spoilt*, and a novel, *The Arizona Game*, which was shortlisted for the Whitbread First Novel award. Her second novel, *Green Man Running*, will be published by Chatto in 2002. She is currently working on a collection of short stories.

Thomas Healy has published two novels, *Rolling* and *It Might Have Been Jerusalem*, and a boxing memoir, *A Hurting Business*. He was born in Glasgow and still lives there.

Desmond Hogan was born in County Galway in 1951. He worked as a street actor in Dublin before becoming a writer. Two of his plays, *A Short Walk to the Sea* and *Sanctified Distances*, were produced at the Abbey Theatre, and his first novel, *The Ikon Maker*, was published in Dublin in 1976. His novels include *Leaves on Grey*, *A Curious Street*, *A New Shirt* and, most recently, *A Farewell to Prague*. He has written four collections of short stories, one of which, *The Diamonds at the Bottom of the Sea*, won the John Llewelyn Rhys Memorial prize, and a volume of travel pieces, *The Edge of the City: A Scrapbook 1976–91*. He lives in County Kerry, Ireland.

Mark Illis has written three novels, all published by Bloomsbury. His short stories have appeared in magazines and anthologies. He is currently working on a new novel and also writes for TV and radio. *There's a Hole In Everything* is one of a series of linked stories.

Jamie Jackson has been writing for five years and is taking a masters in journalism at the London College of Printing. He writes poetry as well as fiction and is currently working on a first volume of short stories.

Panos Karnezis was born in Greece in 1967 and came to England in 1992 where he studied engineering and worked for several years in industry. One of his stories appeared in *Granta 72*. His collection *Little Infamies* will be published by Jonathan Cape in May 2002. He lives in Oxford.

Jackie Kay's most recent collection of short stories, *Why Don't You Stop Talking*, is published by Picador. Her first novel, *Trumpet*, won the *Guardian* Fiction prize. She is a poet and lives in Manchester.

Claire Keegan grew up on a farm in Wicklow. Her collection of stories, *Antarctica*, was published by Faber in 1999. Her work has won many awards including the William Trevor prize, the Rooney prize and the Macaulay prize. She is now living in Monaghan, working on a novel and a second collection of stories.

Christina Koning was born in Kuala Belait, Brunei, and spent her childhood in Venezuela and Jamaica. Her novels include *A Mild Suicide* (1992), *Undiscovered Country* (1998), which won the 1999 Encore award, and *Fabulous Time* (2001). She is working on a fourth novel, set in Borneo, and a collection of short stories.

Nick Laird was born in Dungannon, Co. Tyrone, in 1975 and educated at Cookstown High School and Cambridge University, where he received a first-class degree in English Literature and the Quiller-Couch award for creative writing. He is a commercial litigator for a law firm and regularly reviews poetry and fiction for the *Times Literary Supplement*. He currently lives in Warsaw.

Tim Liardet was born in London and has produced three collections of poetry. The most recent of these, *Competing with the Piano Tuner*, appeared from Seren in 1998 and was a Poetry Book Society special commendation. His fourth collection, *To the God of Rain*, has just been completed.

Douglas A. Martin is the author of the novel, *Outline of My Lover*. It has been adapted in part for the Ballet Frankfurt's production

Kammer/Kammer. He is currently at work on a study of self and representation in the writings of four female authors.

Sean O' Reilly's first book, *Curfew and Other Stories*, was published by Faber and Faber in July 2000 and a novel, *Love and Sleep*, was published in February 2002. He currently lives in Dublin.

Ruth Padel's most recent collection of poetry is *Voodoo Shop. 52 Ways Of Looking at a Poem or How Modern Poetry Can Change Your Life* (out next June) is her selection from her *Independent on Sunday* 'Sunday Poem' column plus an introductory essay, 'Reading Poetry Today'. She is a Fellow of the Royal Society of Authors.

Fiona Ritchie Walker was born in Montrose, Scotland, and now lives and works in north-east England. Her first collection of poems, *Lip Reading*, was published by Diamond Twig in 1999. She is currently studying for an MA in Writing Poetry at the University of Newcastle-upon-Tyne.

Jane Rogers is the author of six novels, including *Mr Wroe's Virgins* (shortlisted for the *Guardian* Fiction prize), *Promised Lands* (winner Writers' Guild Best Fiction Book) and *Island*. She has edited Oxford University Press's *Good Fiction Guide*, and is currently working on a new novel provisionally entitled *Voyage*. She teaches on the Writing MA at Sheffield Hallam University.

Mary-Kay Wilmers is the editor of the *London Review of Books* and is currently writing a book about her family and its role in Trotsky's assassination and other episodes in twentieth-century history.

Copyright information